D0802199

The Girl Who Stole A Planet

by

Stephen Colegrove

Copyright Information

THE GIRL WHO STOLE A PLANET

First Edition: July 2016

Cover design by Lilac
Editing by Alice Dragan (alicedit.com)

Find out more about the author and upcoming books at the websites below:
stevecolegrove.com
amishspaceman.com
facebook.com/pages/Steve-Colegrove-Author
twitter @stevecolegrove

Also by the author:
The Amish Spaceman (2014)
The Roman Spaceman (2014)
A Girl Called Badger (2012)
The Dream Widow (2013)

Table of Contents

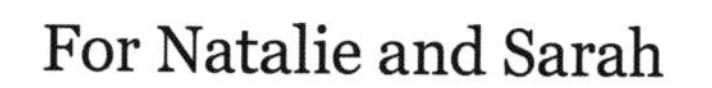
For Natalie and Sarah

Part I

Teenage Thief

1

Of all the orbital prisons in the galaxy, of all the rough-heeled planets that ever shot their violent, rough-heeled trash into orbit, this was the worst. Not just according to popular opinion, mind––they had a bag full of galactic trophies to prove it.

The penal station rotated against the vast panorama of space like a brilliant, four-spoked wheel, a white speck of discipline and free television hanging above the cloudy planetary orb of Kepler Prime. Inside the tubular hull, Detention Officer First Class Nistra tapped on the window of a thick titanium door with his claw.

"And thisss is Prince Treem," he hissed. "The former ruler of Alpha Centauri, who murdered twelve million across four systems. Thisss gender-anomalous filth received one hundred thousand life sentences."

Recruit Officer Flistra bowed his reptilian head and clacked his sharp teeth in respect.

"Yesssssssir."

Nistra pulled down on the jacket of his dark blue uniform and tromped in huge boots to the next porthole.

"Doctor Fistula," he snarled, "designed a virus that wiped every trace of life from the outer rim's third arm. He was given three billion life sentences and a subscription to People magazine."

"Yesssir," said the recruit.

Nistra strode quickly past several doors, dismissing them with a wave of his scaly hand.

"Pop star, pop star, radio DJ ... here we are."

Nistra unsealed the heavy security door with his thumbprint and marched along an empty corridor that had a gentle upward curve. After a full minute of walking, he stopped in front of a hatch covered in diagonal red and yellow stripes.

"There she is," the giant reptile said with a shudder.

Recruit Flistra approached the hatch with small, reluctant steps. A digital placard fixed to the wall caught his eye.

"Armstrong, Amy," he whispered. "Horrible! But I don't see a viewing window, Commander. I mean, Officer. Sir."

Nistra shook his scaly head and stared at the recruit. "Didn't you have maximum security spheres in the outer rim?"

"No, sssir. We didn't, sssir."

"Well, that's what it is––a maximum security sphere. There aren't any windows, because it would interfere with the stasis bubble."

"How do you monitor the prisoner?"

Nistra waved a claw over the front of the door, and a hologram of the interior appeared in mid-air. A pale teenage girl lay on the concave floor of the chamber, both arms around the knees of her orange jumpsuit. A tangled mess of blonde hair covered her face and spread across the bottom of the sphere.

"I don't understand," hissed Flistra. "It looks undeveloped and weak, like a five-toed *poona* who hasn't been given enough slurm."

"Soup brain!" snapped Nistra. "Haven't you been watching the telefeed? She's the most dangerous prisoner in the five square kilometers of this orbiting station! Did you just fall off the galactic shuttle?"

"Actually, sir, I did, sir. You met me in the hangar bay five minutes ago."

"Never mind, then. This is the most destructive, rapacious, and annoying creature that ever drew breath in this arm of the galaxy. It has an appetite greater than a legion of soldiers, a foul stench that can poison the atmosphere of a Class-M planet in fourteen seconds, and a voice louder and more annoying than all the drunken lizard fraternities at the galactic conference of drunken lizard fraternities! It's a vile, disgusting beast from a species that hasn't won a match in the Galactic Cup since the Galactic Cup was invented!"

"My apologiesss, Officer. I don't watch football. Please ssssir, what's it called?"

Nistra opened a mouth full of razor-sharp teeth and snarled.

"My dim-witted, fizz-brained recruit from the outer rim––that's a human teenager."

1995 A.D.
Earth

Amy Armstrong stared out the window at the fog rolling up Forest Avenue, a white, billowing cloud that whipped across the street like smoke from a campfire. She wished it really were smoke and the whole town was burning down, starting with Pacific Grove Middle School.

Amy wrapped a strand of her long blonde hair around a pencil and rolled it all the way from the waist of her blue plaid skirt to above her ear like one of her foster mom's curlers. She was bored, and all the other eighth graders in third period science were bored, too. It was the most boring class on the most boring morning in the most boring school in the most boring city in the entire universe. This would be the deduction of a neutral alien observer, if aliens actually existed and were the kind of nice peeping Tom aliens that liked to watch eighth graders yawn, doodle in their textbooks, and stare vacantly out the window at the occasional over-the-hill citizen walking his or her over-the-hill dog over the hill.

It might have been the fault of the substitute. Mr. Gomez had been a promising young man at one point in his life, with dreams of aeronautical engineering and designing interstellar warp engines, but that was before he checked the wrong box on a college application, triggering a cascade of events that began with a mis-categorized form and ended with a very pale and overweight man with a face like cold butter trying to teach physics to a room full of fourteen-year-old kids.

"Force equals mass times acceleration," droned the tubby Mr. Gomez, and scraped a sliver of chalk across the blackboard.

Amy sighed. She wasn't confused by physics or theories or theorems at all; in fact, she liked math and science. She knew that a television dropped from a second-story window is probably uncatchable, no matter how much your foster brother Tony whispers up to you that "it's all good" and that "he can catch it." The natural laws of the universe did their jobs without question and without dreaming about being someplace else. Gomez probably wanted to be at home watching the Sci-Fi Channel and the teenagers wanted to smoke behind the movie theater at the Del Monte Center or wander over to Asilomar and dig up clams. Amy hated clams and she hated cigarettes. What she liked was a free television. Next time she'd find one on the ground floor.

Mr. Gomez paused and the small portion of the class that wasn't sleeping watched an ambulance flash by the window and disappear up Forest Avenue, siren wailing.

Amy Armstrong didn't have a problem with school. What she had a problem with was anything that got in the way of her very local and very lucrative "property relocation" business. Certain people had a need for a certain type of property, perhaps a nineteen-inch TV-VCR combo. Amy found the certain property and relocated it to the new owner for a fee. The goods she collected in a secret compartment under her foster mom's garden shed had sometimes come into her hands serendipitously, falling "accidentally" into her pocket while on a visit to a schoolmate's house. At other times more planning was required, such as pretending for a month to be Sammie Wong's friend just so he'd invite her to his birthday party and just so she could drop his nineteen-inch television down to her foster brother Tony in the azalea bushes. Tony's shoulder was still sprained and bits of glass still sparkled in the azalea bushes.

A square of folded paper somersaulted through the air and landed on Amy's desk. She unfolded it in her lap, her eyes on Gomez. Scrawled on the note in pencil was, "HELP ME I HAVE SCABIES."

Amy laughed out loud at Helen's note, and then slapped a hand over her mouth.

Mr. Gomez turned from the blackboard and peered down his round, buttery nose at the class.

"What's so funny?"

He leaned over the class roster on his desk.

"Seat twelve––that would be Amelia Armstrong. Miss Armstrong, please explain Newton's law of universal gravitation."

Amy cleared her throat. “The attractive force between two bodies is directly proportional to the product of their masses and indirectly proportional to the distance between them.”

The boys in the back of the room snickered, and the class wag Robert Calcetti spoke up.

“Bodies? She meant boobies!”

“Quiet!” Gomez’s bald head turned crimson and he slammed his chalk in the blackboard gutter. “Thank you, Amy. You are correct.”

Ten minutes later a bell clanged in the hallway, and the drowsy teens sprang up like it was The Final Trump and they were a blue-blazered, plaid-skirted throng of believers heading for the sky.

Amy and Helen squeezed through a hallway lined with slamming lockers, dropped books, and uniformed kids scrambling for their next class. Eighth graders hooted and hollered at the seventh graders, the seventh graders scowled and yelled at the sixth graders, and the sixth graders squirted desperately through the human mob, trying only to survive.

Helen nudged Amy with an elbow and yelled over the din. “Are we still skipping out during fifth period?”

Amy nodded and leaned into her friend’s ear. “Yeah, but I’ll meet you at DMC later. I have to deliver a Sega Saturn.”

The first day of sixth grade, Amy had seen Helen sitting alone in the cafeteria and decided that the short and chunky girl would do for a best friend. She was one of the only Asian kids in the school and a good student, which always helped if you were Amy and had a reputation that needed a boost at times. Lay down with dogs and you get fleas, as the old saying goes. Amy was an unrepentant thief, but she did everything she could to appear as clean as the wind-driven snow.

Appearance was half the battle. Amy kept her blonde hair long and straight, cut her bangs razor-sharp, and flattened the pleats of her skirts with an iron "repurposed" from an open window of Timmy Wilson's house. She always kept her face washed, fingernails clean and short, and spoke in the sweetest and politest of tones when around adults. The few experiences she'd had with the juvenile justice system and authority figures in general had taught her that anyone who acts like a criminal, gets treated like a criminal. Nose piercings and tattoos didn't earn trust with suspicious adults. The problem of looking like an innocent fourteen-year-old girl was that people didn't want to buy a hot Miata from you, but that's what foster brothers were for.

Helen hugged Amy. "See you later!"

"Bye! I'll be there at two o'clock."

Amy leaned against the lime-painted bricks in the hallway and watched the tubby girl twist through the crowd of kids toward her art class. It was funny-- Amy had picked Helen because she looked like the one kid who'd never steal a paper clip, and two years later she was as good at "property repurposing" as Amy.

The bulbous face and brown, stringy octopus hair of Mary Katherine Prezbolewski rose above the heads in the noisy hallway, her great black eyes rolling back and forth over the crowd like those of a hammerhead shark. A pair of spindly seventh-graders trailed behind the mountainous body, carrying her field hockey stick and backpack.

Amy imagined the Earth's gravitational forces shifting with every step of the impossibly huge fifteen-year-old. She gritted her teeth, pulled her shoulders back, and put on her best smile for the giantess.

"Good morning, M.K.," she chirped.

Mary Katherine Prezbolewski slowed to a stop in front of Amy and the black, emotionless eyes glistened down at her.

"Armstrong, you little insect. Where's my nineteen-inch TV-VCR combo?"

Amy shrugged. "It's not the best choice for a birthday present. I've got a slightly used Casio synthesizer your dad would just love. Let's see ... Oh! Does he play golf? I can get you eighteen holes at Pebble Beach or Spyglass, take your pick."

M.K. towered over Amy like a corpulent mermaid, one who smelled like she took frequent showers in mackerel guts.

"Listen, Armstrong," she growled. "When my dad wants a nineteen-inch TV-VCR combo for his fishing boat, he gets a nineteen-inch TV-VCR combo for his fishing boat. It's his birthday today, and that's what he wants. Are you trying to ruin his birthday by not giving him a nineteen-inch TV-VCR combo for his fishing boat?"

"You don't have to keep repeating it, you know. I get it. There's just been a problem with the TV."

M.K. poked a finger on Amy's chest. "If it's not at my house by five today, your little blonde head won't have any other problems to worry about."

Amy beamed. "Thanks, M.K.!"

"No. I mean I'll break you in half, you skinny little Barbie. I'll come at you like Hurricane Hugo!"

The bell rang and Amy sprinted away from M.K.'s oceanic mass and toward fourth period math.

She was ignoring algebra completely and in the midst of considering last-minute sources for a television, including getting a ride to Circuit City, when the ancient brass grille of the intercom speaker crackled above the classroom door.

"Amelia Armstrong to the office, please," came the hollow voice of the office secretary. "Amelia Armstrong to the office."

Amy stuffed her books and papers into her backpack and left the rest of the envious and bored eighth graders with their algebra formulae. She skipped down the hall, certain it was Tony getting her out of school early to help unload some merchandise that had "fallen off a truck." That boy always had something in the works. Just in case it wasn't Tony, she dumped a half-dozen stolen Tupac CDs in the trash and a Mont Blanc pen she'd swiped from Mrs. Pound when the librarian hadn't been looking.

The nurse met her in front of the glass doors of the office. Her face was pale and her eyes didn't want to stay on anything too long, so Amy knew something was up.

"Good morning, Nurse Nelson!" Amy said brightly.

The nurse twisted her mouth. She opened and closed it strangely for a few seconds, as if she didn't know how to begin, and then cleared her throat.

"Amy, your mother had a heart attack."

PACIFIC GROVE spread across the western rocks of the Monterey Bay like green moss on a cold, sea-sprayed wooden piling. It was a town full of perambulating retirees with halos of white hair, a town of driftwood artists, ceramic frog collectors, coconut painters, photographers, golfers, tourists, seagull haters, scuba divers, aquarium lovers, and during the monarch butterfly festival, was packed from Lighthouse Drive to Asilomar with visitors from the rest of California who had discovered last week that they loved butterflies. It was a foggy town with a slow, foggy way of life, which is one of the reasons Lucia Armstrong liked it.

Amy had always been Lucia's favorite among the six foster children, and she hadn't made a secret of it. The other children didn't mind because everyone liked Amy. She kept them supplied with the newest electronic toys and video games, and added the income from her "business" to the household by secretly replacing the staples that everyone needed but nobody kept track of like soap, toothpaste, laundry detergent, shampoo, bleach, toilet paper, milk, eggs, flour, sugar, butter, and pancake syrup. Lucia was neither superstitious nor religious, simply an overworked FedEx driver with six children and too few hours in the day. If leprechauns or fairies or Old Scratch himself were topping up her dandruff shampoo and Tide, she wasn't asking questions.

The school nurse drove Amy up the hill to Community Hospital where she, Tony, and the four little ones watched a team of white-coated doctors and frantically busy hospital staff wheel Lucia out of the emergency room. She was still in her navy blue FedEx uniform. A clear oxygen mask covered her face and a rainbow of wires crossed her body, monitoring her heart, providing intravenous fluid, and displaying the oxygen saturation in her blood.

"Where are they taking her?" Amy asked.

Tony shrugged. "Probably surgery. Lots of knives and lots of blood."

"Stop saying things like that," hissed Amy. "You're scaring the little ones."

The four younger kids--Billy, Anna, Viv, and Eugenia--stood together in a tight pack, their eyes wide and their small knuckles white on the handles of their brightly colored lunch boxes.

"Sorry," said Tony. "I'm sorry. I just ... what do we do now?"

Amy squinted at a television hanging in a corner of the waiting room. "I don't know. But I need to find a nineteen-inch TV-VCR combo."

Tony spread his arms. "Lucia had a heart attack and you want to go shopping?"

"It's a life and death situation!"

"Exactly," said Tony. "I'll take the kids home for lunch. Amy, stay at the hospital. Call the house if anything changes."

LUCIA CAME out of surgery in the afternoon.

Amy felt bad about trying to leave the hospital earlier. She stayed in Lucia's room all afternoon, and left only once to grab a sandwich and once to break into a storage room. No luck in the storage room and the sandwich was too dry.

"Hello, darling," was the first thing Lucia said, her mouth and eyes sleepy from the painkillers, her West Virginia drawl even more syrupy than normal.

Amy jerked up from the chair beside the bed.

"You're awake!"

Lucia blinked slowly. "I'm sorry."

"For what?"

"Scaring y'all. I was carrying a box up the drive of this house on Grand Avenue. It kept getting heavier and heavier, and I started to sweat through my shirt–"

"It's okay, Lucia," said Amy, and squeezed her hand. "You don't have to worry about it. Tony's watching the kids and I'm here if you need anything."

The slow rumble of a laugh traveled through Lucia's sunken chest. She turned her head of short, graying hair on the hospital pillow, causing the plastic cover to crackle noisily.

"Don't tell a mother not to worry," she said to Amy. "Sometimes worrying's all we got."

AMY STAYED with her foster mother until about eight-thirty in the evening, when Tony and the little kids showed up. Visiting hours ended at nine, and then Tony drove everyone back to the house on Pine Avenue.

The street where they lived was long and wide, and a few blocks up the hill from the main drag on Lighthouse. Like that street, Pine ran west to the ocean and east to Monterey, but happily for the residents of the stucco-covered ranch houses, lacked the hustle and bustle of the sidewalk cafes, liquor stores, sandwich eateries, organic breakfast joints, and ceramic butterfly shops of Lighthouse. Although safe from retail shenanigans, the placid environment of Pine Avenue could be disturbed by sirens from the fire department at the intersection of Pine and Forest. Since Pacific Grove was full to the brim with armies of seasoned, white-haired citizens, these pealing disturbances seemed to happen day and night.

Lucia's house was on Pine several blocks west of Forest. A massive three-story house belonging to E.G. Woodley, eminent lawyer and raconteur, had burned to ash in 1912 on the very spot. The parcel never returned to its former glory, but still retained the massive dike of earth that Woodley had had trucked in from the valley to serve as foundation for his mansion. Perhaps he disliked the gravel sidewalks on Pine, or simply wished to rise above the rest of the street. Over the next fifty years the grassy slopes supported dwellings of a more humble nature, until 1963 when Lucia's great uncle Luccesse sold every one of his artichoke fields near Castroville and bought a grocery store in Monterey. He leveled the rickety shacks on the parcel and built a sturdy ranch-style house with four bedrooms. Uncle Luccesse had the money for a grander design that included a second story, but his sister had fallen down a staircase at the tender age of seven, forever prejudicing his opinions on a house with more than one floor.

Upon his death in 1991 the house traveled through the probate system and ended up in the lap of the nearest relative, Lucia Armstrong, who pulled her children out of their schools in Salinas before the signatures on the deed had time to dry. If there was anything to complain about living in Pacific Grove, it certainly wasn't the schools. Uncle Luccesse had let the place go a bit in his dotage, but the cozy heart of the cottage was still there. Lucia and the children pulled off the red clapboard siding and slapped on chicken wire and stucco, painting everything a blinding shade of white. The overgrown front yard was weeded, seeded, and fertilized, and a tall redwood fence sprang up to surround the house on the little hill. The cedar shakes on the roof were replaced with safer asphalt shingles. The rusted garden hut was tossed out and a large, wood-framed shed was built in its place. Painted white, of course.

Tony pulled the car into the driveway at the back, the headlights shining on dark windows and an empty house. This time of night they should have gleamed, should have rattled from Lucia's call to bedtime and hummed from her loud toothbrush commandments. The house was a constant hive of children. Sometimes there were as few as six foster kids like now, but sometimes there had been as many as ten, including a baby. Since Lucia was just down the street from the police department, they quickly got to know her. If someone got clipped for possession or a felony and they had kids, Lucia watched them for a few days or a week until relatives or more permanent arrangements could be made. Amy had been one of those kids, but the difference was that she'd stayed. Nobody liked asking about it because it had been a long time ago and you didn't ask about those kinds of things anyway.

Tony unlocked the house and escaped to his room, while Amy played Lucia's part and led the four younger kids in their bedtime routines. She may have been only fourteen, but she'd learned that people are slaves to the same old patterns, day after day. It made stealing from big, bad adults so much easier when you knew what time they woke up, ate breakfast, went to work, visited the relatives, or played bridge.

Amy took a shower, brushed her teeth and hair, and changed out of her school uniform into an old t-shirt. She turned off the light in her room, climbed to the top bunk, and lay on top of the covers. Eugenia was supposed to sleep in the bottom bunk, but Amy paid her a weekly stipend to stay in Billy and Anna's room and so she could have the room to herself. Amy listened to the squeal of a siren going down Forest while she stared at the glowing stars on the ceiling. The constellations were all in the right places, but it wasn't the same thing as the big sky out in the mountains, or in Carmel Valley. You couldn't make a ceiling spin round and round every night and with the seasons.

She closed her eyes and might have fallen asleep if something hadn't tapped on the glass of the bedroom window.

Amy slid off the top bunk and crept across the room. After three more taps on the glass she grabbed the window sash and pushed it up.

"What's the password?" she whispered at the darkness.

Helen giggled and climbed into the room. "There's no password, silly."

"Just checking," said Amy. "Could be anyone out there." She inhaled in mock fright and held both hands up to her mouth. "Maybe even a boy!"

"Now you're really being silly," said Helen. "Every boy in the school is scared to death of you after you put that dead pelican under Leroy Jenkins's bed."

"He deserved it. Always staring at me in homeroom."

"I think he just liked you."

"The last thing I need is for people to like me."

"Apart from grown-ups, you mean?"

Amy snorted. "Of course. They don't count."

Bedsprings squealed as Helen sat on the lower bunk. She had changed into street clothes--jeans and a long shirt.

"I heard what happened. Is Lucia okay?"

Amy stretched out on the fluffy rug at Helen's feet. "Maybe. She's at the hospital now. She's talking, and I guess the operation went okay."

Helen nodded. "Good. I mean, it's not good that she's in the hospital, but ... aw, you know what I mean."

"Yes, I do," mumbled Amy. She turned onto her stomach and rested her forehead on her arms. "Do you ever wish you came from another planet?"

"Excuse me?"

Amy turned her head and brushed the blonde hair away from her eyes. "It's just so boring around here. Going to the same boring school with the same boring teachers, stealing the same boring crap from the same boring people. Sometimes I dream that my real parents were aliens."

"Blonde-haired, blue-eyed aliens?"

"Maybe. Who knows? I could be a shape shifter. Maybe they left me here to study the human race. Maybe that's why I like physics and astronomy."

"They're jerks if they left you alone without even a beeper or instruction manual or anything," said Helen. "I thought everything was cool here with Lucia. She's never hassled you with too many rules like every other parent."

Amy sighed. "I know, and I do like her. I just feel trapped here. Like I should be doing something somewhere else."

"You and every other member of the human race," said Helen. "You're exactly like my Dad right now. He constantly talks about moving to Australia or New Zealand or Singapore or Bali. I think that might be his hobby––wanting to live somewhere else."

"Yeah," said Amy, and lay her head on the fluffy rug. She watched the long, delicate fibers move with her breath in the moonlight. "Maybe you're right."

"Amy?"

"Yeah."

"Why do you steal things?"

Amy snorted. "It's not stealing--it's 'property relocation.' Anyway, what a dumb question. I do it because I want bigger and better things, like another house for Lucia."

"No. I mean, how did you start?"

"Tony. He saw me trying to shoplift a candy bar, and showed me how to do it without getting caught."

"Did you ever think about ... not doing that? About quitting?"

"And go back to being poor? Never. What's up with the twenty questions tonight?"

Helen shrugged. "Nothing. Well, it's late and everything, so I'll take off. My parents think I'm still at the youth group meeting."

"No problem."

"So how'd the thing go with M.K. and her TV?"

Amy jumped straight up from the rug like a cat on an electric fence.

"She's going to kill me!"

"What? I thought you were going to buy another one."

"I didn't even think about it! I was at the hospital all day."

"What do we do, then?"

Amy pulled on jeans, slippers, and grabbed a puffy jacket.

"To the Bat Cave, Robin!"

***

UNCLE LUCCESSE had been a successful businessman and enterprising figure who looked to the future. In 1963 the future was not expected to be a bright one, and many intelligent people expected radioactive fallout to drastically reduce property values. After the Cuban Missile Crisis many bomb shelters were dug in back yards. Uncle Luccesse was in that group, but he had the time and money to do it right. Since he was digging a new foundation for the house in Pacific Grove, he had the contractors hollow out a rectangular cistern in the back, twelve feet deep and fifteen feet on each side. It was lined with concrete blocks and roofed with foot-wide timbers from an old barn his brother was getting rid of. The air supply could be closed off and had an ingenious filtration system that went through a container of water and required a hand crank. Access was through a metal hatch in the ground that led to a cast iron ladder and a small decontamination chamber. A larger metal hatch, this one vertical, led to the main area of the bomb shelter. Like the other hatch, it had been salvaged from a decommissioned submarine by Uncle Luccesse's brother in Connecticut and transported at an economical rate by a relative in the freight business.

Uncle Luccesse kept the shelter clean, the doors oiled, and rotated the food and water stock regularly until November 1989. With the fall of the Berlin Wall and crumble of the Soviet Union, all the fun went out of having a bomb shelter, and Uncle Luccesse had more time to spend on parcheesi and golf.

After his untimely death in 1991, Lucia took ownership of the property and had no use for the underground space. A bomb shelter was fine for an old man who lived during the Cold War, she thought, but in the modern age it was only good for spiders and millipedes. The garden shed was built directly over the little metal door to keep anyone from getting any ideas. This turned out to be the best feature of the shelter. When eleven-year-old Amy heard about it from Tony, she immediately pried up the floorboards and squealed like it was the fabled El Dorado.

The metal hatches had stiffened but weren't yet frozen with rust. A bit of WD-40 cleared that up. The electric wire Luccesse had run down to the shelter was still hooked up to the house's main panel, although the bulbs had to be replaced. Amy had sworn Tony to secrecy and began converting the underground space for her own purposes.

Amy and Helen crept out of the window and through the moonlight to the shed. Inside, Amy hooked her fingers in a crack where the floor met the wall, and pulled. The middle section of floorboards swung up on hidden hinges to reveal the iron dome of the old submarine hatch. Amy spun the wheel, pulled up, and the old hatch clanked open, filling the shed with the smell of fresh earth, petroleum grease, and the bitter odor of oxidizing metal. The two girls climbed down the ladder in pitch-black darkness, spun open another submarine door, and stepped into the shelter. Amy flipped a switch and the room burst into brilliant pastel colors.

She was still a girl and this was her special place. The floor was painted baby blue, the walls pink, and the ceiling beams crisscrossed in a black and white zebra pattern. Amy had been in a brief unicorn and rainbow phase when she'd discovered the shelter and the walls bore the evidence, covered floor to ceiling in mystical animals and curving single and double rainbows, some with pots of gold and tiny green men.

On the right side of the square chamber stood a pair of cots with sleeping bags, a tall series of shelves packed with purloined books, and a desk with a reading lamp. An old black rotary phone sat on the desk. One of the only things Tony had done for the place was to run an intercom line through the ground up to the house. If anyone got stuck in the shelter, they just had to dial zero and the house phone would ring. Someday Amy wanted to fix it up like a real phone.

On the left side of the room were the shelves of the old food storage, and this was where Amy kept her "repurposed property." The light gleamed on a Casio keyboard, stacks of video games, CDs, tapes, watches, action figures, and piles of comic books.

Helen dropped onto the cot with a sigh. "You're in a tight spot, Amy. Anything on those shelves that might tame the savage beast, so to speak? I mean literally. She is a beast."

Amy put her hands on her waist. "I'm in a tight spot? Once she's done with me, that savage beast is going to eat all my friends starting with you, little Asian smarty-pants."

"She likes games, doesn't she? Give her a whole stack."

Amy thumbed through the plastic cases and shook her head. "None of these are real new. She's probably played them all. I had a couple of consoles and some nice jewelry last week, but sold everything at the flea market on Sunday. Anyway, I don't think even the British crown jewels would make M.K. happy at this point."

"Not even the new Mariah Carey album?"

"No. She thinks I ruined her dad's birthday. Mariah can't fix that."

"How about I stash some weed in her locker and report her like that one girl, what was her name ... Victoria Sanchez?"

"I don't have any weed and I don't like how that turned out."

"Bring her down here and pretend to be her friend, but wait until she falls asleep and put a pillow over her face?"

Amy squinted at Helen. "How much chocolate did you eat today?"

"Couple of Snickers."

"Okay. First of all, she wouldn't fit down the ladder, and second, I'm not killing anyone in my secret stronghold. Think about the smell."

"How about give her an empty box?"

"She'll be even madder when she opens it."

Helen spread her arms. "What if it's full of cyanide? Or even better––laughing gas?"

Amy laughed. "Yeah, that's a good one. Climb out of here and run back to your house, silly girl."

"But what are you gonna do?"

Amy shook her head. "I'll think of something. I always do."

2

Amy tossed and turned half the night, then woke up early and dressed for school. She packed lunches for the four little ones and shooed the groggy children out of bed and into the bathroom. Amy wasn't the best cook, but that didn't matter because Tony was already up. He fixed eggs, bacon, and toast for himself and the kids. Amy wasn't hungry, but had a boiled egg and a few raw carrots.

They usually walked to school, but Tony was going up to the hospital to see Lucia so everyone piled into the station wagon. It creaked and bounced up the street like a houseboat with wheels. Tony dropped the kids off at their school, and then turned back toward Forest Avenue.

"Don't bother," said Amy. "I'm going to the hospital."

"Are you sure? I was going to watch her today. You can come visit after school."

"I'm not going to school today."

"What's going on?"

Amy didn't say anything. Tony kept glancing at her as he passed the school and continued up the hill and out of P.G., the old car swaying in the curves and the pine trees full of morning mist.

They stopped in the hospital parking lot at the top of the hill. The car's engine clanked for ten seconds after Tony turned the key off, but he just sat there.

"Amy, tell me what's going on. If it's about Lucia ... sometimes these things happen. People get sick and we do the best we can for them."

"It's not that. There's a girl at school who's going to kick the living crap out of me."

Tony laughed. "Is that all? Just fight her. Make sure she throws the first punch, though. I know you want everyone to think you're as dewy-eyed and innocent as a newborn lamb."

"She's three hundred pounds! One punch and I'll be dead!"

"That big, huh? What's a girl like that doing in eighth grade?"

"Nothing good, I tell you," said Amy. "She's been held back a couple times. All the social promotion in the world couldn't keep this girl from failing."

"Why's she mad at you?"

Amy rubbed her nose and looked out the window at the cold pine trees around the parking lot.

"I promised a TV to her. That one you dropped."

"Really? Now I feel like it's my fault. Come on."

Tony got out of the station wagon and swung the back gate wide open. He looked left and right, then pulled carpet and a plastic cover off the cargo floor. Around the spare tire lay an assortment of weapons.

Amy gasped. "What are you doing with all these?"

"Protecting myself. It's a thing, you know, since I'm my own favorite person in the whole world."

"Is that a gun? You're only sixteen! You can't have a gun. Where do you think you are--the East side of Salinas?"

Tony smirked. "You're only fourteen. What do you know about Salinas?"

Amy shook her head. "A gun, Tony?"

The teenage boy held up the snub-nosed revolver. "It's only a .38. You can barely kill someone with this. You'd probably hurt them a lot worse if you chucked it at them instead of pulling the trigger."

"I don't think that's true."

"Well, if you don't want to use a gun--which is loaded with blanks by the way--then I have other problem-solvers." He set the gun on the tire and held up a succession of weapons, starting with a switch-blade, an expandable baton, brass knuckles, a strange-looking wooden bat, a huge cherry bomb, and finally a can of aerosol deodorant.

"That's nice," said Amy. "At least I won't have B.O. while I'm beaten to a pulp."

Tony pulled a disposable lighter from his pocket and pointed the deodorant can away from the car. He flicked the lighter, pressed down on the deodorant toggle, and a gout of flame burst from the nozzle.

Amy jumped back from the sudden flash of heat. "Good gravy!"

"Exactly," said Tony. "Only old-school aerosol stuff can do that. I've got a supplier."

"Thanks for the kind thoughts, but I just want to keep all my teeth. I don't want to see my name in the papers or cause an international incident. Taking a weapon to school could make all my problems worse."

"It's just deodorant," said Tony, and sprayed under his arms. "Not very good deodorant, but deodorant."

"Sorry."

Tony shook his head. "Brave girl. I admire your principles. Stop! Don't even think about making that joke." Tony rummaged through the hidden area and held up a pair of black leather gloves. "This is more your style. Silent and deadly."

"Gloves? What are those good for?"

"Quite a bit," said Tony, and tossed them to Amy.

She caught the gloves at her chest, but the unexpected heaviness almost caused her to drop them to the asphalt.

"Whoa! These weigh a ton!"

"Gloves for cops," said Tony. "That's a girl cop size. Designed to put the beat down on degenerates like you and me. Lined with lead on the back and knuckles to make your punches hit hard, and Kevlar mesh on the palms to stop knives. Got them in a trade. The good thing is, they're not illegal and won't get you in trouble."

Amy slid the gloves over her hands. The black leather felt good and weighty on her fingers, like she could hit a concrete wall and just walk away.

"We shouldn't be talking about all this nasty stuff," she said. "Let's go see Lucia."

Tony laughed and closed the car door..

"Oh, Amy. Just like a girl-—always practical."

He put an arm around her and they walked through the blowing mist toward the hospital.

AMY SPENT a few minutes with Lucia, who had been taken off the strongest drugs and was talking just like her old self, then rode down the hill with Tony to school. Amy signed in at the office and then went to second period English.

She knew M.K. would be looking for her between class periods, so when the bell rang she sprinted upstairs to the library, hid out there until the bell rang, and then snuck down the hall to science class. Mr. Gomez was peeved at her tardiness, but she could handle peeved.

Helen tossed a folded note at her when Gomez had his back turned.

I'VE GOT AN IDEA, said the scribbled pencil on the creased paper.

When the bell rang to end class, Amy stayed in the room and huddled together with Helen.

"Did you fix things with M.K.?"

Amy brushed back a strand of blonde hair. "Not yet. I've been avoiding that elephant."

"Her seventh grade spies are everywhere, so don't expect it to last. You should probably do something."

Amy pulled the leather gloves from the waistband of her uniform skirt.

"Tony gave me these," she said. "They're cop gloves. Maybe I can ambush her, give the cow a black eye or two."

"Have you been watching too much television? She'll crush you like a dinner roll. Her body is so massive and the nerves so spread out, it's like throwing rocks at an aircraft carrier. Even if you do hit her first, she won't feel a thing until you're on the floor of the girl's bathroom, probably missing a few teeth."

"Thanks for that mental image," said Amy. "You're such a great friend."

"And the smartest one you have. But enough about me––I've got an idea to keep you from losing your pearly whites or any other body parts."

"Great. I'm very attached to them."

The room began to fill with students for the next class. Amy grabbed Helen's sleeve and pulled her toward the door.

"Come on."

"What about my idea?"

"Let's stand in front of the office and you can tell me. M.K. won't kill me in front of the office. I hope."

The two girls pushed through the rowdy hallway filled with banging lockers and hooting middle-schoolers.

"Okay," said Helen. "M.K. likes video games, right?"

"Doesn't everybody? I already told you I don't have any good ones to trade."

"So you need to re-stock," said Helen. "In homeroom, Calcetti and his buddies were talking about this rich kid they knew, some friend of Calcetti's cousin. They were over at his house last night, and the rich kid has a Super Nintendo."

"I can get one of those at Circuit City. Besides, M.K. already has one."

They stopped in front of the glass windows of the office. Helen glanced left and right, then leaned close.

"This kid has a gold one," she whispered.

"Why are you whispering? I've got a pink one with flowers on it. You helped me paint it, remember?"

"No, it's really gold, the metal and everything. Calcetti said he felt how heavy it was. This rich kid's dad works for Nintendo or something, and it's like the only gold one ever made. The rich kid even showed Calcetti a photo of him holding up the thing with a bunch of Japanese guys in suits."

"Where's the rich kid live?"

"Down in the Highlands, right on the ocean," said Helen. "The big house in the curve, where they're doing all the construction."

"Are you sure?"

Helen nodded. "That's what Calcetti said."

Amy frowned, and pulled a Chapstick from the pocket of her uniform blazer. She rubbed it along her lips and glanced up and down the hallway. Back and forth, left and right.

"All right," she said. "A gold Super Nintendo should keep M.K. off my back. But I have to look at the place first."

"Yeah, of course. You wanna do it after school? I can go with you."

Amy shook her head. "Don't worry about it."

She ducked into a nearby girl's bathroom and did jumping jacks until she was flushed and her uniform blouse soaked with sweat, and then told the school nurse she had stomach cramps. The nurse made her lie down in the medical room for half an hour and sent her back to class. Amy went straight to the girl's bathroom, did jumping jacks, and reported to the office with a fever. After a few rounds of this, the nurse gave in and drove Amy up the hill to the hospital herself.

AMY HAD succeeded in keeping her cute and straight nose perfectly cute and perfectly straight, exactly the way she liked it, and her blue eyes from turning black and blue by Mary Katherine's sledgehammer fists. Tomorrow was another day, though, and she needed the most precious of all treasures to placate the most enraged of all eighth graders. It wasn't like she could just heave any old thing at M.K. and expect her to be happy, even if it was valuable. M.K. had only two hobbies: playing video games and punching middle-schoolers in the face. Amy wanted no part of the latter.

After the doctor had pronounced her a perfectly fine fourteen-year-old, Amy escaped from the emergency room and Nurse Nelson's watchful eye by pleading to stay with her foster mother for the rest of the day. Nurse Nelson was not a kind woman, but luckily happened to be the kind of nurse who hates sick people and hanging about hospitals. The reason she worked at the school was because she very rarely saw any sick people at all, only schoolchildren who made up stories about stomach cramps or a fever. She saw no reason to argue, and in fact left the hospital at a rapid jog due to the dizzying effect of the smell of alcohol disinfectant.

Lucia was sitting up when Amy came to her room.

"There you are, Amy. Is school out already?"

Amy shrugged. "The nurse gave me a note."

Lucia's hug was longer and tighter than normal. When Amy pulled away, Lucia's eyes were wet.

"Stay with me today," she said. "When you left this morning, I felt like I'd never see you again."

Tony stood up from beside the bed. "Don't be silly, Lucia! The doctor said you're getting better and better."

"Right," said Amy.

Lucia shook her head. "It's not about me, Amy. It's about you."

Amy smiled and hugged her foster mother again. "Don't worry. I'm fourteen and I can take care of myself."

Lucia sighed and leaned back in her bed. A pine branch scraped across the window, and everyone stared out at the trees in the mist.

"I know you're fourteen," said Lucia, still looking outside. "But there's a black cloud coming, darling. A cloud I can't see through."

Tony chuckled. "Don't be so dramatic. Everything's fine."

Lucia turned her head away from the window. "Son, could you get me a cup of water?"

"Sure thing."

Once Tony left the room, Lucia's expression changed. Her eyes turned sharp as she stared at Amy and the muscles in her jaw clenched. There was no fear, only a grim determination.

"Amy, I want to tell you something very important."

"What's going on, Lucia?"

"Life is going on, Amy; life, and old age. I want you to promise to forget about me."

"Don't talk like that! You're my mom!"

Lucia shook her head. "That's not what I mean. Amy, the world is full of regular people like me, and brilliant, white-burning stars like you. A smart and pretty girl like you is going to have a massive opportunity land in her lap sooner than you think. No, just let me talk. It might be tomorrow or it might be two years from now, but when that thing happens, don't look back. Don't let me slow down your dreams."

"Lucia, I have no idea what you're talking about."

"It's okay if you don't understand it. Just don't forget it."

Amy had lunch in the hospital cafeteria, and rode home with Tony when he showed up after school. She tried to push Lucia's strange comments out of her mind, and guessed it was just the stress of the heart attack and being in a hospital.

"Can you drive me down the coast before dinner?"

Tony slowed the car to a stop at a red light and glanced at her. "What for?"

"It's a birthday party," said Amy. "For one of my friends."

Tony laughed. "Girl, you don't know anybody down the coast. You're going to steal something."

Amy batted her eyes. "How could I do a thing like that? I'm only fourteen. I don't know peas from carrots."

"I ain't heard lies that big since the last time I fished off the wharf," said Tony. "Well, okay. Just watch yourself and don't do anything stupid."

Amy squealed. She leaned over from the passenger seat and kissed him on the cheek. "You're the greatest!"

Tony sighed. "The whoppers just keep on coming ..."

Back home, Amy dashed to her room and emptied out her drawers searching for a good outfit. She tossed blouses, skirts, dresses, sweaters, slacks, and socks over her shoulder like a deranged pack rat.

"Too young, too young, too old, too boring, too trampy, too itchy, too yesterday, too high school ..."

She finally settled on a short skirt of dark brown corduroy, a tan, button-up blouse, white knee socks, and a brown beret. Into a knapsack went a brown sash covered with merit badges, a bottle of water, a sandwich, a gray blanket, a penlight with red cellophane taped over the end, and a pair of binoculars.

Amy walked a couple of blocks to the grocery on Lighthouse and bought a box of Nerds. She poured the colored rocks into her mouth and dialed Robbie Calcetti's number on the pay phone outside. His mother answered.

"Hello?"

Amy turned the charm level in her voice up to eleven.

"Hello, Mrs. Calcetti. Could I speak to Robbie, please? It's about homework."

"May I ask who's calling?"

"Amy Armstrong."

"One moment. Robert!"

After a long pause, three heavy thumps vibrated in the receiver against Amy's ear.

"Yeah, whaddya want?"

"Robert, it's a girl. Be polite!" came the muffled voice of Mrs. Calcetti.

"Sorry," he said. The phone rustled and the teenager's voice came through clearly. "Whaddya want ... please?"

"Robbie, this is Amy. I heard you went to a party last night."

"So?"

"A dear, close friend of mine wanted the name of the birthday boy."

"Why should I tell you?"

"Because I'll give you a bunch of comics. I've got a whole stash from my brother."

"Even Namor the Submariner?"

"The whole series," said Amy.

Robert sniffed. "If you're stupid enough to give away comics, I'll take 'em. The kid's name is Frankie Yamagashi. He lives in the Highlands, across the road from that hotel in the curve, whatever it's called."

"I know. Thanks, Robbie."

"Wait! What about the comics?"

"Keep your pants on. I'll bring 'em tomorrow."

Amy hung up the phone and walked home.

SOUTH OF CARMEL the mountains come straight to the sea.

This is not a beachfront paradise. This is not a place where Nature whispers that she loves you. This is a place of gray rocks older than mankind, rock soaked black in the surf and made razor-sharp by the wind. This is a place where experienced swimmers drown in riptides, divers tangle in the thick seaweed, and stones cut your feet to shreds on the way to the beach. This is a place to lose your way in the midnight fog and stumble off a cliff. This is the dark, wintery soul of a state that has no winter. Even on the best days full of sunshine when the water is sapphire and you can see twenty miles down the coast to the lighthouse, the mountains and rocks and sea are still there, waiting for the fog to come back and your mistake to happen. Sharp and tough-barked pines cling to the mountains next to the sea, and between these trees are houses.

Amy didn't care about all that crap; she just wanted a Super Nintendo made of pure gold.

Tony had dropped her off a half mile north of the place on Highway 1, and she walked the rest of the way. He'd said he'd pick her up at ten.

A dozen pickups and white vans were parked along the side of the road near the house. Through the fence Amy saw a two-story mansion of gray stone and huge windows facing the ocean. A platoon of workers hammered on a skeleton of fresh wood next to the house--someone had obviously decided that the obscene amount of square footage in the place wasn't obscene enough. Amy squinted through the pines and guessed there were two dozen rooms inside. She had no problem stealing from fat cats, but more rooms meant security systems, or guards.

Amy crossed Highway 1 and climbed the rocky, pine-covered slope of the opposite side. She found a comfortable little niche on the shadowy side of a boulder, pulled out her blanket and binoculars, and settled in for a long wait.

Around four-thirty the construction crew left all at once with a burst of tired but jovial Spanish and joined the other cars speeding up the highway toward

Monterey. The wrought iron gate across the driveway clanked and opened with a steady, motorized hum, and a black Mercedes drove out, an Asian woman behind the wheel and a teenage boy in the back seat.

Time crept by slowly, but Amy was good at waiting. Patience and a cute nose were the best qualities of any girl, Tony always said. Knowing the girls he'd dated, Amy didn't believe a word.

A large orange tabby stopped at the white-painted fog line at the edge of the road. He looked left and right, and then slunk across the road toward the house with his tail low to the ground. The sun dipped behind the clouds in the west and changed the sky to brilliant orange and red. Lights came on in the other houses but Frankie's stayed dark.

A white pickup with the gold badge of the Monterey County Sheriff's Office slowly drove by.

Amy hurriedly kicked off the blanket and pulled her beret lower on her head. She arranged the sash covered with patches over her shoulder and pointed the binoculars at the cedar and pine trees across the road.

Gravel crunched as the white pickup pulled into the tiny parking area in front of the house. A tanned deputy in forest-green pants and a tan shirt got out and walked across the road, the leather of his gun belt squeaking with each step.

"Hey there, little girl," he said.

Amy smiled. "Hello, officer!"

"Are you okay up there? Do you need any help?"

"Actually I do. Have you seen any condors around here? I need one more bird for my merit badge."

The deputy laughed. "A condor? You have to go fifty miles down the coast to see one of those. How about I give you a ride home? It's getting dark."

Amy cringed inside, but kept up her smile. The cop was going to put her in a bind.

"I don't need a ride, officer! I can walk."

The deputy glanced across the highway at the half-dozen cliffside houses.

"Where do you live?"

Amy started to groan in frustration, but turned the sound into a giggle.

"Frankie Yamagashi's house right there," she said. "I'm his cousin."

The deputy looked her up and down for a moment. At last he nodded.

"All right," he said. "Don't stay out here too long, and be careful when you cross the road."

"I promise!"

The deputy got back in his pickup and pulled out with a pop of gravel. Amy waited until his brake lights disappeared around the bend, then stuffed everything into her knapsack and scampered down the rocks. She hid behind a tree until a quiet gap appeared in the traffic, and then dashed across the road to a clump of cinnamon-barked manzanita bushes. Covering her face from the sharp branches, Amy crawled through the shrubbery until she found a dark space next to the redwood fence safe from passing headlights.

She relaxed among the tea leaf and pine smell of the manzanita, and went over her options. The deputy would be back, and he'd forced Amy to give up Frankie's name. She hoped he wasn't good police; the kind who'd knock on doors and scope out her story. If a one-of-a-kind game console disappeared from the Yamagashi house, that little blonde Girl Scout with the binoculars would be front and center for any questions.

Amy sighed. This is what happened when you did anything at the last minute. If she walked away, Mary Katherine would break her nose. If she got caught, she could be sent to a group home or another foster family. If she snatched the gold console and gave it to M.K., she'd just be another slave to the giant teenager, who'd threaten to tell the cops.

Ideally she'd have time to case the house, find the location of the console, and maybe leave another gold-painted SNES as a decoy. She'd make friends with this kid Frankie, find out the family travel patterns, and maybe wait for a weekend or a vacation.

But sometimes you had to suck it up and put on the big girl panties, and it looked like this was one of those "sometimes." Amy thought she could handle any blackmail Mary Katherine threw her way. She might even have time to double-cross her or steal the console back before Frankie noticed it was missing.

Amy stuck her hands into the cop gloves and felt the bottom of the redwood fence for a loose board or gap. Twenty feet along the weather-beaten fence she found a depression in the earth and a wobbly board, probably where that orange cat slipped through. Amy checked but it was too narrow to squeeze through even for her slender body.

She stuffed the Brownie sash into her knapsack and pulled a pair of black jeans over her legs, then tied her blonde hair into a ponytail, pinned it up with a barrette, and covered it with the brown beret.

Amy stood up carefully in the thick shrubbery, listening after every snap of a twig for a sudden bark or a footstep. She stretched her arms, hopped up, and felt barbed wire at the top of the tall redwood fence. The sharp prongs didn't penetrate her leather gloves, luckily. Amy folded the wool blanket along its length about six times, and then jumped up with her arms extended to lay it over the top of the fence. She still hadn't heard anything suspicious from inside, so leapt up and pulled herself over the top, using the layers of the blanket as protection against the barbed wire.

The slim teenager dropped behind a lilac bush. She pulled her blanket off the fence and squatted in the dark, watching and waiting.

At the bottom of a slope covered in pine trees, twilight framed the house against a gray ocean. The deep bass and rumble of waves crashing on the rocks was much louder than out on the street, and the moist earth beneath Amy's feet seemed to vibrate with each regular, unending boom. A brick path wound through the trees, and the air was full of the smell of flowers and pine needles. Apart from the glow of walkway lights and a spotlight at the main door, the majestic house lay dark and silent.

Amy scanned the entire area with her binoculars. A security camera swiveled maliciously above the double red doors of the main entrance. Amy spotted other cameras at the corners of the house.

After ten minutes, nothing had changed. Amy searched the ground around her feet, and then tossed a rock at the main entrance. The pebble cracked on the sidewalk and bounced away. Amy hit the red door on her third try. Still no response. She crept through the trees and threw a handful of tiny stones at the closest window, one after the other. Nothing.

Amy waited in the shadow of a big cedar and thought over the problem. The security cameras at each side of the house panned back and forth, but as they swept away from Amy and toward the ocean, created a blind spot around the wooden skeleton of the new construction. Another camera should have covered that area, and must have been removed while the work was going on. Amy waited until the cameras rotated back to the sea, then sprinted across the garden and into the building site.

She crouched with her back to a concrete wall waiting for a yell or footsteps, but heard only the creak of pine branches lifting in the breeze and the rumble of the ocean.

Bare plywood covered the floor of the addition, dotted with scraps of wood and a thin blanket of sawdust. The woody, moist smell of fresh-cut lumber tickled Amy's nose, and above her head, the dark rafters were framed against a purple sky.

Amy felt around the wall and touched the hinges of a door. The knob turned freely but the door wouldn't budge, even with Amy's shoulder and all her weight against it. Something had jammed it in place, intentionally or otherwise. There was no sign of a keyhole and the wooden door sounded hollow against a faint knock of Amy's knuckles, so she guessed it was jammed for security.

A pigtail was always useful on jobs because it was basically a tiny crowbar. Amy took one from her knapsack and slid the flat end beneath the half-inch gap in the bottom of the door and the kicker plate. The pigtail knocked against something a few inches from the door jamb. Amy started from the other side and worked the pigtail back and forth until the thing popped away and the door swung freely. She pushed the door and inside on the linoleum floor lay a rough-cut wedge of wood––a cheap doorstop. Amy crept inside, shut the door, and put the wedge back in place.

Boxes of ceramic tile and construction tools were stacked around the dark room, and it was full of the chalky smell of drywall. Vertical smears of spackle marked the unpainted walls. Amy moved through the room at a crouch and avoided the windows crossed with blue painter's tape.

A clear plastic curtain blocked passage into the main house. Nearby, a sign in flowery letters proclaimed, "Please Wear Shoe Covers," and pointed to a wicker basket.

"Don't mind if I do," Amy murmured.

She took a pair of the white cotton sheaths from the basket and slipped them over her shoes. Amy slowly pushed through the plastic and gasped in shock.

She'd been through a mansion or two in the last few years, but nothing like this. Huge paintings of cowboys and Western landscapes covered the walls, and the ceiling glowed from hidden lights at the cornices. The floor was waxed hardwood, and overstuffed leather furniture waited around the room on fluffy rugs. Across the room and to the left were dark wooden doors and a mahogany staircase. To the right lay the foyer and the red doors of the main entrance.

Nothing but the regular tick of a clock broke the silence, not even the high-pitched whine of a television. In Amy's experience, the only people left in a dark house would either be sleeping or watching television.

Amy scanned the room for cameras, saw none, and then crept through the rooms in the first floor. A house like this probably had a playroom for video games, foosball, pool--a space for kids to hang out. She could have asked Calcetti where the gold SNES was, but that was like yelling "I WANT TO STEAL IT" over the public broadcast system.

Rich places like this were more like a museum or a house on another planet. They could afford a maid, a good one who actually cleaned things. The rooms smelled of lavender and clean metal and leather, not like the places that normal people lived. Normal houses smelled like the people and things inside them, which meant pizza, ripe cantaloupe, cat urine, and bleach.

Amy found a kitchen, dining room, library, exercise room, office, sunroom, conservatory, garage, and several bathrooms on the first floor, but no playroom and no gold Super Nintendo.

She worked her way carefully up mahogany steps to the second floor and poked her head into luxuriously appointed bedrooms filled with more paintings and huge beds covered in puffy down comforters.

The fourth door was ajar. Amy listened for a moment, then pushed it open a bit with her gloved finger. Through the crack she saw a bed covered with a rumpled Spiderman blanket and a *Dumb & Dumber* movie poster on the wall.

"Bingo," she said, and crept inside.

G.I. Joes and a spray of tiny plastic weapons covered the red carpet as if Little Big Horn had broken out at the Hasbro factory. Posters of Schwarzenegger and the Lethal Weapon series covered the walls. A bookshelf was loaded down with a battalion of Transformers in the midst of robotic conflict; some hanging by white string, plastic guns extended, and others sprawled in the agony of defeat. The room was filled with the disgusting stench of a teenage boy: Cool Ranch Doritos, model glue, and body odor.

A neon blue leather sofa stood at the foot of the bed and faced a huge, thirty-two inch television in a black entertainment center. Purple and lilac Super Nintendo controllers lay on the carpet in a tangle of wires. Amy followed the trail of cords to a glass cabinet beside the television, where a golden, blocky treasure reflected the crimson shine from her flashlight.

"Double Bingo!"

Amy opened the glass door. She unplugged the power, video, and all four controllers from the gleaming Super Nintendo, and then pulled it off the shelf.

"Yowza," she whispered, and set the console on the carpet.

It weighed a ton and Amy was glad she had the cop gloves to protect her fingers. She wondered if the thing would rip through the bottom of her knapsack. The best thing would be to hide it inside the knapsack and carry everything in her arms. It wouldn't be easy, but nothing about today had been easy.

A swish came from outside the room and Amy flattened against the side of the bookshelf. The door creaked open and the large orange tabby padded inside, his green eyes wide and striped tail held straight up. The cat trotted past the bed and went straight to the gold Super Nintendo on the carpet. He bent down to sniff it.

It was just a cat. Amy let out a loud sigh, and released all her nervous, clenched-up tension.

The cat sprang three feet straight up and landed in the tangle of controller cords. It hissed and spat as it squirmed in the cables for a few seconds, causing Amy to giggle.

The cat freed himself from the cords with a frantic somersault, and bared his teeth at the laughing girl.

"What's so funny?" said the cat.

3

The cat had spoken in a man's voice with a strange, unfamiliar accent. Amy glanced at the television-- still off--and looked around for a clock radio that had probably just switched on.

The orange tabby walked up to the golden Super Nintendo and sat on top of it. His huge green eyes watched Amy and the tip of his tail switched back and forth.

"Are you deaf? I asked you a question," said the cat.

Amy could have sworn she'd seen the pink lips move. She knelt over the orange-striped feline.

"Must be some kind of Japanese toy," she murmured. "Man, this kid is loaded."

The cat sniffed.

"I'm not a toy, stupid girl, but it doesn't matter. You've only got five seconds."

"Five seconds?"

The cat shook his head. "I swear there's an echo in here."

The air crackled with heat and the smell of burnt toast. Blue lightning popped around Amy and formed a dome of energy with the cat at the center. Sparks and white flame cut through the purple sofa and back wall and curved through the television, which exploded in a shower of glass and flame.

Amy was a sharp and practical girl and not the type who screamed at the sight of a Neiman-Marcus catalog, or any catalog for that matter. When the room disappeared in a whirl of oily smoke and was replaced by a vast panorama of stars, spinning planets, flashing comets, and nebulae, however, it was quite reasonable for her to have a reaction.

"Good gravy," she whispered.

A freezing pain spread through her body. Everything––the circle of carpet, the orange cat, the stars, Amy's hands and fingers––faded to white. All that was, was not, and all that was not still wasn't anything.

Amy blinked sleepily at the red carpet pressing roughly on her cheek. Could she have changed her perfectly respectable standing position with very little slouch for a less dignified position of lying on her face? She realized this was the case.

Something jabbed her in the chin. Amy raised her head and a tiny plastic rifle fell to the carpet. She sat up and brushed a battalion's worth of miniature weapons from her blouse and jeans.

She was surrounded on all sides by a white, brilliant nothingness, not counting the circle of carpet below her. The strange blue lightning or welder's arc or whatever it was had cut through every single object in what she guessed was a perfect dome ten foot in diameter. This included a corner of the purple sofa, part of the bookshelf and wall behind it, and the left side of the television. Tendrils of smoke curled up from the back of the sliced but still upright cathode tube.

Amy crawled forward to get a better look, but the floor below her knees rocked and crackled. Like a house of cards, the television and all the strangely cut objects crashed to the carpet or tumbled to the glowing white floor with a deafening clang.

At least, it looked like a floor. Amy crawled unsteadily to the edge of the carpet and banged her metal pigtail tool on the white surface. It sounded like metal; not steel, but maybe aluminum. She knelt on the edge and carefully stepped off. The floor felt sturdy like aluminum, but was inscrutably white.

Amy walked around the circle of carpet and the broken objects. The carpet had rocked back and forth because it lay on top of a half foot of wood, electrical wire, and broken drywall. A perfect ten foot sphere had been taken from the house, including part of the ceiling from the room below.

Either she was dreaming or someone had gone to a lot of trouble to play a prank. It was probably meant for that Frankie kid, and she'd triggered the mechanism instead of him. But it was too good, too real, and most importantly for a joke--nobody was laughing. Amy scanned the walls for windows or mirrors, but nothing broke the featureless, glowing whiteness around her.

She sat on the red carpet and had a picnic with the rest of the food from her backpack. Sometimes she could wake herself up from a bad dream by just wanting to wake up. Amy squeezed her eyes shut and "wanted" really hard, but nothing happened. She raised her water bottle and squeezed the last drops into her mouth with a crackle of plastic. Maybe she'd been hit by a car. All important places had a waiting room--why not heaven?

A click and whir came from above her head. Amy looked up to see four tentacles spurt from the ceiling. Each was as thick as her forearm and covered in silver, articulated plates. A large, multifaceted sapphire adorned the tip of one tentacle, but the others ended in three gleaming talons.

A squealing, clattering yowl came from the ceiling, like a cat in steel garbage can rolling down a gravel driveway. An artificial voice began to speak.

"Props 386749001--"

The strange voice continued to read out numbers for a few seconds, giving Amy time to pull out her can of Mace. Whoever was pulling this stupid prank wouldn't be laughing with a face full of Mace.

"--0991. Primary valuable secured by Operator Badge SF063. Secondary valuable scan begin."

Blue light shot from the sapphire and waved like a hyperactive flashlight over the carpet, broken material, and Amy.

"Secondary valuables identified."

The clawed arms sifted through the remains of the bookshelf and grabbed a pair of novels. Another arm plucked a Super Nintendo controller from the carpet. The tentacles disappeared into the ceiling with the objects, and then sped down to Amy.

She sprayed half a second's worth of Mace at the gleaming claws before one of them ripped it out of her hands. The straps of her backpack jerked and Amy felt herself being lifted into the air.

"Let me go!"

She coughed, trying not to breathe the Mace, then slipped out of the straps and landed on her feet on the carpet. Above her head the tentacles rooted through her backpack.

"Get out of my stuff, you creep!"

The tentacles pulled out the Brownie sash and dropped the backpack, which landed with a heavy thunk in front of Amy. The clawed tentacles disappeared through a port in the ceiling with the merit badge sash, and left a single, sapphire-tipped tentacle hovering over Amy's head.

"Biomat scan initiated," said the trash-can voice. "Biomat detected. Event sound waves analyzed. Spoken language detected. Query: Are you sentient?"

"Stop playing around, you idiots," yelled Amy. "I'm going to call the police!"

"That response is invalid. Query: Are you sentient?"

"Yes!"

"Cognitive verify: What is the frequency of the spin-flip transition of a hydrogen atom?"

"I'm not even in high school! How should I know that?"

A sound like tin cans banging together came from the ceiling. Amy couldn't decide if it was a problem with the speaker system or the laughter of an insane computer.

"All right," said the voice. "I'll give you an easy one. Who won the Galactic Cup in 3316?"

"The Galactic Cup? Are you serious?"

"I know, it's really too easy," said the artificial voice. "But I need your answer."

"At least give me some choices!"

"Negative. Multiple answer questions are for the sentience-challenged."

Amy sighed. "Galactic Cup. I don't know ... Alpha Centauri?"

The tin can sound vibrated the room and the single tentacle waved back and forth.

"I can't breathe ... Alpha ... Centauri ... it's too hilarious. Sentient scan ended. No intelligent life detected. Gamma radiation cleansing in ten seconds."

The tentacle whisked up through the ports in the ceiling, and the white walls in the room deepened to red.

"Wait! I didn't mean that! I meant, uh, Procyon!"

Amy scanned the featureless room for a means of escape. She took off a glove and dashed along the walls, using her bare fingers to feel for gaps or notches in the smooth surface.

"Five seconds until gamma cleansing."

The room shook and tilted wildly, throwing everything into the air. Amy slid to the bottom of the rectangular space and dodged the wood, carpet, and other debris that crashed around her. The air in the room felt warmer and hummed with power.

"This isn't funny anymore!"

Amy leaned against a nearby surface. Blue lines sparkled to life where the bare skin of her palm touched the wall, and formed the outline of a rectangle two foot by one foot. The lines popped and a tiny door swung inside, bringing a gust of air that smelled of sulfur and grease.

Amy was a thin girl and had no problem diving head-first through the dark and narrow opening, especially when it seemed she was about to be roasted alive. She reached back into the room and grabbed her backpack just as the small door slammed shut and a crackling roar came from the other side.

The space she found herself in was cramped and dark. Amy tried to sit up, and banged her head on a low ceiling.

"Flying forks and fanny packs," she hissed, rubbing the top of her head.

She took out the pen light with red cellophane taped over the end. The crimson-colored light reflected off the flat gray walls of a shaft that went on for thirty or forty feet. In the dust Amy saw the paw prints of a cat and long, shiny scratches, as if a heavy weight were being dragged along the metal.

"That little thief! He's got my Super Nintendo."

Amy squirmed forward on her elbows and knees. The metal walls narrowed drastically after a point, and she was forced to shove the backpack ahead of her and turn sideways, although she couldn't bend her knees and had to pull herself forward with one arm. The tunnel angled to the left, and after twenty more feet the paw prints led straight to a featureless white wall.

No locks, keypads, or handles showed anywhere. Remembering what had happened before, Amy pressed her bare palm to the white surface. A neon maze of blue lines spread from her hand, creating a door that slid up. Dim light and a clanking, rumbling sound poured inside.

Amy squeezed sideways out of the doorway, stopping for a second as the metal button at the front of her Levis caught on the edge. She sucked in her stomach and worked her hips back and forth, at last pushing against the outside wall and yanking her waist free.

The floor outside was gray and felt slightly sticky and rough at the same time, like tacky sandpaper. A faint aroma of rotten eggs mixed with the clean smell of machine oil and a strange animal musk. The auditory soup of a busy city was stirring somewhere nearby, with a thousand different events and conversations taking place at the same time.

Amy got to her feet and almost fell down again in shock. If there hadn't been a metal cable at waist level that's exactly what would have happened, although she would have tumbled over the edge and fallen five hundred feet.

"Oh, brother," she breathed.

Before her lay an impossible city. It was a mishmash of objects, materials, and construction styles, as if a thousand cultures and time periods had been thrown together. The stone walls of medieval keep stood shoulder-to-shoulder with the red bricks of American Federalist houses and the peaked roofs and jade tiles of Japanese dwellings. Rickety shacks made from planks of gray wood and covered in tar paper faced Italianate mansions, at least fragments of them. The lack of consistency extended throughout the city, and many of the buildings were a mixture of materials and objects, reinforced by tall silver poles at each corner. The vertical bow of a battleship pointed to the sky, with doors and windows hacked into the gray metal. A treehouse covered the branches of a giant oak, and stood next to the red and yellow fabric of a Mongolian yurt. Fragments of New York brownstones rose several stories, the silver poles at each corner their only obvious support.

Under a variety of streetlights strolled a menagerie of cats and dogs. Amy searched the distant specks of color as they wandered over dirt lanes, brick alleys, and asphalt thoroughfares, but saw nothing bigger than a terrier. A few of the dogs pulled small wagons piled high with boxes of goods. Amy guessed this was some kind of weird, fancy-pants zoo, but she couldn't see a single human being. Where were all the visitors?

A gigantic fan of metal rafters supported a dome over the city, all pointing to a glowing needle of a building at the center of everything. The bright, thread-like tower served as a light source and disappeared into mist at the uppermost heights of the dome. Vast terraces surrounded the perimeter of the city, like balconies around the atrium of the galaxy's largest Marriott. Each level of terrace was graduated––slightly wider at the lowest floor and as narrow as an Italian balcony at the highest, near the metal supports of the dome.

Amy counted five terraces between her and the dome. She looked down and fought back another wave of vertigo. Below her feet were another thirty or forty floors and a scattering of cats and dogs trotting along the terraces.

"Wake up, girl," Amy whispered. "Just wake up."

A flash caught Amy's eye a dozen levels below. A brown and white Corgi pulled a small wagon loaded down with a golden, rectangular object; the point of Amy's original mission.

"Well, I can't stand around all day, even in a dream."

Amy searched the terrace and found another line of paw prints and scrapes. She followed the faint trail along the curving balcony for a hundred feet or so, until it stopped at another of the narrow white doors. The prints of the cat continued for another twenty feet and disappeared into another door. The cat had bypassed at least a dozen doors before stopping at these two.

Amy sat down with an exasperated sigh. She leaned back against the brushed metal wall and stared at the vast urban conglomeration beyond the terrace. What did a cat want with a Super Nintendo? Why these doors and not the others? They didn't look any different. And why weren't the cats and dogs fighting like cats and dogs?

The door the cat had disappeared into whisked open and the orange tabby emerged. He scraped his back feet against the floor a few times to kick away something imaginary and filthy, then walked to the edge of the terrace all prim and proper, his tail held high. Amy watched as the cat sat on his hind legs and gazed over the city. The orange and yellow fur on his back shook with a giggle, one that turned into a full-blown peal of laughter; a very human and un-catlike sound.

"What's so funny?" Amy asked.

The cat jumped into the air, banged his head on the ceiling, and made an unfortunate somersault that ended with him hanging off the edge of the balcony, scrabbling desperately for a purchase with his front claws.

Amy jumped forward and pulled the cat to safety by the fur on the back of his neck. The orange tabby spat at her and backed away, ears flat and tail low.

"Don't touch me," he growled. "I don't like being touched!"

Amy pouted. "What a crabby kitty. Stop hissing or I'll smack you with a shoe."

The cat shook his head. "Only five seconds and you're threatening me with violence. I suppose that's normal for someone like you."

"Someone like me? I just saved your life! That's twelve feet to the next level, twenty-four if you bounced!"

"You're the one who scared me!"

Amy was surprised at how quickly she had become used to talking to a cat.

"Give me that gold Super Nintendo and we'll call it even," she said. "And don't even think about using that old cat trick of looking cute when you need something."

The cat blinked at her slowly with his green eyes.

"That particular prop is halfway through the city by now. Corgis make for the worst dinner companions and fastest delivery drivers."

"I want it back."

"You can't have it," said the cat. His jaw dropped and eyes widened. "Wait a minute! You're supposed to be dead!"

"I hope not. I've got a date with a game console."

The cat sniffed. "I could have sworn you didn't make it through the remat process. You certainly sprawled across that carpet like a dead human. Nope, definitely dead. I've been around the block a few times and you were as dead as a five-toed *poona* on his wedding night."

"I was sleeping. Did that ever cross your mind?"

The orange tabby licked a paw and gave the fur behind his ears a brisk swipe.

"Sleeping? Don't throw your strange technical terms at me. I'm not one of those operators who claim to know everything about humans. I suppose I'll add that to the list. One question: can you sleep without a head, and all that red goop everywhere? Most of the humans that have come back with me were missing a few parts, and definitely had lots of red goop. Can I also say you're very noisy creatures?"

Amy swallowed. "That's definitely not sleeping."

"Human biology is so boring," said the cat with a yawn. "Must have been why I slept through the class. How did you get out of the remat chamber? Those Service Employees guys are supposed to scan for secondary props and burn out the foreign biomat. Don't tell me they shut down the unit again." The cat bared his fangs in a grim smile. "Those union jokers; I remember the last time they went on strike. Nothing got cleaned for weeks. Nick brought back a French wardrobe with some idiot human inside. A team of dogs hauled that heavy thing almost to C Sector before he jumped out. Scared the poop out of everyone, I'll tell you that for free."

"Some tentacle with a blue eye talked to me and tried to cook me alive. I found a door and squeezed outside."

The cat gasped and held a paw over his nose. "But how? All portals are surface-coded by job and operator function. You're just some dumb human who wandered inside. With nothing about you on file, there's no way the portal should've worked! You should be monkey bacon right now!"

"I'm not lying. Watch this."

Amy touched the nearest white rectangle on the wall. Blue lines spread from her bare fingers and the bright door slid up with a swish, revealing a tunnel.

The orange cat leaned forward, his mouth open. "Impossible! That's private and for ... never mind."

"Don't ask me to explain it. I'm just dreaming in a made-up fantasy world."

"There's something very odd about you," said the cat. "First the not-being-dead thing, and now this door-opening thing. I need to do some serious thinking, but before that, it's lunch time. There's absolutely nothing to eat on Old Earth."

"What do you mean, Old Earth? Wait!" Amy pointed to the city beyond the terrace; the vast hodgepodge of castles and temples, cats and dogs, ships and shacks. "Tell me what this place is before you get some kibble."

The cat tilted his head and gazed at the city. "That's Junktown. It's the most magnificent pile of garbage in the galaxy."

"Why were you laughing at it?"

"I wasn't laughing AT it. I was laughing BECAUSE of it. Junktown is the most amazing place I've ever been. It's the center of the largest, most impressive ship that will ever roam the stars; a ship commanded by the most intelligent and powerful being to draw breath. If the waveform of highs and lows in galactic history could be tracked, I can say without reservation that this is the highest point."

"What's the lowest point?"

The cat bared his fangs. "The birth of the inventor of SpaceBook, without a doubt."

"This is a spaceship?"

"I think I said that. Didn't I say that? I keep forgetting what tiny ears you monkeys have."

Amy hopped up and down. "I've always wanted to go into space! Show me a window or a porthole or something."

"The nearest observation deck is on the other side of Junktown," said the cat in a sour tone. "I'm not taking time out of my schedule so you can plaster your big nose across a window. It's all black and stuff, so use your imagination. Do you have one? Seriously, I'm just checking."

"But what kind of spaceship is this? What are all these animals doing here? Where are all the people?"

"Questions, questions, questions," said the cat. He walked away from Amy, his tail held high. "This is the largest robbery in the history of the universe."

4

Amy followed the cat along the terrace and through a three-foot-high door the cat opened with his paw. The walls of the square room brightened with light as the cat stepped inside. It was still too small for Amy's comfort, and she had to crawl inside and sit slightly sideways with her knees bent.

"Is this where you eat?"

"Don't be silly! This is an elevator."

The white doors slid shut and Amy felt her weight lift a bit. The doors became transparent and Amy watched levels of the terrace slide up as the elevator descended. An English bulldog waited at one level with a leather harness strapped to his body and a four-wheeled, red wagon behind him piled high with grinning plastic pumpkins.

"The largest robbery in the history of the universe," said Amy. "And you're stealing Halloween crap?"

"One cat's trash is another cat's treasure. I'll be honest––some operators aren't very good at props."

"Props?"

"Property Relocation Operations," said the cat. "'Props' for short. A job comes from the Lady and filters through the chain of command to the operator. We launch, find the prop target, and call for a return. The target gets transported, maybe with a few secondary items, and junkies take the leftovers to Junktown."

"Launching and returning? But I didn't see a spaceship or any kind of rocket."

"This isn't the dark ages! Remember the sphere of energy around you and the unfortunate not-dying part? That was a return, or a 'remat.' We launch the same way. It's called a 'demat.' Don't think I'm telling you because I care. I just don't like it when people use the wrong words."

"People? But you're not a person."

"Please. From the smell of things, I'm more of one than you are."

The levels crept upwards past the transparent door of the elevator. A dachshund waited patiently at one level, his green wagon empty.

"Let me get this straight," said Amy. "A talking cat teleports down to Earth from this spaceship, finds something to steal, and teleports back with plastic Jack-o-lanterns or a gold Super Nintendo?"

"Number one: I'm not a talking cat, and two: I'm just following orders. If the Lady wants a gold Super Nintendo, the Lady gets a gold Super Nintendo, even if I have to land in the ocean and get chased by Earth dogs for three days."

"Are there any other kind of dogs?"

"Don't get me started," said the cat.

The levels passed one by one, and Amy wondered if they'd ever reach the bottom.

"Why haven't I seen any people around?"

"The Lady thinks humans are boring, and it's easier for a cat or dog to sneak around places."

"It sounds like a whole lot of effort just to steal a few things."

The cat blinked his green eyes at Amy. "There's the pot calling the kettle black. You wanted to steal that golden blocky thing, too. Unless your name is Frank Yamagashi, the human who lived there. Are you a male or female? I can never tell which is which."

"I'm a girl!"

"Well, here I have a girl thief who is jealous of a much better thief."

"You destroyed that bedroom and probably the house! How is that a better thief?"

"Ah, well," said the cat. "What they don't know won't hurt them."

"I should stop eating so much cheese at dinner," said Amy. "I've had strange dreams before, but this takes the cake."

"Don't even joke about eating cheese. What is this 'dreams' you keep mumbling about? Is it a disease? Does it mean you're dying? That would make everything easier."

The transparent door changed back to white and whisked open. Amy crawled out to a wide hallway lined with paintings that ranged from bizarre Cubist work to Dutch masters. A number of cats and dogs were trotting along the hallway, and all stopped and stared as Amy got to her feet.

She followed the orange cat toward a buzz of conversation and scrape of ceramic tableware. The air smelled like vanilla mixed with fresh rubber. Expecting a cafeteria or restaurant, Amy walked through a doorway and stared at a room full of animals. Cats and dogs lay on cushions scattered around the room, each with a bowl of glowing blue beans nearby. On the far wall were a stack of bowls and a series of silver machines that looked like expensive coffee makers, but with more silver tubes than she remembered.

The conversations in the room halted completely, and all eyes focused on Amy.

The orange cat raised his voice. "Don't worry, it's just a delivery from my last job. You wouldn't want an old salt like me to starve to death, would you?"

"No," yelled a black-furred terrier. "We want you to hang yourself!"

The room burst into hoots and raucous laughter.

“Or jump off the tower,” yelled a black and white tuxedo cat.

The animals rolled on their cushions and squealed with mirth.

“Or tell the Lady to get stuffed,” shouted a high-pitched beagle.

The room turned deadly silent.

“I didn’t mean that,” said the beagle. “I was going to say ... he should get stuffed to death!”

The other animals looked away in disgust, and picked up the threads of their interrupted conversations. Murmurs and the clink of metal on ceramic filled the air again.

The orange tabby walked to a stack of bowls on the floor and pushed one below a strange ‘coffee’ machine. He pressed the clean white front of the machine and a stream of glowing beans poured into the bowl.

Amy bent down and sniffed the blue oblong shapes. “Smells like a new car.”

“Excuse me,” said the cat and pushed his bowl away from Amy. “It’s very rude to sniff someone’s Re-Carb, especially when he hasn’t eaten for a week. Feel free to get your own bowl, but it may or may not be incredibly poisonous to humans. Who can keep track of all the things that can kill such a silly species? Not me.”

“In that case, I’ll pass.”

The cat shook his head in disgust. He pushed the bowl into a corner of the room and lay on an empty cushion. Amy sat cross-legged on a pillow nearby.

“So, next in this dream or nightmare or whatever, you’re going to tell me you’re not really a cat, and these aren’t cats and dogs. You’re all a bunch of ancient aliens in disguise, stealing crazy things from Earth to make a super weapon that will destroy the universe.”

The cat scooped glowing beans into his mouth with a paw.

"That's a funny story," he said. "You're funny for a human. All the rest I've met are either throwing things at me or screaming about missing body parts. Do humans make money by telling funny stories? You'd be good at that."

"So you're alien cats and dogs? Not like it matters, because I'm basically talking to myself at this point."

The cat popped more of the beans into his mouth. "Aliens? You mean those human-eating things from the movies? Nobody eats humans around here, especially me. Even the thought makes me sick. If that weren't the case, I'd have bitten a few chunks out of you already--my stomach was growling louder than a platoon of schnauzers today."

"Not an alien like that. I mean from another planet."

"We're all from different planets: Tau Ceti, Gliese, Kapteyn," said the cat. "This isn't some backwoods flea circus from the galactic rim. Only the best and brightest are picked to work for the Lady. I admit we've got a few dozen Russian shorthairs that never do anything but wander around Junktown all day asking for a cheeseburger, but that's nepotism for you. And Russian shorthairs."

Amy watched as the cat finished the last of the glowing beans, then licked his paw and cleaned his face.

"That was good," he said. "I can probably go for a week on that."

"An alien moggie that eats poisonous glowing beans," said Amy. "I'd hate to see what comes out the other end."

The orange cat flattened his ears. "That's private!"

"I hope so."

The tabby curled up on the cushion and rested his head on his front paws.

"Now that I've got my energy back and it's obvious you aren't going to be dead or lose your body parts anytime soon, I suppose I should introduce myself. The name is Sunflower."

Amy giggled. "Strange name for a cat!"

"My parents were free-thinkers, and didn't follow the rules of normal cat society."

"Hippies?"

The cat blinked slowly. "If that's the human word for cats who live out of their transport vehicle and make money selling leather hats made in the back of that vehicle while high on catnip, then yes, they were hippies."

"Well, Mr. Sunflower, I'm Amy Armstrong."

The green eyes squinted up at her. "But you said you were a female. 'Amy' is a boy's name! In fact, it's my father's name. Do you even know what gender you are?"

"I already said I was a girl, and I haven't changed since then!"

A Jack Russell terrier that had been eating near-by poked his black nose into the matter.

"Hey, Sunflower," he said with a Midwestern American accent. "What year is this human from?"

The orange cat sniffed, and rested his chin back on the cushion. "O.E. 1995."

"There's your problem," said the Jack Russell. "Girls had boy names back then, and the other way, too. Skippy-dippy!"

"Thanks, Betsy," said Sunflower. "I remember now."

"So tell me," said Amy.

Sunflower sighed. "Old Earth humans gave their female children names like Alice, Linda, and Moneesha. These are obviously male names, but whatever. Humans like to coddle the females in any litter. They thought that by giving the females a different name, the female would stand out from the other humans. Strange names and unique spellings weren't enough, and as time passed, they stole names from the males in the litter. Frances, Terry, Billie––those were all male names that were given to females. Over the course of a few hundred years, females took over all the male names, so the males had to take what was left: unfashionable female names like Alice, Linda, and Moneesha. Now, in the year––what year is it, Betsy?"

"3317," barked the male terrier.

"In the year 3317, the trend is slowly rotating the other way. Happily, it's only a few social outliers who think it's fashionable to call a female Jessica."

Amy shook her head. "The year 3317? Everyone always said I had a good imagination. Maybe I should eat some of those glowing beans. You're supposed to wake up if you die in a dream, right?"

"That's exactly what happens," said Sunflower.

Betsy barked. "You don't want to do that. It would be bad. I take that back. It would be very, very, very, very, very, very––"

"Can it, you twit," growled Sunflower.

"Aww, don't be mean to Betsy," said Amy. She stuck out a hand to stroke his furry brown and white head, and then jerked it back when she realized it might not be polite.

"Betsy's not being nice," said Sunflower. "He just knows how much of a mess your body would make when it explodes everywhere."

The Jack Russell terrier wagged his tail.

"I see," said Amy.

The pale lilac glow of the ceiling in the cafeteria changed to red and the air filled with a buzzing sound like a massive swarm of hornets. All the animals including Sunflower and Betsy jumped off their cushions and ran pell-mell out of the room.

Amy dashed after the cat and terrier as they galloped down the corridor.

"A fire alarm?" she yelled. "Or alien attack? Is it battle stations?"

"Worse than that," shouted Betsy, his pink tongue lolling from his jaws. "Emergency inspection!"

The trio stopped at a corner to catch their breath.

"It's the Lady," said Sunflower. "She'll send me back to prison if I'm caught with an unregistered prop, especially a live one. I'm NOT going back to prison."

Betsy wagged his tail and stared at Amy. "Can't we just leave her?"

"Have some principles, dog! This is an inspection, not bingo at the old dog's home!"

"Sorry."

"Where's your cart?"

"Parked on level five," said Betsy. "But I don't want to get in trouble again. You're always getting me in trouble!"

"Too late for that," growled Sunflower. "Take us to the cart."

"Okay, but we can't use the elevators."

"To the emergex, then!"

Amy held out her palms in the flashing crimson light of the corridor. "Maybe I should just stay here. I don't want to cause a problem."

"At the risk of repeating myself––too late for that," said Sunflower. "You seem like a smart human who wants to continue not being dead, so come on!"

The orange tabby sprinted down the corridor and touched a panel with his paw. He darted inside an opening with the terrier and Amy on his tail. The blonde girl followed the cat up a narrow set of spiraling stairs on her hands and knees. Sunflower waited for Amy at the fifth landing and led her onto the terrace.

"Where's that silly dog?" hissed Sunflower. "If he ran off, I'm going to put milk in his water dish."

Amy felt the floor vibrate beneath her hands and heard a furious whir. Betsy galloped up pulling a large, four-wheeled cart, attached to the dog with a black harness and two silver poles.

"Climb in," said Sunflower.

"She looks too heavy," panted Betsy. "A hundred and sixty pounds, I bet."

Amy stamped her foot. "I'm a hundred and five!"

"Don't be silly," said Sunflower. "She's skinny and weak, and almost dog-size. You won't have a problem, but if you do, I'll be there to help."

Betsy laughed. "A cat pulling a transport cart? That's funny! You're funny!"

Amy lay on the scratched steel floor of the cart and Sunflower covered her with a white blanket. The cart jerked forward. Amy used her rucksack as a pillow and to keep the top of her head from hitting the front of the cart. She squeezed her knees to her chest and wrapped her arms around her shins, and was completely hidden by the blanket.

The cart turned and stopped. Amy heard the swoosh of doors closing, and everything became quiet.

"We're in the elevator," she heard Sunflower whisper.

"I know," said Betsy. "Why are you telling me that?"

"Quiet! I'm talking to the human!"

The cart creaked and leaned a bit to one side. Amy squealed as a substantial weight thumped onto her ribs.

"Sorry," came Sunflower's voice. "I have to ride on you for a minute."

"You're so heavy! How can you weigh that much?"

"See what I mean about cats?" murmured Betsy. "Always looking for a free ride."

"Keep it quiet, both of you. We're at street level."

The elevator bounced and stopped moving. Amy heard the door whisk open, and the cart jolted forward.

The buzzing alarm was gone. Amy heard the creak of Betsy's harness, the smooth rub of the wheels on the waxed floor, and the echoes of animal feet in the corridor.

The cart picked up speed and swerved through several corners. It stopped without warning and Amy was squished uncomfortably to the front of the cramped space. Sunflower dug his claws into her side to keep from flying away, and Amy had to bite a knuckle to keep from screaming.

"Sorry about the quick stop," whispered the cat. "Betsy tried to get around the queue, but there's another group of inspectors."

Amy heard a faint metallic voice; one that came closer each time the cart inched forward.

"Operator BL8519," said the voice. "What is your prop destination?"

Amy heard Betsy clearing his throat. “It’s not a prop,” said the Jack Russell terrier. “It’s junkmat for my place in town.”

Amy held her breath as she saw a blue light move over the blanket.

“Expose the junkmat,” said the metallic voice. “Extricate from the transport carriage, Operator SF063.”

Amy felt Sunflower’s weight shift slightly on her ribs.

“It’s just a load of rubbish,” said the cat. “Is that you, Tony? I thought I recognized that voice, even through the speech chopper.”

The metallic voice brightened. “Sunny! How are you doing?”

“Fantastic, now that I’ve heard from my favorite lady. Where have you been hiding all this time? I haven’t seen you for months.”

The machine voice giggled, or at least, made a thrashing sound that Amy hoped was a giggle.

“I haven’t been hiding anywhere, Sunny. I’ve been pulling double shifts since that space debris hit sector four.”

“We should have drinks sometime. I’ll give you a call.”

“Sure thing, Sunny. Oh--what about this transport? I’m getting foreign biomat readings.”

“It’s nothing to crinkle your beautiful little whiskers, Tony,” said Sunflower. “Betsy’s last prop exploded everywhere, and it’s just leftover cleaning agent. On my honor as a fellow classmate, it’s all safe.”

“Okay, Sunny, if you say so. Take care!”

The cart jolted forward and the blue light disappeared. Amy let out the breath she’d been holding.

Betsy picked up his speed to a trot and the wheels bumped and whirred.

"Looks like someone's got a date," Amy heard the terrier say.

Sunflower growled. His weight left Amy's ribs, much to her relief, and she heard the patter of soft paws beside the cart.

"Inspector Tony," Sunflower murmured. "I always hated that cat."

THE WHEELS shuddered and jolted over patchwork asphalt and brick streets. The creaking of Betsy's cart joined other sounds coming through the blanket: clusters of conversation or shouting, the smack of hammers, the roar of compressors, the hiss of water spraying on concrete.

The rubbery, new car smell had disappeared after the cart had left the maze of corridors. Amy breathed an aroma of wet stone, fresh plaster, cigarette tobacco, ancient grease, and new paint.

The sizzle and smell of frying meat caused Amy's stomach to grumble, and she lifted the edge of the blanket. The little buildings that passed her eyes were made from such a wild variety of materials that it seemed like the aftermath of a fantastic hurricane, where the residents had simply hammered together anything that had landed on the ground regardless of size, shape, color, whether it belonged on a fishing boat, or was a fishing boat. One shack would be lit by Christmas lights, the next halogen, and the third by gleaming hoops of neon. In front of another building were ten lava lamps, nailed to a board and hung upside-down. A mix of dogs and cats trotted along the sidewalk. Others curled in doorways or on high windowsills.

The cart stopped briefly, and then crossed an intersection. Amy saw a line of dogs waiting patiently in the street, all harnessed to carts with cargos of strange machinery and boxes. On the next block stood a building that seemed formed of glue, with bulbous pink columns and an irregular, rounded dome. Dogs and cats reclined in clear, bubbly windows with bowls of the glowing beans. Amy smelled the same rubbery aroma as in the cafeteria.

Something whirred by in the air, probably a bird. Amy pulled the blanket back a little further and looked up. Tiny red, purple, or green lines zipped past and were framed against the distant rafters and cloud-obscured dome of Junktown like colorful shooting stars. Amy couldn't tell what it was: bird, robot, or supersonic moth.

Amy lay back in the bottom of the cart and closed her eyes. She should write all this crap down when she woke up. Helen said her mother did that kind of thing; kept a dream journal. Amy had never had any dreams worth writing down, and definitely nothing like this. She thought about Lucia in the hospital, and hoped she was okay. Things were going to be rough for a few weeks while she recovered. That was another thing that was supposed to wake you up from a dream: thinking about the real world. It certainly wasn't working for her, and Amy wondered if her brain was a double-crossing cheat, since all the rules for waking up from a dream were in her head, along with the dream that was causing the problem. It was the mental version of Schrödinger's cat, and she was feeling more and more like the cat.

The cart bumped over potholes and swerved around corner after corner. At last it shuddered to a stop, and Amy heard Betsy's gruff voice.

"All out that's getting out!"

"Hush up, silly dog," hissed Sunflower. "Keep the blanket on, human, and follow me."

"Don't step on his tail," said Betsy. "Cats hate that!"

"Quiet!"

Amy slid across the metal cart and followed Sunflower's orange-striped tail across gray asphalt to a battered green door. Sunflower pushed at a moldy brick to reveal a brass key, then stood on his hind legs and unlocked the door. The cat led Amy into a human-sized hallway and through a series of dark rooms covered in frayed, patchwork rugs.

Amy bumped her head on something and fell to her hands and knees on a rough brown carpet.

"Ouch! Can I take finally take this thing off?"

"You're still wearing that? You could have dropped it ages ago," said Sunflower.

Amy ripped off the blanket and blinked in the darkness.

"Hit a light switch or burn a candle or something," she said. "I can't see a thing."

"Yes, master. Can I get you a bowl of diamonds and gold, master?"

Wood creaked as he pushed open a small window. The room brightened and Amy found herself in a ten by ten room. A fluffy round mattress lay in one corner. The blue-painted walls were covered in fixtures of human hair care: brushes, combs, barrettes, hair clips, and bobby pins. Tiny strips of wire or globs of clear jelly kept the items stuck to the walls. Against one wall stood a low bookshelf made from particleboard and loaded down with a pile of colorful cloth.

"I guess you like hair accessories," said Amy.

Sunflower looked away. "It was like that when I moved in."

"The guy who lived here before didn't take his stuff?"

"It wasn't a guy," said Sunflower bitterly. "The Lady sent her to a place where nobody takes anything, and nobody comes back."

"I'm sorry," said Amy.

Sunflower left the window and trotted across the room to the doorway.

"Stay here and don't make a sound," he said. "I'm going out for a minute."

Amy pointed to the mattress. "Is it okay if I take a nap?"

"Remind me again––is that when you lay down and pretend to be dead, or is it when you're really dead? There's no point for me to find human food if you're going to be really dead."

"Pretending to be dead."

"Good."

"But this entire spaceship and everything in it is probably going to disappear," said Amy. "Everybody knows you can't sleep inside a dream."

Sunflower stared at her for a long moment, then walked out of the room. Amy heard his voice from the hallway.

"I'll never understand humans ..."

5

Amy flew over the greens of Spyglass and Pebble, arms outstretched and a snow-white gown of fog streaming behind her, the morning air full of the smell of freshly cut lawn. She dodged the gray-green limbs of coastal pines as she flew to Carmel Beach and felt the mist of breakers on her face all the way to the rocks of Point Lobos.

She continued south, past vertical cliffs topped by magnificent parlors of stone and glass. A column of black smoke and orange flame boiled from the roof of the largest mansion, transforming into a powerful vortex that pulled at Amy. She tried to escape, to fly away, but the smoke jerked her back like an angry leash. Amy spun down and down through the gas and roasting flame to the bedroom of Frankie Yamagashi.

Her foster mother lay on the Spiderman quilt, her hospital gown covered in a pile of wires and clear tubes, all melting, dripping, burning. Amy pulled at the horrifying mess in an attempt to free Lucia, but even more wires dropped from the ceiling.

Lucia shook her head and grabbed Amy's hand.

"Wake up," she whispered.

The walls of the room collapsed and smothered Amy in a soft and warm darkness. It smelled like a strange combination of cheddar cheese and wet dog.

"Get closer," she heard Betsy say.

A high-pitched voice spoke near Amy's ear. "Like this?"

"No. Under the nose."

"How about inside? She's got such a huge nose, poor dear. I could probably shove all of it in."

"Whatever works," said Betsy. "You know everything about humans, not me."

Hummingbird wings buzzed at Amy's cheek. Something that smelled of stale cheese scraped across her upper lip and into her left nostril.

Amy batted the thing away from her face and sat up, her eyes wide.

"Who's sticking things in my nose?"

The hummingbird thing flew into a dark corner and Betsy barked, his front paws spread wide.

"Not me! I'm on guard duty," he said.

Amy pulled an orange Cheeto from her nose and tossed it at the Jack Russell terrier, who spun in a circle and barked again.

"You did, too. I can see the bag."

"Where?"

Amy pointed at the open bag of Cheetos on the floor. "Right there!"

Betsy whined and hung his head. "I didn't do anything, I swear!"

"Who was it, then?"

"Me!" squeaked the high-pitched voice.

A pile of neckties twitched on the floor and a hummingbird crawled out. It leapt into the air and buzzed toward Amy.

Only it wasn't a hummingbird. Wings beat the air to a blur just like a hummingbird, but in front of the blur floated a pale woman six inches high. Her blonde hair was pulled back to a ponytail and she wore a tiny pink blouse, white miniskirt, and white sandals.

The tiny woman crossed her arms and twisted her red lips into a scowl.

"You almost killed me. Be careful with those giant hands!"

"Ooookay," said Amy. "Talking cats and dogs, and now a fairy."

The flying woman gaped at Amy. "What did you call me?" She buzzed down to the bag of Cheetos and grabbed one, brandishing the snack food in her arms like a bulbous orange spear.

"Calm down, Nick," said Betsy. "She didn't mean that."

The tiny woman flew up and jabbed the Cheeto at Amy's nose.

"Ow!"

"Words hurt, but so do snack foods," said the fairy woman.

Amy blocked the cheesy spear with her palm. "I'm sorry. What should I call you, if 'fairy' isn't the right word?"

"Call me Princess Nick, commander of the skies, deadliest woman alive, and most beautiful creature in the quadrant!"

"You're very beautiful, Princess Nick," said Amy. "I love that outfit, especially the cute little skirt."

The flying woman dropped the Cheeto and beamed happily. "Thank you! I'm the cutest thing in twelve systems but the animals around here couldn't give a compliment to save their lives."

"Hey! I'm no animal," said Betsy. "I don't wear clothes. How am I supposed to know what's good and bad in fashion?"

"Shut up! You'll put the human off her dinner. Eat more, now. Aren't you hungry?"

"Cheetos? That's my dinner?"

Nick tossed her blonde ponytail. "Of course! Nobody in Junktown eats that human food. It's icky and low in energy. Sunflower dropped by and said he had a human pet, so I grabbed a few bags and flew over. I can tell you're starving, poor dear. Just look at your filthy and lifeless hair."

"Ooo, nasty," said Betsy. "Do you think that's normal for a human pet?"

Amy ran her fingers through her hair self-consciously. "Human pet? That's not right. It's against the Bill of Rights or the Magna Carta or something."

Nick pouted. "I don't understand. Sunflower saved you from the inspectors, you're sleeping in his bed, and you don't belong to him?"

"He's the one who got me into this mess!"

"She's from Old Earth," said Betsy.

Nick laughed and flew in a circle. "Of course she is! How else does a human get on the ship?"

Amy sighed. She pulled a handful of Cheetos from the bag and popped them into her mouth. She grimaced at the texture, but swallowed.

"These must be a year or two old," she said.

"I know," said Nick. "They'll make your skin glow. Eat up! Human food is yummy-yummy, put it in your giant tummy-tummy."

"Cheetos aren't supposed to be chewy."

Nick pouted and put her fists on her waist. "Why are humans so picky about their food? Do you know all the things I had to trade for this? That's a bucket full of clothes right there!"

"Did I say it was awful? I mean fantastic. Do you have any water?"

Betsy nudged a plastic container at Amy's feet. "Here you go. Water, I think."

"Is it fresh? Has it been boiled or decontaminated or whatever?"

The terrier hung his furry brown and white head. "No. I'll send it through the cleaner. Where did I put my manos?"

Betsy stuck his front paw into a wide silver bracelet. The band tightened around his leg and four metal fingers and a thumb popped out of the surface, making it appear as if the dog had grown a mechanical hand.

"What on earth is that?" asked Amy.

"It's a manos, of course," said Betsy. "And not from Earth."

Amy watched the terrier pull the container of water out of the room with the hand on his paw.

Nick circled the room until the door shut completely. "Clean water is very important for humans," she said. "I forget that sometimes."

Amy leaned back on a cushion. "So what do you do in this wild and crazy dream world, Princess Nick? Are you the Lady everyone's talking about?"

"Absolutely not! Don't even make a joke about that."

"Sorry."

"Apology accepted. I'm a sprite. I work in Gems and Minerals, Floor Twelve."

"So you steal diamonds and rubies, that kind of thing?"

"Not anymore. I used to be an operator like Betsy and Sunflower, but I got promoted to curator. It's a nine-to-five schedule, and better for watching my human. What did Sunflower call it? Oh, right––a desk job."

Amy grabbed a handful of Cheetos and tossed them in her mouth. "Must be a tiny desk."

"Is that a joke?"

"No. So I take it you're from the planet Zooberon like the rest of these talking cats and dogs, who steal things from Earth but aren't from Earth and aren't aliens?"

Nick shook her head. "Poor girl. You still think it's a dream."

"What else?" Amy sniffed the air, then grabbed the front of her blouse and smelled the fabric. "One question: do you have showers in space?"

"My human thought it wasn't real, either," said Nick. "For at least a month after I saved him he kept muttering in a cute little voice that it was a nightmare. Then came the anger, the questions, trying to get me to send him home no matter what. It was so cute! Now he lays around all day and never talks to me at all, not even for cheesy treats. Do you think he's getting old?"

"Maybe you should take him home. I mean, where you found him."

"Haven't those two boys told you anything? There's no way to go back."

"Sunflower said this was the year 3317. It sounds like he's been bouncing between here and Earth all the time, so why can't you go back?"

Nick shook her head and rubbed her tiny hands together.

"I keep forgetting you're from Old Earth, with out of date Old Earth knowledge implants."

"I don't have any knowledge implants!"

"Even worse," said Nick. "You probably believe in magic, unicorns, an afterlife, and silly things like time travel. Launching into the same timeline as your own can't work because of the conservation of matter. Chronology is irrelevant to the universe––what matters is your 'matter,' one place at a time."

"But how are you stealing things from the past?"

"It's not the past. Get away from that idea. Instead, think small. The wave form of a photon or any molecule can have a number of different states, none of them predictable."

Amy nodded. "Quantum suicide."

"Are you sure you don't have a knowledge implant? Anyway, to sum up the theory, any possible change in state creates a copy where the change did not happen."

"Mirror universes?"

"Kind of. We don't travel through time; we shift into alternate universes, then return to our original universe, or state. It's how we can steal the Hope Diamond over and over, even though it was never stolen in our universe. It's not always in the same place, unfortunately. Some of the time it's radioactive and some of the time surrounded by ... I don't know what to call them. A nasty horde of shambling humans with open mouths."

"Zombies?"

"No. Tourists! That's the word. This one time Betsy and I––"

"But, it doesn't mean you can't return. The alternate universe exists somewhere."

"I guess it does, but the amount of energy needed to return there is exponentially higher than a random demat. That means the Lady won't allow it, and that means it's impossible. The Lady runs an efficient business."

"Really? It sounds like the biggest flea market in the galaxy."

The tiny eyes of the sprite popped and she looked around frantically.

"Fleas? Where?"

"I didn't mean real fleas. I meant a kind of market."

Nick sighed. "That's good. Be careful with the 'F' word. We haven't had an outbreak for three years, but it's still a touchy subject."

"So what kind of place is this, anyway?"

Nick landed on a nearby cushion. "This is the largest powered asteroid slash spaceship in a quadrant filled with massive spaceships. We're orbiting Kepler Prime, the home planet of the sauropods, the most ferocious traders in the entire galaxy. Even though the Lady has protected the secrets of her demat and remat technology, she still has to make a profit. A thousand employees in a powered asteroid slash spaceship don't come cheap, especially when you add 401k and dental."

Betsy backed into the room pulling the square container. "Water's here!"

"And that's why we can't launch back to the same dimension," said Nick. "The bottom line."

Amy poured water into a cup and took a cautious sip. It tasted like copper.

"The home planet of the sauropods," she said. "Did you just make that up?"

Betsy tilted his head. "Make up what?"

"If anything sounds like an evil alien, it's 'sauropod.' "

"There aren't any such thing as aliens," said Nick. "Didn't you tell her, Betsy?"

"I never had time! There was the inspection, and when we came here she just lay down and closed her eyes for hours!"

Nick buzzed into the air and hovered beside the terrier. "Humans have to do that every day," she said. "It's like I'm the only person around here who pays attention!"

Amy brushed the Cheeto dust from her fingers onto her black jeans. She stood and stretched with a sigh, her hands pressing on the low ceiling.

"Well, my little animal friends, this has been fun and everything, but I really need a shower. My face and neck have felt icky and nasty since I woke up. It's probably some alien goop trying to take over my brain."

"That was me," said Betsy, wagging his tail happily. "I gave you a bath with my tongue."

"Gross! Why?!!"

"You looked so pitiful on the cushion," said Betsy. "Laying there with your mouth open and not moving. A little bit of drool ran from the corner of your mouth. I licked it up, but more kept coming, so I thought what the heck, and cleaned the rest of your face."

Amy covered her mouth and bent over. "I'm going to be sick!"

"Betsy's the one who should be sick," said Nick. "Human mouths are full of germs!"

"I don't know about that," said the terrier. "But she hasn't brushed in a while."

Amy coughed into her sleeve. "Stop talking! I'm going to need industrial-strength mouthwash."

"What is ... mouthwash?" asked Nick. "I might have it at my apartment. I've got lots of strange jars and bottles of Old Earth stuff."

"A miniature *poona* would be cheaper," said Betsy.

Nick shook her head. "I can't stand the smell."

"All right, let's take a walk to your place," said Amy. "Where's my rucksack?"

"Here," said Betsy, and pulled the bag from under a pile of neckties.

Nick clapped her tiny hands and beamed. "This is so exciting! You can meet my human."

"I don't have a mirror," said Amy. "Does anyone have a mirror?"

Nick beamed. "You want to look shiny and healthy for the other human. It's so cute!"

"Not even. I just don't want to be a muddy hobo with a face full of garbage."

"You look fine. Not up to the beauty standards of a sprite princess, but fine for a human."

"Thanks, I guess."

"Maybe they'll have puppies," said Betsy. "Wait! Humans don't have puppies. They lay eggs."

"Don't be stupid," said Nick. "They have tiny things called rug rats."

"Nobody's laying eggs or puppies or anything," said Amy. "If your human touches me, I'll punch his or her atoms into the next dimension."

Betsy gasped. "Wow! Humans are powerful."

Amy checked the contents of her pack: metal pigtail, binoculars, miniature flashlight, and brown skirt. She swung the strap over her shoulder.

"Let's go."

Sunflower trotted into the room, the end of his orange tail switching back and forth.

"Nobody's going anywhere."

"Why not?" asked Amy, Nick, and Betsy in unison.

Sunflower sat on a cushion and scratched his neck with his back leg.

"That inspection was just the beginning. Junktown and all of C Sector are full of patrols, all of them looking for an illegal human. Orders are coming straight from the Lady."

Nick crossed her tiny arms. "Any human, or just her?"

"The order just says 'human,' but it's probably her."

"But they could be looking for my human! It's always getting out and wandering around Junktown. I have to go back!"

"Calm down, Nick."

"Don't tell me to calm down. You've only had your human pet for a day, so what do you care? I've had mine for years!"

Amy brushed a lock of her blonde hair back over one ear and adjusted the brown beret on her head.

"I thought I'd never say this, but the flying fai––I mean, Nick––is right," she said. "We need to check on the other human, and I want a shower. Both very important and extremely critical things are at Nick's place."

"You know what the Lady will do if she catches us," murmured Sunflower. "She'll make us disappear."

Amy shrugged. "I wish I could wake up and this whole dream would disappear. Do you have a better plan?"

Sunflower shook his head. "Not right now. I guess we'll go to Nick's place, even though we'll probably be caught on the way and tortured and banished to another dimension."

"Yay!" shouted Betsy and Nick together.

"You know you're pulling the cart again, right?" said Sunflower.

Betsy dropped his head. "Awww ...."

6

Amy hugged her knees and folded into a tight ball at the bottom of Betsy's cart. A blanket flew over her and blocked out the light, and the little dog-powered vehicle squeaked out of the alley.

"Try not to move," whispered Nick's high-pitched voice. "I'm sitting on your head."

Amy thought over her situation as the wheels of the car whirred and jolted through the streets of Junktown, past rubbery smells, murmuring voices, and crowds of padding feet. If this was a dream, she should have woken up already. Was she having a delusional episode? Is this what happened to people when they were in a coma? Maybe she'd been hit by a truck. Maybe M.K. had sat on her. The possibilities were endless and the probabilities few. Would it be crazy to accept everything as real, or crazier not to?

After several sprints, gallops, and not a few panicked swerves the cart bumped to a stop.

"Quick," whispered Sunflower. "We're here."

Amy threw off the blanket and climbed out. The black, murky shapes of tall buildings rose above her in the darkness, and were framed against the mist of the dome's high ceiling. Below her feet, large patches of bright lavender glue covered the asphalt.

"Keep going," said the terrier, Betsy. "I've got to take off my harness."

Amy ran deeper into the shadowy lane after the dim shapes of Sunflower and Nick. The buzzing sprite hovered near a battered green door, looked left and right, and then dove into a tiny hole in the graffiti-covered brick wall. Metal clicked and clacked on the other side, and the door shivered.

“Push!” came Nick’s strained voice.

Amy put her shoulder to the metal door and forced it open just enough for her to turn sideways and squirm inside. Sunflower trotted after her without a problem.

“Mommy’s home, Philly-Billy!” screeched Nick. “Come and meet the guests!”

The sprite buzzed away, and Amy stared at the cat.

“Philly-Billy?”

Sunflower blinked his green eyes. “What’s the problem?”

“Never mind.”

A broken chandelier hung from the middle of the ceiling and glowed with a dim light, although half the crystals were broken or missing. The room was packed with enough jars, bottles, and boxes to make a hoarder squirm. The walls were painted a bright shade of purple and a fluffy pink rug covered the floor, but neither were easily noticed under the piles of unopened snack food boxes, shampoo bottles, jugs of purified water, and all manner of hair brushes and human clothing.

Amy pulled a red-and-white canister of shaving cream out of a box.

“Is this for Nick's human?”

Sunflower lay on the floor next to a massive case of Hostess Sno Balls.

“I don’t remember,” said the orange tabby. “It’s got short hair. Is short hair a female human or the other kind of human?”

“It could be either one!”

The cat yawned. “Well, you’ll find out soon enough.”

Amy heard Nick's high-pitched, girlish laughter in another room.

"But I'd rather not see them," moaned a male voice in the posh nasal tones of the English countryside. A few of his open vowels cracked lower, the sure sign of an adolescent with a changing voice.

As soon as he spoke, Amy ripped off her beret and pulled her blonde hair out of a ponytail. It never hurt to look good, especially if you needed to twist someone around your little finger. She grabbed a hairbrush and stood in front of a tiny mirror, brushing her hair quickly with long, lightning-fast strokes so that it hung straight down and across her blouse. Nick and the boy continued to argue, so Amy pulled off her shoes and jeans and jumped into her brown skirt.

"I'm glad someone's excited," murmured Sunflower.

"Shut up, cat!"

She'd just zipped up the side of her skirt when Nick flew into the room.

"Bless my cute little peepers," said the winged sprite. "You've cleaned yourself up."

Amy shrugged. "I don't know what you're talking about."

A teenage boy shuffled through a doorway. He was pale and tall, with black, slicked-back hair that almost touched the ceiling. His white shirt and dark blazer hung so loosely on his skinny shoulders that he reminded Amy of a stick insect from a nature program. His mouth was wide, his nose long and straight, and his brown eyes large and liquid. When he caught sight of Amy, his cheeks flushed.

"My word! You didn't tell me it was a girl!"

Nick spread her tiny arms. "Does that matter? You should be happy to see her!"

The teenager glanced left and right in a panicked, last-minute search for escape, but settled for sticking his hands in his pockets and looking down at the floor.

Amy stepped forward with her hand out.

“Hello! I’m Amy Armstrong.”

The tall boy cringed and stared at Amy's fingers in horror, as if she held an invisible hatchet. After a long pause, he stuck out a bony palm and shook her hand weakly.

“Greetings,” he said. “I’m Philip Salisbury.”

“I like your accent. You’re British, aren’t you?”

“English, actually.”

“I thought British and English were the same thing.”

“The United States and California are the same, I suppose?”

Amy clapped her hands. “That’s where I’m from! California, I mean.”

“That’s perfectly wizard!” said Philip, and smiled. “I’ve never met anyone from there.”

“Look at them, getting on so well,” Nick whispered in Sunflower’s ear.

Philip waved angrily at the tiny sprite. “Stop talking about me! I hate it when you talk about me!”

“Philly-Billy! You have guests, so be nice.”

Philip sighed and slumped his shoulders. “Sorry.”

“I love British television shows like Monty Python and Red Dwarf,” said Amy. “What’s your favorite?”

“Pardon me. My favorite what?”

“Television show.”

“Is that a kind of play? Like the queer little boxes with moving pictures the cats and dogs watch?”

Amy crossed her arms and squinted at Philip. “Wait a minute ... when were you born?”

“I beg your pardon!”

"Everybody knows television," said Amy. "Especially in 1995."

Philip's eyes grew wide. He stepped forward and grabbed Amy by the shoulders. "Crickey--1995! So you can tell me what's happened! I was brought to this horrid, mad place in 1889. My disappearance would have been plastered across the world and noted in history books. My father was the Duke of Marlborough, largest landowner in Yorkshire!"

Amy pushed Philip's hands away. "1889? You've been here that long?"

"It jolly well feels like it. No, that was the year I was kidnapped."

"More like hitchhiked," said Nick. "It still makes me giggle when I think about it!"

Philip sat on a box of toilet paper rolls, his shoulders slumped and head bowed.

"In any case, I've been in this beastly madhouse for two years. Ellie's forgotten me already, I know it."

"Ellie?"

"Yes. She's the only one who ever cared about me."

"I'm sorry, Phil. A lot of things happened between 1889 and 1995, and I don't remember anything about a Duke's kid going missing. The Lindberg baby, yeah, but that's as close I can get."

Philip twisted his mouth into a frown. "You must be thinking of goats. The son of a duke and heir to Clarence House is certainly not a kid!"

Amy put a hand on her hip. "Sure about that? You're starting to sound like one."

Philip turned red, but before he could say anything, Sunflower spoke up.

"The two of you are talking about years and history as if you came from the same dimension, and that's definitely not the case. Philip's disappearance wouldn't be part of Amy's history."

Amy shrugged and turned to Nick.

"Sunflower said you have a shower. Could I use it? I really need to wash up."

The blonde sprite hovered in front of Amy and giggled.

"Shower? You mean a pet cleaning room. Of course I have one! It was such a waste of money, though. Philly-Billy never wants to use it."

"I going to jolly well scream if you don't stop talking about me," growled Philip.

Betsy trotted into the room and shoved the door closed with his butt. "Who's talking about me?"

"Nobody," said Sunflower. "Ever."

"Awww ..."

Amy stamped her foot. "Quiet! While I'm scrubbing dog spit off my face, you three come up with a plan to get me back to 1995. That's MY 1995, and I want to go back in one piece."

Sunflower jerked his head up. "Impossible!"

Amy raised both hands. "Miss Armstrong is now taking a shower and all questions must be submitted in writing."

Nick buzzed around Amy's head. "Come with me, Amy Waymee! We'll scrape off every bit of disgusting human filth and dog filth and other strange filth you're covered in!"

"Okay, okay. I'm not that dirty. You make me sound like a hobo."

Amy followed the tiny hummingbird woman along a dim, shoulder-wide hallway. The breeze from Nick's buzzing fan of wings shivered hundreds of cellophane snack bags and bits of newspaper tacked to the walls. Amy glanced over the scraps as she walked, but saw nothing more than advertisements for dish-washing detergent and something called 'Spacom.'

Nick turned left into a small, swampy-smelling alcove and pointed at the open lid of a top-load washing machine.

"There you go," she said brightly. "Cleaner for human pets!"

Amy groaned and covered her eyes. "That's a washing machine, but not for people. It's for clothes."

"It works for people, too! Philly-Billy sits on the top and sticks his legs inside. He rubs water over his skin and everything. It's so cute! I have to use the 'Delicate' cycle, or he gets sick and starts yelling, though. Do you want him to come in here? You two pets can take a bath together!"

"No!"

Nick pouted and whipped her blonde hair back and forth. "You don't have to yell. The human soap is on the shelf and human water in the bucket."

Amy bent down to sniff the water. "Is it clean?"

"I sterilized it this morning."

Amy sighed. "Please shut the door. Humans don't like to be watched."

"But I have to turn on the machine."

"Shut the door!"

Nick slumped her tiny shoulders and buzzed away.

A variety of towels and cleaning products lined the shelves of the alcove. Spic-n-Span, Dove dish-washing liquid, and Toilet Duck sat next to bottles of shampoo and hair gel. Amy smiled to herself, thinking about the horrible bathing experiments Philip must have gone through. A rich twerp like that couldn't have drawn his own bath even in his own time, much less in Junktown with cleaning products from different centuries. The experience didn't seem to have made him a nicer person, however.

Amy piled her clothes on top of the washing machine and took a sponge bath with shower gel, water, and a washcloth. She shampooed her hair with a bottle of something that had expired in 2001, twisted a towel around her wet blonde hair, and dressed in her underwear, skirt, and blouse.

As soon as she stepped out of the "pet cleaning room" and into the hallway she could hear a maelstrom of voices.

"I've never heard anyone say anything that disgusting and stupid in my entire life," squeaked Nick. "You take it back right now!"

"I won't," said Sunflower. "That's the only way it works. By hiding him for so long, it's clear you choose your pet over the Lady."

"That's not true!"

Amy walked back into the cluttered room. Sunflower was sitting on the pile of toilet paper rolls, the end of his tail twitching. His green eyes glared at Nick, who buzzed circles around his head. Betsy and Philip were nowhere to be seen.

"What's not true?"

Nick clenched her fists and flew to Amy.

"Aargh!" she screamed. "This stupid cat! He says I have to give up Philly-Billy!"

Amy shrugged. "You'll find another human. Maybe one that's nicer and better-looking."

"I heard that!" yelled Philip from his room.

"No! Philly-Billy is the first human I met, and you're the second. There haven't been any others!"

"I'm sure there will be more. How old are you?"

Nick's face turned crimson and she buzzed away to Philip's room.

Sunflower shook his head. "Never ask a sprite how old she is."

"Sorry!" Amy yelled after Nick.

Cartons of Hostess Sno Balls trembled, and Betsy crawled out.

"Is the yelling over?"

Sunflower licked a paw. "Almost."

Amy grabbed a pink Sno Ball and ripped open the clear packaging. Checking the expiration date would only make things worse.

"So what's the plan to get me out of here?"

"An illegal prop like a human pet leaves the *Dream Tiger* only two ways," said Sunflower, and blinked lazily at Amy. "If you aren't counting capture and death."

"Or death and capture!" said Betsy, his brown tail wagging.

"You'll be caught eventually," said Sunflower. "The Lady would incinerate you or toss you out an air-lock, or both."

"She'd incinerate you," said Betsy happily. "The airlocks are too far away."

Amy shook her head. "Philip's been here for two years and nobody's bothered him. Why are you so worried about me getting caught?"

"We don't know," said Sunflower. "The Lady is a cruel mistress."

Betsy barked. "Don't you dare say that!"

"Fine. We don't know why the Lady allowed Nick's human to roam Junktown freely, and never sent inspectors after it. The Lady has her own reasons, and far be it from us to question them. Right after you showed up, though, all inspectors were put on alert and she's been combing the entire ship from top to bottom like a mother looking for a lost kitten."

"Or a sauro looking for his plasma rifle," said Betsy.

"Why?"

Betsy giggled. "Because he loves killing!"

"Not that. Did I set off an alarm or something? Why does she want me and not Philip?"

Sunflower shook his head. "Maybe the Lady was fine with one human, but when another shows up she thinks it's an invasion. We've had problems with sauros lately, and maybe she thinks you're a spy. Or, since Philip is one kind of human and you're another ..."

"Another what?"

"One of you is a boy and the other a girl," said Sunflower. "Don't make me try to remember which is which. It's not like you're a cat or anything."

"I'm a girl, okay? I'm the opposite of my name!"

"Awkward," said Betsy. "I thought you were a boy. My face would be so red if it wasn't covered in fur."

Amy chopped a hand through the air. "Cut the crap, okay? How do I get off the ship?"

"Right, sorry," said Sunflower. "Anyway, with the inspectors out, you're going to get found. Even with your magical ability to open any door on the ship, we can't run from hiding place to hiding place forever."

"It's not magic. I don't know what it is, but it's not magic."

"Well, I was trying to explain it using words you could understand."

"I understand!" barked Betsy.

Amy sighed. "Continue."

"Using that ability to open doors, you can get me into the engineering section, and I can link all of the demat cores into one channel. With that much power and quantum jiggery, I can probably demat you to the right dimension."

"Say what?"

Sunflower sighed. "Human version: I can send you back in time."

"Okay. What's the catch?"

"The catch?"

"The negative. The huge problem with this plan."

"Oh," said Sunflower. "Well, security will lock down everything and I'll probably be arrested for treason, so we only get one chance. That means you have to pick one year to demat to, and the other human is out of luck."

"That sucks. What else could we do?"

Sunflower blinked. "The Lady keeps several small craft in the hangar for shuttling cargo. We could sneak you onto one of those, but you wouldn't survive on Kepler Prime. That's the planet we're currently orbiting. The Lady's personal cutter, *White Star*, is docked outside the asteroid. It's a big and fast ship and can take us anywhere we want to go, even the human systems. The problem is, it's been powered down for decades. We'd have to find a way to restart the engine core, fill the stores and tanks, and charge the oxidizers, among a million other things. What to do ... what to do ..."

"I can't fly a spaceship!"

"Finding a pilot is the least of your problems. Astrogation is taught in elementary schools these days, and *Starman Jones* is a very popular book."

"What would I do on the human planets in 3317? They're a thousand years beyond my time. They probably drink methane and use thought waves to communicate instead of talking."

"They don't talk much," said Betsy. "They're too busy watching television!"

"It hasn't changed as much as you think," said Sunflower. "Humans are very simple."

Betsy wagged his tail. "They eat cheese! It's weird."

"Okay," said Amy, with a shrug. "I guess that's an option."

"Maybe not," said Sunflower. "It's more dangerous than linking together fifty demat chambers, each with the power of a sun. Worst of all, it creates a problem that can't be solved by your magical, door-opening hand."

"What problem is that?"

The orange cat jumped down from the pile of toilet paper rolls and walked across the cluttered carpet. He sat in front of Amy.

"To access her personal ship, you'd have to kill the Lady."

7

Betsy scampered out of the room with his tail between his legs, while Amy backed away from the orange tabby.

"I'm not doing that," she said. "Even in a dream."

Sunflower watched her calmly. "Do you remember my apartment? You asked about the cat who used to live there, and I said the Lady made her disappear. What I didn't tell you is that she was my wife. I gave myself a year to find her, and if I couldn't get any answers, promised myself to either quit this job or take a hunk of cheese up to the Lady and blow both of us to bits."

"That's horrible! You're not going to do it, are you?"

The cat stretched out and laid his chin on his paws. "The year is up, and that golden toy from Old Earth was my last prop. Now I have to decide what to do."

"Even if the Lady is as bad as you say, I don't want to murder her. I'm not that kind of person."

"Maybe not, but if the Lady catches us you'll be the kind of highly incinerated person who fits in a trouser pocket."

Philip stomped into the room. "All of this is stupid and pointless. My father is the Duke of Marlborough and you have to consider my plan first."

"Exactly," said Nick, from her perch on Philip's shoulder. "Listen to Philly-Billy! He wants to stay with me."

"Actually, no. I demand to be taken home. The American girl can stay here."

Nick jumped off Philip's shoulder and corkscrewed wildly through the air. "What?!!"

Sunflower flattened his ears. "You want her to die? If she stays, that's what will happen. Also, the only way you can go back home is with her help. She's the only one who can open the right doors."

"I didn't consider that," said Philip. "I ... uh, I'm sorry. I suppose all of you think I'm a frightful toff, demanding this and demanding that."

"Oh, I don't mind," said Amy. "You're just being a boy. How old are you?"

"Fifteen."

"Well, I'm sixteen," lied Amy. "That puts me in charge, even though my father wasn't a duke. I say we have a vote, American style."

"My little pet has to stay," sobbed Nick. "I can't live without him."

Sunflower sighed. "I'm sure you'll go on somehow. Camille in Accounting has wanted a date with you for years."

"Male sprites are so icky! I want Philly to stay here."

"That's obvious," said Amy. "Staying is Nick's vote. Phil wants to go back to 1889, so that's his vote."

Betsy scrambled back into the room and knocked over a box of empty water bottles.

"Take Amy home!" he barked. "I like her the best!"

"There's Betsy's vote," said Amy. "How about you, Sunflower?"

The cat brushed by Amy's leg and lay on an old sweater. "Humans are stupid cheese-eating monkeys who are bad at football," said the cat morosely. "But Amy is the best one I've met, and we can't do any of this without her help. I would vote for taking her home, but we have a better chance of surviving if we steal the Lady's personal ship, the *White Star*."

Philip bowed from the waist. "Good show, and I suppose that's the end of it. Amy will certainly vote for herself, so we're going to 1995."

"Wait!" Amy held up a hand. "It's my turn, and I say we take Philip home."

The teenage boy clapped his hands and jumped up and down. "Hurrah! What a first-rate girl!"

Betsy jumped in the air. "I change my vote to whatever Amy just said!"

Sunflower gaped at Amy. "What in Saint Fluffy are you talking about?"

"Phil's been stranded here for two years, and really misses his family. I've always wanted to see England, and with everything I know about history I can be a millionaire in no time at all."

Sunflower shook his furry head. "You still think this is a dream, don't you? You'll never see your family again."

Amy nodded. "You're right; I do think it's a dream. Kind of a weird one, but still a dream."

Nick sobbed on Philip's shoulder as the tall teenager shook Amy's hand.

"Thank you," he said. "I'd give you a proper hug if you were a chap. As it is ..."

"Good idea, Phil. Keep your hands to yourself."

Sunflower sighed. "This day has turned into such a burning furball of joy."

Oblivious to the unfolding drama, Betsy chased his tail.

***

AMY AND PHILIP shoved expired snack foods and bottles of purified water into a pair of rucksacks, along with silver and copper coins that Philip said they could use for money in England.

Betsy dropped Amy and Sunflower off at a plain section of wall and sped away, the wheels of his cart squealing.

"Where's he going?" hissed Amy.

"To transport Philip to Demat 3," whispered Sunflower. "Didn't you listen to the plan?"

Amy held her stomach. "I was too busy throwing up Hostess Sno Balls."

"It's your own fault for eating that garbage. Why can't you eat ReCarb like a normal cat or dog?"

"Because I'm not a cat or dog!"

"It was a rhetorical question."

"This is the first time I've been asked a rhetorical question by a cat, and I don't know if I should be happy or sad about that fact."

Amy held her palm on the wall. Lines of glittering blue fire spread from her fingers and the surface turned warm. The hatch hissed up and out of sight.

Sunflower shook his head and trotted inside. "How do you do that?"

Amy followed the cat on her hands and knees through a narrow tunnel, her shoulders brushing the dull gray walls as she crawled forward. A blue light glowed ahead. Amy squirmed out of the tunnel and stood up in a cramped space that was packed floor to ceiling with towering racks of vertically-arranged, thin obsidian blocks. Pinpoints of blue light throbbed on the face of each inch-high slab. Yellow cables sprouted from the back of each slab and covered the floor like a tangled mess of string.

Sunflower poked his head from behind a towering rack. "Over here!"

Amy stepped carefully over the wiring to a green iridescent screen and keyboard, hidden inside an overflowing thicket of cables.

"A computer! Do you want me to type something?"

Sunflower's tail twitched. "Of course not. That's just for decoration or whatever. Push your arm inside and try to find a pressure sensor."

Amy wrinkled her nose at the rubbery, plastic stench, but shoved her hand into the bird's nest of wires. Her fingers touched a flat, cool surface.

"Got it!"

"Press your entire hand on it."

"Okay."

The computer beeped, and lines of green code scrolled down the display.

"Transmat access granted," said a smooth female voice.

Amy gasped. "Lucia! What's she doing here?"

"Transmat Operation Control, build version 1.41005. My parameters include oversight and technical--"

"Stop," said Sunflower to the display. "Amy, that's not a real person. It's a 'Tic-Toc.' "

"A what?"

"Terminal Interface Computer, Transmat Operation Control."

"Do you have a query?" asked Lucia's voice.

"Why does it sound like my foster mom?"

"I couldn't tell you," said Sunflower. "Tic-Tocs are used in other places around the ship. It's a voice control system."

"It's just weird!"

"I understand what you're saying," murmured the orange cat. "But time is running out and we need to focus. Now, repeat after me: Transmat operations, root access request."

"Transmat operations, root access request."

"Working," said the computerized voice of Lucia. "Root access granted."

"Wow," said Sunflower. "I didn't think that would work. Okay, repeat exactly what I say."

The cat read off a lengthy series of orders, all inscrutable and full of strange terms to Amy, who spoke them to the iridescent screen of the Tic-Toc. She finished with the last phrase and the flashing blue lights on all the obsidian slabs changed to lavender.

"That's it!" said Sunflower. "Run! We've got only two minutes!"

The cat dashed out of the control room and through the narrow tunnel. Amy dove after him and crawled as fast as she could to the exit. She held her palm to the door's surface and squeezed outside.

The shambles of Junktown rose beyond the terrace, but Betsy was nowhere to be seen.

"Never trust a dog," growled Sunflower. "Come on!"

He bolted along the terrace like a furry cannonball, tail flying and with Amy right behind. Seconds later the cat plowed straight into a terrier who'd just turned the corner with his cart.

"Sorry I'm late," panted Betsy.

"Shut up! No time," hissed Sunflower, and untangled himself from Betsy's harness.

Amy jumped into the cart and it started to roll at a high rate of speed, one that Amy would have thought impossible for such a little dog. She held tight to the blanket to keep it from being torn away by the hurricane of air.

The cart jolted and slid to a stop, the rubberized wheels squealing black skid marks across the surface of the terrace.

"We're here," panted Betsy. "But there's an inspector up ahead!"

Something pulled the blanket off Amy.

"Get inside Demat 3," said Sunflower. "I'll take care of the inspector."

Betsy giggled. "Another date with a cat you don't like?"

"Shut up, dog."

Amy scrambled out of the cart and pressed her hand to the pale wall. A large section slid up; much larger than the tunnel she'd crawled through when she first came to the spacecraft and big enough for a human to walk upright. Amy sprinted down a hallway and opened another door to the brilliantly white dematerialization chamber.

A red circle fifteen feet in diameter was painted on the floor. Philip sat across the chamber with his back to a wall and his arms around his knees. He looked up as Amy stepped into the room.

"Finally!"

Amy walked to the red circle. "You've waited two years. What's a few more minutes?"

"Sorry. It's just ... I'm so close to finally escaping this place. To going back home."

Amy sat in the center of the red circle and crossed her legs.

"I guess I can understand that," she said. "Come over here, Phil. Red is usually bad news, but in this case I think it's where we have to sit."

"You're probably right."

Philip plopped down on the red circle a respectable distance from Amy. He watched her carefully.

"What's happened to England?" he asked. "Since 1889, I mean."

"A couple of horrible wars. England has lost pretty much all of her colonies. You don't even have Canada."

"Is that a joke? Who rules the world now? Germany? France? Please don't tell me it's France."

"Nobody does, and it's complicated," said Amy. "It doesn't matter, anyway. The history of my Earth is not really the history of your Earth. Things could turn out differently, especially with me around. Maybe I can stop the war from happening in 1914. Who knows?"

Philip snorted. "If you think a pair of teenagers can change the course of nations, then you're either the bravest or maddest girl I've ever met. A cat has more chance of becoming king!"

"A pair of teenagers? I didn't say anything about a partnership. I've got my thing, and you've got your 'Dukeship' or whatever."

"I understand," said Philip. "In any case, I'll make sure you're given proper compensation for taking me home. I just wish I knew how they were."

"Your family? Me, too."

Philip sneered. "No, not them. That's the best part of this whole affair: not seeing any relatives for two years. A shower of greedy bastards, all of them."

"Okay ..."

"I miss Ellie. Ellie and the dogs."

"Is she your mother? Your ... girlfriend?"

Philip stared at Amy so hard she thought his eyes crossed.

"Crickey, no! Ellie's my horse. Oh, the magnificent times we used to have back in the day. The dogs baying ahead, Ellie and me crashing through the forest, suddenly vaulting over a stream. There was never a finer steed, nor another place I'd rather be. You certainly wouldn't understand if you don't hunt."

Amy shook her head. "Your whole sob story was about a horse? I would have voted for the spaceship!"

"She's a fantastic animal. Maybe someday you can meet her." Philip glanced down at Amy's outfit. "Not socially, of course."

Amy made a gagging sound. "Fine, whatever. Not to change the subject or anything because you're boring me to death, but how did you end up here?"

"I was hiding inside my father's French wardrobe. Thunder and lightning suddenly filled the air and I was transported to this ghastly place. The tiny flying girl saved me, but I don't know how I feel about that. She provided me with food and a place to stay, even though it wasn't to my liking. On the other hand, she considered me a pet. Me! The son of a Duke!"

"Why were you inside the wardrobe?"

Philip looked puzzled. "I was hiding from father, of course."

"You haven't seen any other humans for two years?"

"We're not in the proper quadrant of the galaxy to meet humans, and even if we were, the Lady only allows 'Class E' beings on her spaceship."

"Class E?"

"The 'E' stands for 'Enlightened.' It's a long story. Believe me, I've had time to study how the ship works and the beastly state of the galaxy. Nick brought me magazines she'd find here and there, or would trade for them. She even forced me to watch the Galactic Cup last year. Great gumdrops, what I'd give to see a proper cricket match."

"Tell me more about these weirdo cats and dogs."

"Haven't they told you anything? I would have thought Sunflower had talked your ear off about Tau Ceti already. It's his homeworld, and all the cats from there never shut up about it."

"Tau Ceti? That's a planet, right?"

Philip nodded. "At some point in our history-- Old Earth's history, as everyone here likes to say--the capability for traveling through the stars was made possible through a remarkable engine. I came across a book in Cat French about the subject. Even 'normal' French isn't my best subject, but I was able to read most of it."

"A light speed engine?"

"Even faster. However, the engineers at the time were in the midst of an ethical quandary--the engines gave off dangerous, invisible energies that would have sickened and killed any human crew long before they reached their destination."

"You mean radiation? Gamma rays?"

Philip spread his hands. "You obviously know more of the natural sciences than I do, and it could have been that. Because of the danger, a mixture of automatons and animals were sent in place of men. These weren't just any old mongrels and Toms scooped from the back alleys of Shoreditch; only the healthiest animals with good breeding and high intelligence were chosen. The scientific boffins did something to the brains and bodies of the animals to increase their odds for survival. They even taught them to talk in a rude manner."

"A spaceship full of cats? I don't buy it."

Philip shrugged. "You're sitting in a spaceship full of cats right now, but I'm just repeating the claims from the book. That first ship was a test to see if humans could survive the journey. Automatons and machinery would do all of the work."

"Okay, fine. Continue, please."

"Four massive ships were launched, each with thousands of animals of different breeds. Cats were sent to Tau Ceti and Gliese 667, and dogs to Kapteyn and Herodotus--originally named HD 85512. All of the ships completed the long journeys and the animals thrived."

"What about humans? Did they fill another starship with a bunch of pedigreed, well-bred people?"

"That's a perfectly wizard idea, but no," said Philip. "Another great vessel was completed, but before it could launch a terrible war consumed all the nations on Earth. Fire rained from the skies and destroyed all living things, including mankind. Ten thousand survivors packed into the last star vessel and left for Alpha Centauri."

"That's horrible!"

Philip shook his head. "It's even worse than you think. None of the survivors were any good at football, or even had the gene for being good at football. Mankind hasn't won the Galactic Cup for two hundred years, since the competition began."

Amy squinted at the teenager. "Are you seriously talking about soccer? The human race was almost destroyed and that's all you care about?"

"Try to get anything done around this ship when a match is on. I'll tell you the answer--it doesn't get done. Dogs are especially mad about it."

"How does a dog play soccer, anyway?"

"With his head, of course! They're obviously better than humans, for reasons I just explained."

Amy sighed. "Okay ... tell me what happened to the cats and dogs, the ones shot off to Tau Ceti."

"Only cats were sent to Tau Ceti."

"Whatever!"

"From what I read, something happened during the journey between the stars. Maybe it was the energy from the powerful engines, maybe it was something else on the new worlds. The intelligence of the animals tripled and kept going. They taught themselves how to read from the great libraries on the starship and to create tools like that artificial hand, the 'manos.' The colonies thrived and expanded in population. Colleges sprang up. Cat and dog scientists researched how to tame the new planets and their resources. With Earth gone and the humans on Alpha Centauri struggling to survive, the animals saw themselves as the new masters of the universe. They changed their bodies using science I don't understand, to the point where the internal biology of a cat or dog in 3317 is unrecognizable from one born on Earth."

"Basically, supercats who talk and eat glowing stuff," said Amy.

"Yes, I suppose so."

"They still speak English. Why not use a cat language or speak in meows? Didn't you say that book was in Cat French?"

Philip nodded. "French-speaking communities of animals did develop on the new worlds, but seemed to be limited to academic circles. The majority of the dog and cat population on all four planets chose English because an Earth billionaire paid extravagant bribes to put a set of grammar books called 'GlobalEnglish' on the colony ships. The animals liked the drawings and bright colors, and chose to study English."

"What's taking Sunflower so long ..." murmured Amy. "Oh! I just remembered––what about aliens? Had to be some nasty aliens on those new planets."

"There's no such thing as an alien."

"What about the sauros?"

"It's boring."

"You say that like we've got something else to do."

Philip sighed. "They're carnival horrors."

"Really?"

"The sauropods are biological automatons made for entertainment by the owner of a cat carnival on Gliese six hundred years ago. He was a shockingly brilliant former scientist, but unfortunately for the galaxy, too smart for his own good. With no samples of Earth reptiles available, he made a decimal point error and gave the Sauros brains that were ten times larger than normal. A pair of the godless creatures stole a star craft and the recipe to make more lizard men. Thousands were suddenly appearing like frogs after a rain. There was a war on Gliese, cats versus sauros. Eventually the lizards retreated to Kepler Prime, an Earth-like planet that orbits the star Kepler 22."

"But we're orbiting Kepler Prime right now! These lizards sound dangerous."

"Sauros aren't that bad," said Philip. "They love beating other creatures into a pulp, but even more than that, they love to trade and making piles of money. They'd make perfectly good Englishmen if they weren't so cold-blooded. And reptiles. And biological automatons. Actually, that's very English."

"Did you just make a joke?"

Philip nodded. "I think so."

"Are the little flying sprites the same thing? Circus freaks?"

Philip grinned. "No, the sprites started as a joke, and came along later than the lizards. The advanced dog civilizations on Kapteyn and Herodotus became very nostalgic about the old days on Earth and their close relationship with mankind. Dogs had advanced so much in the period after the great war that humans on Alpha Centauri actually found them annoying to have around. Instead of chasing cars or chewing up the furniture, dogs were stealing the family hovercraft and flying to IKEA."

"Oh, no! That's sad."

"I suppose. In any case, several leading lights of the dog business community traveled to Tau Ceti, one of the cat homeworlds, and secretly arranged for the cat scientists to develop an artificial 'pet' human as a companion for dogs. Research into artificial life had been banned for a hundred years since the start of the sauro wars, but the cat scientists still agreed to the project, mainly because cats never turn down an opportunity for a prank. When the first shipment arrived at Kapteyn and the tiny sprites flew out of the transport, the dogs were shocked. The cats had agreed to develop low-intelligence, artificial humans of normal size, and here were these tiny, well-dressed fairies. It was all broadcast live on the largest cat networks, with the highest viewership for decades. Sudden death from apoplectic laughter was not uncommon that day among elderly cats."

"It doesn't sound that funny."

"True, but you're not a cat."

"So what did the dogs do?"

"Oh, you know dogs. They're the most agreeable and easy-going race in the galaxy, and laughed almost as hard as the cats. They bought even more of the sprites than I think they would have, simply because it make them chuckle. The tiny sprites were used as maids and repair workers at first, and after the Sprite

Emancipation Act, were given freedom to live and work as they pleased."

The exit hatch swished up and Sunflower slid headfirst across the floor. His front legs bumped against Amy's leg but the cat stayed prone and stretched out in utter exhaustion: eyes closed, ribs heaving in and out, and jaws open.

"What happened?" asked Amy.

"Can't talk ... no time," gasped the cat. He raised his voice. "Demat 3 ... reroute to Tic-Toc ... Tic-Toc, do you receive?"

The air hummed with static.

"Receiving and operational," said Lucia's computerized voice.

"Tic-Toc ... execute command ... 'Cat's Paw.' "

All the surfaces of the room changed from white to sunshine yellow and the floor began to vibrate.

"Sit closer," gasped Sunflower. "In ... center."

"You're going with us? I thought it was just me and Philip."

"Can't launch ... without operator," wheezed Sunflower. "Looks like ... you're stuck with me."

"Can I hold you on my lap?"

The orange cat opened his eyes a crack and looked at Amy. "Yes, but no petting."

Amy lifted the limp animal into her lap while Philip squeezed closer, his shoulder touching hers. The surfaces of the room changed from yellow to emerald green. "PREPARE FOR DEMAT" and "HAVE A NICE TIME" flashed across the walls.

"At least the future has a sense of humor," said Amy.

The walls faded back to white and the text disappeared. The vibration in the floor stopped.

"Excess mass detected," intoned Tic-Toc's voice. "Remove twenty-five point one kilograms excess mass before demat."

"*Poona* droppings," hissed Sunflower. "I forgot about the weight limit. Toss those backpacks outside the circle."

Philip gasped. "What the blazes? We'll have no food or currency at all!"

"It's the bags or you. Take your pick."

Philip kicked his pack outside the circle and Amy tossed hers at the wall. Her binoculars, jeans, flashlight, and can of Mace were inside, and the only tool she had now was the pigtail in the back pocket of her skirt.

"Excess mass detected," intoned Tic-Toc. "Remove four point eight kilograms excess mass before demat."

"Get rid of everything," snarled Sunflower. "Shoes, belts, extra clothing!"

Amy kicked off her sturdy Mary Janes and Philip did the same with his shoes.

"Excess weight detected. Remove two point two kilograms excess mass before demat."

"If it's not one thing, it's another," growled Sunflower. "Clothes off!"

Amy clenched her jaw and stared at the cat in her lap. "I'm not doing that. Take me to the Lady instead!"

"I'll never understand humans," said Sunflower. "We don't wear clothes. Why do you have to?"

Philip sighed and stood up. "Anything for queen and country," he mumbled. "Look away, you two."

Sunflower snorted. "A cat can look at a king."

"He can also have a shoe thrown at him," said Philip.

Amy turned her head while the tall teenager stripped off his trousers and sweater and flung them out of the circle. He sat next to her in a thin undershirt, white boxer shorts, and white socks.

"I bet those stupid shirts and pants make your monkey brains smaller," said Sunflower.

"At least I don't have fleas."

"How dare you," whispered the cat.

"Prepare for demat," spoke the computerized Lucia. "Have a nice time."

The walls changed to yellow, then green, and the floor vibrated and clattered like a lawnmower over a pile of aluminum cans. The red circle rose into the air, and Amy reflexively grabbed Philip's arm for support. Sunflower lay on her lap, eyes closed and limp. A dome of blue lightning crackled over the two humans and cat, outlining the red circle precisely. The hair on Amy's forearms stood on end and everything smelled of carbon and lavender. The entire universe shrank into the mass of a single snowflake, and exploded.

THE STRANGE CREATURE spun like a bobbin in the center of a gleaming, madly whirring sewing machine, the bent silver needles of its eight legs clacking on dozens of keyboards in a circular pit. Hundreds of holographic rectangles curved around and above the pit, displaying blue lines of scrolling data, static images of red circles, or video feeds of Junktown, the terraces, and warehouses full of categorized objects. Beyond the floating holograms of market reports and action figures in the original packaging, a web of black and yellow cables covered the floor of the circular room, all humming with power. The glowing squares of more traditional screens covered two-thirds of the curving walls and were broken by a segmented window, beyond which lay the gentle curve of a cloud-covered blue planet and a vast, magnificent star field.

If the creature was human, it had been a long time since it had strolled into Burger King and ordered a shake. The eight silvery, spidery legs sprouted from the sides of a meter-wide obsidian sphere. A human torso sprouted from the top, her arms crossed over a green and gray striped sweater, as strangely inappropriate as a dress on a cat. The woman's long white braid waved behind her back as the spidery needle-legs hammered at the keyboards and jabbed at the holographic displays. Wrinkles creased her face and deep shadows hollowed her eyes. Liver spots dotted her collarbones and sharp sinews pulled and tugged beneath the wrinkled skin of her neck. Pinpoints of light blinked and throbbed beneath the surface of that skin, like Christmas lights under a sheet of waxed paper.

The creature moved quickly and with an unnatural speed for one so large. The ancient, spotted skin of her face held eyes that were large and blue; liquid gems that had seen the galaxy but had forgotten it and like a child, wanted to see it all over for the first time.

Triangular yellow symbols flashed across the holographic screens, and were replaced a few seconds later by a video feed of two human teenagers sitting on a red circle in the middle of a white room. An orange tabby sprinted into the circle, and after a frantic bit of pack-tossing and pants-removal, a dome of blue energy crackled around the three beings. As the circular platform rose higher, the dome of blue lightning revealed itself as a sphere.

A hundred screens turned crimson and screamed with warning triangles, red this time. The silver legs of the strange creature ceased tapping as a high-pitched warble drowned out the electrical hum in the air. The old creature smiled as the sphere of lightning flashed and the screen turned black. All the displays around the creature followed suit as everything in the room lost power. Outside the segmented window the blue planet blinked into nothingness, leaving only empty space and hundreds of orphaned satellites.

Seconds later, the panels along the walls glowed back to life and the holographic displays flashed on in clumps of two and three. The silver needle-legs of the creature rattled the keyboards around her control pit as she checked on systems and restarted those that had failed.

After all the warning triangles were gone, the creature rubbed her wrinkled hands in a very human gesture of relief. She focused on the video feed of a grim procession crawling through the streets of Junktown.

Four spheres of liquid metal floated in the middle of the screen, each with a dozen silver tentacles dangling in the breeze of their travel. These mechanical monsters surrounded and prodded forward a brown and white terrier and a tiny flying woman with hummingbird wings. A menagerie of cats, dogs, and sprites trotted and flew behind the prisoners.

The metal octopi escorted the two prisoners through vast suburbs of junk to the center of the surreal metropole, where every structure seemed as out of place as a square Earth hammered into a round universe. They stopped at a thin and brilliantly gleaming ivory tower, which stretched from Junktown into the rafters and mist far above.

A male sprite broke from the crowd at the base of the tower and flew to the tiny blonde woman. He hugged her tight and spoke a few words before the tentacles waved at the sprites and forced them apart.

A pair of tall doors slid open at the base of the needle, and the inspectors pushed the terrier and the blonde sprite inside. The tiny woman waved at the crowd as the doors closed, and the pair were left alone.

The blue eyes of the half-human, half-machine creature watched a video feed of the elevator ascending the tower. After the two endured a bath of cleansing mist and torrent of air from the drying fans, a pair of metal doors slid open in the wall of the creature's chamber.

The Lady turned and smiled yellow teeth at the two animals.

"Hello, my children," she said warmly.

Nick and Betsy knelt and touched their noses to the plush white carpet.

"Good day, Lady," both said.

The Lady waved a wrinkled hand.

"I see that all three made it to the demat chamber in time, as I requested."

"Yes, Lady," said Betsy.

"You're such good doggie. Nicky, you've been good, too. I put five hundred gold stars in both your accounts. You may also choose any one item from the collection. Don't be naughty––only terrace five or below!"

Nick raised her head and grinned. "Thank you, my Lady!"

"Yes, thank you," barked Betsy. "You're the greatest and we love you so much!"

The Lady smiled and tilted her head.

"Now, now. None of that. Once you have a break and do some shopping, please get back to work on your other little projects."

"Other little projects?" asked Betsy, his tail still wagging.

"Silly dog," whispered Nick. "My spaceship thing and your inspector-robot thing!"

"Oh, yes. My inspector-robot thing. I'll work so hard on that and you'll be very proud, my Lady!"

The Lady smiled. "I know you will, Betsy. Now, scoot. Scoot!"

The terrier and tiny sprite dashed back into the elevator. The door closed behind them with a swish.

The Lady turned back to her video feeds and streams of data. In the empty space where the cloudy blue orb of Kepler Prime had rotated only a few minutes before, a sauro fleet popped into view one ship at a time. The red streaks of residual warp energy speared across the screen and formed the dangerously pointy hulls of battle cruisers.

"Amy Armstrong," murmured the Lady. "The girl who stole a planet."

Part II

London, 1889

8

The smell came first. Amy wrinkled her nose at the sharp stench of urine, human waste, rotten cabbage, wet tobacco, coal dust, and mildew. She lay on her side in complete darkness, covered by the overpowering miasma of foul odors.

"Did I land on a garbage dump?" she groaned.

Philip spoke through the impenetrable gloom and something touched Amy's shoulder. "Bravo! You're awake. Before you ask--"

Amy rubbed her eyes. "What's wrong with me? I can't see anything!"

"I'm in quite the same state. The cat said it was a possible side effect of the travel. Apparently it happens if you aren't an 'operator,' as he said, along with a few other impolite things about humans."

Amy sat up with Philip's help. She crossed her arms and shivered as a cold breeze rattled something that sounded like wooden shutters. A church bell tolled, low and mournful. A squadron of tomcats yowled at each other.

"Sunflower?"

"He went to find something," said Philip. "I wouldn't be surprised if he ran off and left us here to die. Never trust a cat--traitors to the last breath."

"That's not true. Sunflower risked his life for us, and now he can't go back. If he was going to stab us in the back it would have happened before we teleported or time traveled or whatever."

Philip sighed. "Sorry. I suppose I'm being an absolute pill. It's been so long since I was home, that I'm looking for bad news."

A clip-clop and sound of rolling wood clattered in the distance and faded away. Amy guessed they were in a narrow space or a back alley.

"Can we find someplace to sit that's warmer? Someplace that doesn't stink like the boys' bathroom?"

"That's a superb idea," said Philip. "But the cat said to stay here. If we wander blindly around the streets we'll likely be trampled by a carriage."

"Is this London?"

"I'm not quite sure. I heard a few Cockneys pass by and an Irishman, but we could still be anywhere."

Amy's teeth chattered. "Anywhere? How about an asteroid spaceship full of talking cats and dogs?"

"They were Irish cats and dogs, in that case." Philip grabbed Amy's hand. "Hush! Someone's coming."

Heavy footsteps slapped the wet bricks of the lane.

"Well, well. What do we have here?" said a deep voice with a heavy English accent. "A pair of begging lovebirds? A little squirrel with his pretty bit of jam?"

"Tramps on the run is more like it," said another male voice. "Not a shoe between them and rags for clothing. Leave 'em be, Dick. They'd be sleeping in the doss if they'd a farthing between them."

Amy heard Philip clear his throat.

"You're quite right, chaps," said the teenager. "We've completely lost all our traveling money. If you'd be so kind as to lead us to the nearest police constable, I give you my word that a reward of twenty pounds will be sent to you by my father."

"Constable? Are you blind?" asked the first voice.

"As a matter of fact, we are."

Amy felt a breeze as something waved in front of her face.

"That's a good one, Dick," said the second voice. "They can't even tell who we are."

"Let's drag them over to Cherry's place," said Dick. "She pays good coin for a healthy pair of chickens."

"What year is this?" blurted Amy. "Where are we?"

"Blimey," said the second man. "The boy's posh and the girl's American. Maybe they really are lost, Dick. Bring 'em to Cherry and we'll be clapped in irons before the week's out."

Dick laughed. "You must be joking. They'll never be found in that warren."

Amy carefully shifted her sitting position on the bricks of the alley, and touched the pigtail in the back pocket of her skirt. She could do some damage with the small crowbar if she weren't blind.

"Leave us alone, you filthy pigs," she said. "You'll be sorry if you don't."

"Nobody talks to me like that," growled Dick. "Not even a pretty pullet like you."

Hands grabbed her arms and jerked Amy to her feet.

"Unhand her, you brutes!" yelled Philip.

Amy heard a smack and the sound of shoes scraping and cloth ripping. Dick still held her by the arms. His breath puffed in her face; a foul wind of rotting meat and yeasty alcohol.

"I warned you," she said.

Dick laughed. "Warn me? You moppet."

From the way he gripped her arms and the location of his voice, Amy had a good idea of Dick's height and the location of one particularly sensitive area. She stepped forward and kneed him in the groin with all her strength. Dick screamed in pain and bent over, letting go of Amy's wrists. Unfortunately for him, Amy wasn't done. She searched blindly through the air with one hand until she felt Dick's hair, then smashed him in the temple with the pigtail she held in the other. Dick crumpled at her feet like a sack of wet potatoes.

"Bloody hell," said the other man's voice. "What did you do to him?"

Something hard struck Amy across the cheek. She fell to the slimy bricks of the alley, her face numb and red dots of pain sparkling in her blinded eyes.

"My father has money," yelled Philip. "I promise he'll pay you whatever you want."

"Indeed he will," said the second man. "After I box your ears!"

"Stop!"

Sunflower's command dangled in the air and everyone stopped what they were doing, like tiny kittens grabbed at the back of the neck. Amy rubbed her cheek and tried to stare through the red and black film over her eyes.

"Who said that?" asked the man who had hit her.

"I did," said Sunflower. "Look down."

"There's nowt but a big old Tom here shaking his tail."

"Surprise!"

Sunflower yowled and the man screamed. Amy heard a flurry of steps, a loud thump, then and a splat. She crouched on the bricks, left hand stretched out and the other ready to strike with the metal pigtail.

"Get back," she snarled.

"I wouldn't worry about him," said Sunflower. "He's not moving. Is that dead or sleeping?"

Philip groaned. "Either one is fine with me."

"Oh, and you're welcome," said Sunflower.

Amy listened to the delicate blip of the cat's paws on the wet bricks. "What did you do to him?"

"Nothing. I just jumped in the air a little. He was so scared that he ran into a wall. Didn't I tell you that humans are stupid?"

"Thanks. I think they were going to sell us into slavery or something awful."

"Steady on you two," said Philip. "Slavery was abolished fifty years ago in England. Unless we're in the East End of London. We're not in the East End of London, are we?"

"Probably," said Sunflower, and sniffed the air. "Ugh. Most definitely."

"What year is it?"

"How would I know?"

Amy cleared her throat. "From a newspaper?"

"Exactly," said Philip. "From a newspaper."

"I don't have time to stop and read a paper! I may not have majored in Old Earth history, but I don't think that's something cats did."

Philip sighed. "Yes, that would be a sight."

"What do we do now?" asked Amy. "Two blind beggars stuck in London with a sarcastic cat."

"Correction: a genius cat with a pair of under-dressed and shivering blind beggars," said Sunflower. "Help me pull the clothes off these dead humans."

"I think they're just sleeping," said Philip. "But it's a first-rate idea!"

Amy heard things sliding over the wet bricks and rustling cloth.

"I'm not wearing those smelly clothes," she said. "First tell me why I can't see anything."

Sunflower sighed. "I told your boyfriend. I hate repeating myself."

"The name's Philip, actually."

"I told Philip Actually that blindness is a rare side effect for someone new to demat. I don't see why you care that much anyway. Just use your other senses."

"Smelling my way through London is not exactly my cup of tea," said Amy, and giggled. "See what I did there? London? Tea?"

"I don't understand," said Philip.

"We can sit here and have a pleasant little chat," said Sunflower. "Or we can steal the trousers and jackets from these dumb humans before they wake up!"

Amy waved a hand through the darkness in front of her face.

"How are we going to walk around while we're still blind?"

The sound of rustling cloth stopped.

"That's a good point," said Sunflower.

"I know," said Philip. "Some of the blind beggars have dogs that lead them around. We can tie a rope to the cat."

"Whatever," said Sunflower. "Pull off these boots, and be quick about it!"

"Now look here, cat--it's a bit hard when I can't see anything."

Amy heard the same wooden clatter echo on the bricks and fade away.

"What's that sound?"

"It's a wheeled transport," said Sunflower. "Pulled by horses. Ugh. Don't even get me started on horses."

With the cat's help, Philip stripped the first thug. Amy's fingers and toes were numb with cold, so she pushed down her disgust and crawled over to the man she'd smashed in the head with the metal pigtail. She was glad to feel his chest moving as she stripped off his scratchy jacket and draped it over her shoulders.

She jerked off his filthy trousers, pulled it up her legs and over her skirt, and stepped into cavernous leather boots. A big, floppy hat draped over her blonde hair.

"Something's coming," hissed Sunflower. "Grab me and run!"

"I can't see or hear anything," said Amy.

"You wouldn't! You barely have ears, little monkey girl. Now hold me!"

"What about the string idea?"

"No time!"

A furry weight dragged down the front of Amy's jacket and she wrapped her arms around the cat.

"Grab my coat, Philip."

"Where? I can't--oh, I've got it!"

Philip grabbed the hem of Amy's jacket. She held Sunflower with one hand and the waist of her oversized men's trousers with the other, and clomped briskly along the lane in her oversized leather boots.

"Go straight," breathed Sunflower in her ear. "A little left now, straight on for twenty more steps ... get ready to make a sharp right turn ..."

Amy stepped into a breeze that tossed her hair and blew away the stench of the alley, replacing it with the musty smell of horses. The sharp taste of tiny coal particles crunched between her teeth and something sweet hung in the air like the smell of licorice. A group of seagulls screamed high above. Hooves clopped and wheels in need of grease squealed and clattered. Men muttered to themselves, walked by with a rapid tread on pavement, sniffed or coughed in the cold air.

Amy froze as the ground shook and she heard a loud rumble.

"You're fine," Sunflower whispered in her ear. "Keep going."

Pinpoints of cold water collected on the back of her hands and face as Amy walked through what must have been a thick mist. The feeling reminded her of home. She bit her bottom lip and led Philip faster through the street noise.

"Is it night-time?"

"Indeed, it is," hissed Sunflower. "A night as dark as the Lady's heart and almost as cold. Stop for a moment."

The cat squirmed out of Amy's grip. She heard a metallic clang and rustling fuss nearby.

"There aren't many travelers apart from the carriages," said Philip, from behind Amy's shoulder. "It must be the dead of night."

"Or the middle of nowhere," said Amy.

"What a queer thing to say! It's physically impossible to be 'nowhere.' "

Metal cans rattled. "You've obviously never been to Cincinnati," said Sunflower. "Here, grab onto this."

A strip of something that felt like rope or twisted cloth fell into Amy's hand.

"The other end is tied around my neck," said Sunflower. "Hold on to that and I can lead you around. Don't jerk it and don't let go."

Philip groaned. "This is absurd! What if I'm recognized?"

"Do you have a better idea? Both of you silly monkeys are as blind as a newborn *poona*."

"That's not exactly true," said Amy. "I can see blobs of black and red. Maybe it's clearing up!"

"That doesn't mean anything. Talk to me again when you can see the smirk on my face."

"Take me to my parents, you beast!" blurted Philip.

"All right, all right. I thought the English were supposed to be polite."

Amy held the bit of rope and Philip gripped her jacket as the cat led them through the streets. Groups of men and women passed with the sharp smell of tobacco smoke, speaking with thick English accents and laughing at the sight of beggars led by a cat. More carriages rolled by on the street to Amy's left as they walked, and on the right poured a torrent of piano music, singing, and the sour smell of spilled ale. Fuzzy white orbs joined the red and black shapes in Amy's sight as she listened to the men's voices.

Up the apples an' pears, and across the Rory O' Moor,
I'm off to see my dear old Trouble and Strife.
On the Cain and Able, you will always see
A pair of Jack the Rippers and a cup of Rosy Lee.
What could be better than this -
A nice old cuddle and kiss -
All beneath the pale moonlight.
Then some Tommy Tucker and off to Uncle Ned.
Oh what a luverly night tonight.

"We're definitely in England," shouted Philip over the music. "Let's ask the chaps inside what year this is."

"Step inside and look stupid if you want, but there's really no need," said Sunflower. "I found a newspaper. Sit against the wall and hold it so I can read the thing."

Amy's fingers touched painted wood and she slid down against the slick surface. Sunflower pushed a bundle of damp paper into her hands and stepped into her lap. The world in her eyes was still a nebulous red, white, and black, but Amy was able to spread the pages and hold them up for the cat. Men in heavy boots passed by on the sidewalk and entered the pub, the slam of the wooden door shivering the wall at her back.

Horses clomped and carriage wheels bounced over what sounded like cobblestone. Amy listened to the speech of the men passing by and thought she heard Irish, German, and Italian accents. The quiet murmur of women's voices and a faint shuffling sound floated to her from the other side of the street. The men in the pub began a new song.

My Bonnie lies over the ocean
My Bonnie lies over the sea
My Bonnie lies over the ocean
Oh, bring back my Bonnie to me

Bring back, bring back
Bring back my Bonnie to me, to me
Bring back, bring back
Bring back my Bonnie to me

"Turn the page," said Sunflower.

Next to Amy, Philip stirred. "What's taking so long? We simply need the date."

"Sorry," said the cat. "I found a very interesting article on a cure for intestinal parasites in dogs."

Amy groaned. "Tell us the date!"

"March 17, 1889. Right on the front page."

Philip gasped. "That can't be right! That's only two days after I was kidnapped."

Amy looked toward the sound of Philip's voice. "Isn't that the point?"

"I was living in Junktown for almost two years. Shouldn't I come back two years later?"

"You'd have a lot of explaining to do," said Sunflower. "They're not going to believe you lived in a spaceship with dimension-hopping cats and dogs."

"That's as may be, but I'd have less to explain than now. I've grown three inches and gained twenty pounds!"

Sunflower sighed. "Do you think they'll really notice? Humans don't like their children very much, I've heard."

"They'll definitely notice. It's only been days to them."

Shoes scraped across the pavement.

"Here now," came the slurred voice of an old woman. "Is that a cat you'd be speaking to?"

"Of course," Amy replied to the red and black blob. "He's a time-traveling cat from the future with a really bad attitude."

"He is, is he?" The woman hiccupped. "You're a right smart one, darling. That'd make a stuffed bird laugh. Good night and God bless."

Amy heard a few uneven steps and a crash.

"Humans are weird," said Sunflower. "Especially humans who drink alcohol."

"You took the words right out of my mouth."

"We're back home in England," said Philip. "But where, exactly?"

"The newspaper is something called 'The London Standard,' " said Sunflower. "If that gives you a clue."

"Smashing," said Philip. "Hail a cab and speed us to King's Cross! We'll be home in a few hours."

"That's a cool story and everything," said Amy. "How are you going to pay?"

Philip sniffed. “I had a handful of shillings and gold crowns in my backpack but this vile cat forced us to leave all of that behind. It doesn’t matter in the slightest, because the whole of England must be up in arms at my kidnapping. Find a constable and we’ll be neck deep in biscuits and hot tea before you know it!”

“Turn the page, please,” said a bored Sunflower. “What was your name again?”

“Philip Salisbury, son of the Duke of Marlborough.”

“There’s nothing about a missing duke’s son. Or any missing boys.”

“I’m not a boy! I’m a man, you filthy, flea-bitten beast!”

Amy waved blindly and pushed Philip away from the hissing cat. “Stop fighting, you pair of idiots!”

“Amy, please listen to my idea. Give my father’s name to any respectable citizen or police officer and they’ll grant us safe passage.”

“There’s nothing safe happening at this hour,” murmured Sunflower. “And I’ve never trusted police in any dimension. They remind me of inspectors, and inspectors remind me of awkward dates.”

Amy sighed. “What exactly is your plan then, Mister Smarty Cat?”

Sunflower’s fur twitched under her hand. “I don’t know. I thought I’d help you two get settled then wander down to Egypt. I hear they worship cats.”

“Maybe a few thousand years ago. Philip, do you know anyone in London?”

“Of course, but it would be unspeakably boorish to wake them at this hour.”

“You’d rather freeze to death on the street?”

"Given the choice between embarrassing myself and––" Philip gasped. "Did anyone see that? A rainbow! What could it mean?"

"It means your eyesight is coming back," said Sunflower. "Were you born this dumb, or did you grow into it?"

Amy folded the newspaper and slid it beneath her as a cushion over the cold pavement.

"Any relatives, Phil?" she asked.

"Relatives? My word, Kensington! Why didn't I think of that before?"

"Is that a home for troubled boys like you?" asked Sunflower. "Because I've got better things to do. Hiking to Egypt, for one."

"No, no. We have a house in Kensington. My family comes down to London every year for the season."

"Will anyone be there?"

"Definitely. At the very least, Anthony will be at home."

"I hope he's a good cook with plenty of food, because I'm starving," said Amy. "Let's go."

"He's not a cook at all; he's the groundskeeper. I'm certain we can find something in the pantry. Where are we in London?"

"Don't ask me, I'm as blind as you," said Amy. "Sunflower, can you see any street signs?"

"I see a human face on a building with the word 'tobacco' underneath."

"That doesn't help."

"How about 'Aldgate High Street?' "

Philip sucked in a breath. "Good God! We're in Aldgate? That's the East End!"

"So?"

"We're lucky if we make it out alive. This is the Ripper's neighborhood!"

Amy laughed. "Jack the Ripper? That's a story made up to scare children."

"I'm afraid you've been misled," said Philip. "But even if the ghastly murderer isn't real, there are a thousand other ways to get sliced, robbed, butchered, walloped, or kidnapped in the East End. Even constables have to travel in pairs! It's full of thieves, scoundrels, and immigrants, a rotting pit of filth widely known as the most dangerous area of London!"

"Lots of cats, though, if that's your thing," said Sunflower. "The place is crawling with them. I bet I've seen a hundred so far."

Amy stood up. "Let's not hang around. Spit spot and clip clop, as you English say."

"But we're blind. You can't walk from Aldgate to Kensington, where the house is. How exhausting, not to mention that we'd be run over by a hansom cab. They're notorious for that kind of thing."

"We need money for a cab, I guess," said Amy. "How much is a cat worth?"

"That's funny," said Sunflower. "Don't quit your day job."

"I'm fourteen. I don't have a day job."

"Don't stop being fourteen then."

"I don't understand," said Philip. "You said before that you were sixteen."

"I wish I was sixteen. I also wish I wasn't blind and freezing to death!"

Amy took off her floppy hat and slapped it on the ground in frustration. Steps walked past on the pavement and she heard a dull clink of metal.

"A couple bob for you, poor dears," said a man's voice, and the door to the pub slammed.

Amy reached into the hat and felt a pair of coins still warm from the stranger's pocket.

"Did someone just give me money?"

"That's exactly what happened," said Sunflower.

"This is unacceptable," hissed Philip. "My family has never begged for money. Not for such small sums, at least. I'd rather be trampled in the street than stoop to that level."

"Um ... you're sitting outside a pub on a filthy street in stolen clothes," said Sunflower. "Begging is a step up."

"Shut your mouth, you flea-bitten mongrel!"

"Quiet, both of you," said Amy. "Philip, why don't you look at this money like a temporary loan? If it makes you feel better, you can come back later and hand money out to everyone."

"What a superb idea! I say, Amy, you're just a girl but you've got a first-rate mind."

"Just a girl?"

Philip ignored her question. "Yes, it's a plan. I'm not begging. I'll certainly return and help a few of these degenerates pull themselves out of their filthy, primitive existence."

Sunflower chuckled. "Sounds like what I'm doing with you two."

Amy collected money in her floppy hat as the pair sat forlornly at the door of the pub, listening to the sounds of the street and the shuffling, murmuring women. Occasional giggles and the laughter of men broke over their soft voices. Sunflower curled up in Amy's lap and put on his best wide-eyed 'hungry kitty' face for the benefit of the passers-by. The proprietor of the pub came out after a while and gave the two teenagers hunks of bread and a bowl of milk.

"Poor little moggie," he said with a smile, and swayed his bald, sour-smelling bulk back inside.

Amy's eyesight had improved to the point that she could make out vague shapes. She watched Sunflower's orange blob sniff the bowl.

"What in the name of Saint Mittens is that?" asked the cat.

"It's milk," said Amy. "From a cow."

"Lactic bovine excretions? Does that human know what lactose does to a cat?"

Philip laughed. "I'm certain he does, because he gave it to you."

Sunflower backed away from the bowl of milk. "Have either of you heard of tri-nitro toluene?"

"I know!" blurted Philip. "A city in Siam. My father went there once."

"It's dynamite," said Amy. "A nitrate explosive."

"One of you is correct, and it's not the ugly one called Philip."

"Hey!"

"Don't be offended," said Sunflower. "I'm certain that the dogs on Kapteyn would be pleased to see you."

Amy held up her hands, which now appeared as two white blobs in the darkness.

"Hold on. What's this have to do with milk?"

"The bodies of cats from Tau Ceti and Gliese 667 have been biologically altered over a thousand years. During that thousand years we endured exposure to radiation, alien bacteria, and *poona* scat but absolutely none of us drank bovine milk. When the Lady began to recruit cats as property operators, we discovered that milk causes a reaction in our bodies similar to activated TNT. It was an ice cream social. It wasn't pretty."

Amy laughed. "That's a joke, right? You get a little gassy."

"If by gassy you mean the milk would kill me and a ball of fire would vaporize everything in a hundred meters, then yes--I get gassy. Preserved lactose is even worse. Have you heard of the Tunguska event of 1908?"

"The huge meteor that exploded over Siberia?"

Sunflower shook his head. "Operator Cindy Williams. Poor cat skipped his nutro-break before the mission and ate a ball of mozzarella. Poof! No more Cindy Williams. Also, no more Tunguska."

"How did he get a ball of mozzarella cheese in Siberia?"

"He was probably wearing it as a hat. Williams was a strange dude."

"I can see my fingers," said Philip excitedly. "I can see again!"

Amy bit into the hunk of bread. It had been covered or soaked in some kind of meat drippings, which gave it the flavor of roast beef. The blurry shapes of carriages rattled across her field of vision, and coins dropped into her hat.

"Thank you!"

The vague shadow of the benefactor walked away and Amy saw a pointed white tower across the street. Dark shapes moved from left to right at the base of the pale structure.

"Is that a church in front of us?"

"Maybe," said Sunflower. "A group of human females are walking a circle around the building. The sign next to the entrance says 'Saint Botolph's,' whatever that is. I find 'The Dog and Pony' much more appealing, mainly because the sign has a dog pulling a wagon."

Philip stirred. “The Dog and Pony?”

“That’s the name of the human ReCarb center we’re currently sitting outside.”

“Tell us about this Lady of yours,” said Amy. “Is she a cat?”

“She is neither a cat, dog, or a sprite,” said Sunflower sadly. “The Lady might have been human a long time ago, but that’s like saying a cat who ate cheese used to be a cat. She doesn’t care about anything except stealing things and making piles of cash.”

“What’s wrong with that?”

“What’s wrong with a *poona* who crosses the road? Absolutely nothing until he’s smashed under a speeding eight-wheeler. The Lady is absolutely fine, until she’s not. If you go up against her she’ll crush you into dust.”

“Why did you take a job with her?”

The cat sighed. “The Lady is the wealthiest being in the galaxy. To set foot on her asteroid is the dream of billions on the civilized planets and to work for her is beyond imagining. We travel across dimensions, see things that no other cat or dog has ever seen, have our bodies uplifted with technology beyond belief ... I was the number two student from Tau Ceti that year. The second best of ten billion.”

“Who was number one?”

Sunflower was quiet for a moment. “She’s gone now. It doesn’t matter.”

“Was it your wife?”

“I don’t want to talk about it.”

Amy’s vision shifted in and out of clarity. Across a slate-gray cobbled street stood a brick church. The moon gleamed on a white bell tower and a line of women in dark dresses who walked slowly around the building. Her eyesight dropped to fuzziness again.

"I never thought bread could be this delicious," said Philip, as he chewed on the crust.

Amy glanced down at the green-eyed cat. "Uplifted with technology? Does that mean you have implants?"

Sunflower laughed. "Of course! You think I could survive all those demats without bone-strengthening and cellular mapping? The germs I'm exposed to on Old Earth would kill a normal cat. There's also no way I could return to the Lady without a Thor in my chest."

"A what?"

"A Thoracic Transponder," said the cat. "It's about the size of a bean, tracks my location in dimensional space, and allows me to call for a remat. A rematerialization, for the lay cat."

Amy's vision sharpened again. The darkness of the city surprised her, since she thought that electricity had been invented by 1889. A gas-powered street lamp gave a dim illumination to the front of the church and the pub. Few other lights shone anywhere, apart from a lantern at the door of the pub and candles in the windows of the church. A chestnut mare clomped by on the cobbles, driven by a cloaked figure who sat behind the small passenger compartment of a black, two-wheeled hansom cab, a lantern swinging from the side. The strong musk of horses trailed after the cab in the breeze. Across the street at the church, a man in a short brown coat with the lapels pulled up around his ears approached the circling women. He walked away with one of the females on his arm, bringing down a storm of squeals and cat-calls from the rest.

"So you've got a tracking device inside you?"

"Why are you so surprised?"

The sidewalk rumbled as a porter passed, shoving the handles of a wooden cart loaded down with heavy brown sacks. The cart left a faint trail of white flour.

"Can the Lady use that to find us?"

Sunflower snorted. "She'd never do that. You don't realize the massive amount of energy it took for all three of us to launch to this dimension. The Lady is parsimonious to a fault, and she'd never waste a joule of energy to come after a couple of underdeveloped humans and a runaway operator."

"I would."

"It's lucky you're not the Lady, then."

Philip raised his head. "Do either of you smell something?"

"I smell half a million somethings," said Sunflower. "Most of them the disgusting product of a human body."

"Not that. I smell lavender."

"You're right," said Amy. "I smell it, too."

The air above the street vibrated with an extremely deep, modulating hum. A sphere of blue lightning popped into existence, crackling like a forest of dry twigs and casting a sapphire glow over the cobblestones and the church. The people along the sidewalks looked up with pale expressions of shock.

Sunflower cleared his throat. "I, uh, may have spoken too soon."

The women at the church screamed and ran pell-mell, clutching purses to their chests as they fled in terror. Men poured out of The Dog and Pony, stared at the ball of lightning for a nanosecond, and then followed the example of the women, although with slightly less screaming and slightly more shouting.

With a final gigantic crack the lightning disappeared and left a cloud of white smoke. Out floated a large chrome ball with dangling metal tentacles tipped in sharp claws. At the end of one particularly thick tentacle glowed a sapphire light.

Sunflower took a second or two to say a few things that a cat should never say unless an inspector has just appeared in front of him and the cat really, really didn't want that to happen.

The final of these choice phrases was:

"Time to run, kids!"

Amy grabbed her hat and stuffed the cold money in her pocket, ignoring the few coins that tinkled across the sidewalk. She picked up Sunflower and pulled Philip to his feet.

"Which way?"

"Any way!" yelled the cat.

Amy ran as fast as she could away from the shining blue light of the inspector, holding Sunflower and the waist of her pants with one hand and leading Philip with the other. The lanes were narrow and black as octopus ink, and in the oversized boots she expected to stumble and fall at any moment. As the sapphire beam of the inspector chased them deeper into the dark warren of desperate women and foul-smelling men with broad yellow grins, Amy wondered if getting caught by the Lady wasn't the worst that could happen.

A wave of panicked Londoners fled the floating metal octopus, which hummed a mechanical tune to itself while it scanned the departing humans. It was just as well that all the people were too busy running for their lives or hiding under beds to listen to the melody from the flying machine––the song wouldn't be written until the next century.

I come in last night about half past ten

That baby of mine wouldn't let me in
So move it on over. Rock it on over
Move over little dog, a mean, old dog is movin' in

The singing monstrosity followed the crowds around a corner. The street became quiet again, like the eye of a hurricane.

A brown and white Jack Russell terrier trotted down the center of the deserted cobblestone street. Not a soul was left on the street or in a window, but any that might have peered outside would have laughed out loud at the sight of a small dog with a strange leather pack on his back and a series of metal strips around his head. He sang the same little tune as the inspector, humming the chorus while he trotted along the street. A microphone sprouted from the dog's headset and bounced in front of his nose. A glass rectangle on a metal stalk hung over his left eye and glimmered with a tiny video feed.

"Go straight," said the dog. "Left a little. Faster! No, the other left! Blast these stupid machines."

"Identify target for blasting," said a metallic voice near the dog's ear.

"Cancel order." Betsy sighed. "I hate this thing so much."

"Identify target for hating," said the voice.

"Great gobs of goofy gumdrops," snarled Betsy. His claws scrabbled on the gray stone as he leapt into a gallop.

9

Amy stopped and gasped for breath against a dark and slimy wall. She wondered if the whole city smelled like wet garbage.

"Did we lose them?" asked Philip.

"Lose who?"

"The men with the blue torches. Did we outrun them? I'm sorry, but I still can't see clearly."

Sunflower peered over Amy's shoulder. "We're not running from any humans. We're running from an inspector."

"I see," said the teenager, and his jaw dropped. "Wait––that can't be right!"

"Don't even go there," said Sunflower. "I know better than you that inspectors don't launch into another dimension. It's never happened."

Amy wiped sweat from her nose. "Why couldn't it? There's a little sprite driving it around, right?"

"What a silly idea! Inspectors are floating cameras, not a joyride for drunken sprites. Don't you remember what happened back at the ship? They're remotely controlled by cats and dogs at a special command center. Pretty boring, actually, and not my style."

"What IS your style, then? Rolling around in trash and being sarcastic?"

"I don't roll around in trash!"

"I say, will the two of you please keep your voices down," whispered Philip.

Sunflower rolled his eyes. "Even if somehow it's being controlled across dimensions––a scientifically impossible feat––sending an inspector is a violation of the Lady's rules on the highest level. We're not supposed to attract attention by flying around with silver waving tentacles. The Lady never wants us to break cover!"

"Obviously she's changed her mind," said Amy.

Philip laughed. "The right of every woman!"

"I hear you, brother," said Sunflower. "Females be craaazy, right?"

Amy crossed her arms. "Could the two of you please stop acting like interdimensional morons and focus on what's happening?"

Sunflower rubbed an ear with his paw and watched a beam of sapphire light flash above the buildings at the end of the alley.

"The inspector has got a bead on my thoracic transponder," he said. "It's on a high-band radio frequency. Surround me in something thick and the signal won't connect."

"It can follow you through dimensions but not brick walls?"

"The portable module isn't as powerful as the huge detector coils on the ship."

"How about a lead box? Does that work?"

"Very funny. I know what happens to the cat in that story."

"It's been a pleasure knowing you, Mister Sunflower," said Philip. "Fare thee well, and may angels watch over you."

Amy stared at him. "What are you talking about?"

Philip shrugged. "The inspector is following the cat, not us. If he gives himself up we're scot free."

"How could you do that? He's the reason you're in England and not throwing up fossilized Twinkies in Junktown!"

"Steady on there, Miss Armstrong. If someone's for the chop, it's got to be him. He's only a cat after all."

"I can't believe I thought you were a nice guy. You know what? If that's how you think, you can leave now. Find your own way back to Binketee-boo or whatever stupid tree house your family lives in."

Philip hesitated. "Miss Armstrong, I'm not going to abandon you. I am a 'nice guy,' as you put it, and I want to get us out of this sticky situation as quickly as possible."

"The boy is smelly and stupid, but has a point," said Sunflower. "You two are free to escape. I'll distract the inspector."

Amy held the cat tighter in her arms. "I'm not leaving you."

"In that case," mused Sunflower. "Are there any tunnels or caves nearby? That might block the signal even more than these brick walls and narrow alleyways."

"The tube, but it's a vile, disgusting place," said Philip. "Full of smoke, rats, and murderers."

"Sounds like home," said Sunflower. "You should put that on the official website."

"What's a website?"

"All right, you two," said Amy. "Let's head for the tube. What's under the ground of London can't be filthier than what I've seen above. I hope the rest of the country isn't like this."

Philip gritted his teeth. "I resent the implication–"

"And I resent ever meeting you," hissed Sunflower. "Lead us to the tunnels, human."

***

THE TWO TEENAGERS and dimension-traveling cat fled from the searching blue light of the inspector drone. They tried their best to follow the darkest alleys and keep to the shadows, away from the panicked clusters of people and growing crowds.

East Enders continued to pour out of the closely packed rows of brick houses like bees on fire, impelled by the sights and sounds of their more southerly neighbors running pell-mell through the streets. The men were in shirtsleeves, the women in long dresses, and the children wore scraps of everything, but rarely shoes.

None of the frightened crowd wore pajamas, and Amy wondered how they dressed so quickly. She realized, shamefully, that these were the only clothes they owned.

Philip had recovered his eyesight faster than Amy, and it became his turn to lead her by the hand through the crowds of fleeing people.

"Those robots can't really hurt anyone, can they?" she shouted to Sunflower, who ran beside her on the cobbled street.

"They're not robots," said the cat. "Drones. Remotely controlled machines."

"I'm not scared of them," said Philip. "Should I be scared?"

"Always," said Sunflower.

"Come on," puffed Amy. "It's not like they have killer laser beams or anything."

The street shook with a massive explosion, throwing all three to their hands and knees. Chunks of brick rained from the sky and smashed or bounced across the gray cobblestone.

Sunflower blinked his green eyes. "Any other questions about killer laser beams?"

Amy watched three children taking shelter in a nearby doorway, their eyes wide with fear. She realized that many of the dark houses were filled with children, and weren't as empty as she'd thought. The two smaller ones--a boy and girl--looked about eight and clutched at the waist of a blonde girl in a patched and worn forest-green dress. Her arms circled the shoulders of the two smaller children, but the hard eyes and grim line of her mouth told Amy she meant business.

Amy felt a pang of melancholy. The exciting time-travel dream had suddenly ground to a halt, and she saw a reflection of herself in the pale teenage girl whose life was filled with dirt and pain and toil. Amy pushed the feeling away and jumped up with clenched fists.

"This Lady of yours is crazy!"

Amy pulled Philip to the side of the street as a huge crowd of panicked East Enders fled from the blue light.

"She's a lot of things, but crazy isn't one of them," said Sunflower, after he dodged the legs of the people in the crowd.

"Sending a robot across space and time to burn two teenagers with laser beams isn't crazy?"

"There's so much wrong with that statement, I don't know where to begin. The Lady always has her reasons and a logical plan of action. I don't agree with her most of the time and I'd probably blow her to bits if she was in front of me, but even I realize that she doesn't act on a whim."

Philip raised a hand. "Excuse me? If we don't get moving we'll be the ones blown to bits."

Amy couldn't help from staring at the three children nearby, and shook her head.

“Why?”

Philip tilted his head. “Um ... because getting blown to bits is quite painful?”

“No. Why am I still dreaming about any of this?”

Amy cinched the huge trousers around her waist and walked toward the three children.

Sunflower groaned. “Blessed Saint Mittens and his three legs, what is she doing?”

Amy fished around in her pocket and held out a hand to the children.

“Please leave us alone,” said the blonde girl. “We haven’t a farthing and not a scrap worth stealing.”

Amy said nothing, and left a pile of silver and copper coins on the stoop at the feet of the three children. The grimy and quick fingers of the older girl swiped at the money and it instantly disappeared into her pockets.

“What game is this?” she asked, glancing between Amy and the earth-shaking flares lighting up the sky.

“It’s a gift,” said Amy.

She turned and sprinted down the street after the receding shapes of Philip and Sunflower, and caught up to them at the back of a crush of people in a narrow alley.

“Are you two trying to ditch me?”

ƒ“Absolutely not,” said Sunflower. “We were ... scouting ahead. That’s it!”

The cat jumped onto Amy’s shoulder, and she felt the soft pressure of his paws on top of her floppy hat.

“Hey! What’s going on?”

“That’s what I’m trying to find out. These ignorant humans are stopped for some reason.”

Philip cleared his throat. “Ixnay on the alkingtay,” he whispered. “People are beginning to stare.”

"I hope they've seen a cat before. Wait––do they eat cats around here? Is it London or China that does that?"

Amy pulled him off her head and held him at her chest. "Both, if you don't keep it quiet!"

"These people care about me when there's an inspector shooting killer laser beams at them?"

Philip huddled close to Amy and the cat, trying to shield them from staring eyes.

"I know what you're saying, old stick, but humans are quite good at ignoring the obvious."

Sunflower nodded. "I believe that completely."

A flurry of shouts came from behind Amy, and the crowd shoved her forward. Amy held Sunflower with one arm and pulled up her baggy trousers with the other.

"Great! We're packed like sardines and I'll die covered in cat hair," she said. "Did you see what's blocking things up ahead?"

"Nothing but other humans in dark blue uniforms and tall hats," said Sunflower. "Is that the cat-eating squad?"

"I hope you find out, one way or another."

"Friends, my sight is clear now," said Philip. "And I see the only way out of our troubles."

Sunflower nodded. "I know exactly what you're thinking––let the inspector kill all the humans and hide under their bodies!"

Philip pointed at the nearby wall. "We must go up!"

"Are you sure you can see?" asked Amy. "It's at least thirty feet up to the roof."

"That's nothing," said Philip, with a laugh. "I've scaled higher places in Yorkshire. One time cousin Tubby bet that I couldn't climb the spire of a church in his village. That was the day after I climbed up to his window and--"

"Hey! It's the geezer what nicked our gear!" yelled a male voice behind Philip.

A pair of bare-chested men pushed through the crowd.

"It's those two thugs," hissed Amy.

"Come on, then!"

With Sunflower clinging to a shoulder, Amy followed Philip through the crowd to the side of the alley. The bricks in the wall might have been red at some point, but were black and crusty now. Amy bet the wall was covered in green mold and soot and other nasty things. Philip grabbed a window ledge, pulled himself up, and began to climb.

Sunflower stirred behind Amy's neck. "What's the hold up? Go!"

"I'll tell you! One, my pants are going to fall off. Two, I'm wearing a skirt."

Sunflower sighed. "A pair of humans are about to kill you, the inspector blowing apart the city is less than a hundred meters away, and you're worried about someone seeing your underwear in the dark. Drop those pants and climb!"

Amy shucked off the oversized trousers and grabbed onto an edge of brick. She climbed as fast and carefully as she could, hand over hand after Philip, who amazingly had almost made it to the top. Moving from window to window, ledge to ledge, Amy climbed the precarious face of the building. She'd done this kind of thing before, but not with a killer robot and grown men in pursuit.

"Watch out, Amy!"

Philip waved at her from the roof. Amy glanced down to see the two half-naked men clambering up the brick wall. She stuck her leg out, shook her foot, and dropped a leather boot square in the face of the nearest climber. He plunged fifteen feet into the crowd below, causing a storm of jeers and angry screams.

"Want the other one?" yelled Amy.

"Nice one," Sunflower murmured from her shoulder.

The second boot missed, but it was just as well. With all his weight to balance and thick fingers, the other thug climbed like a pig compared to Amy, who was sure-footed without the clumsy boots.

Near the roof Philip grabbed Amy's hand and pulled her up. Sunflower jumped off her shoulders with a gleeful shout.

"That was fun!"

The air was gray and misty on the roof and smelled of coal. Philip had collected a few roof tiles, and he and Amy dropped them on the heads of the men still trying to climb up the wall. Amy's first shot smacked into the second thug's bare head, and she clapped her hands.

"You're good at this," said Philip, and smiled.

A sapphire beam flashed across his face.

"Target acquired," said a voice like an aluminum can being shredded.

The silver orb of the inspector flew through the columns of chimney smoke, its tentacles waving madly only fifty feet from the teenagers.

"Run!" yelled Sunflower, and followed his own advice.

Amy and Philip sprinted across the slate tiles after the cat as crimson beams tore through the air, exploding brick and wood and turning the rooftops into a horrible, fiery apocalypse.

***

BETSY TROTTED under a wooden cart and collapsed. The dog panted with effort and his long tongue drooped from his jaws.

“Why do they have to run so fast?” he gasped.

“Query,” said the mechanical voice from a tiny speaker on Betsy’s backpack. “Do you wish for an increase in velocity?”

“No! It’s dangerous on those rooftops, and I don’t want them to fall. Slow down and shoot behind them.”

“Standing order is not to harm target.”

Betsy sighed. “That’s why I said to shoot behind them.”

He wished for a moment that he could’ve switched places with Nick, who was supervising the cleaning and refit of the Lady’s personal ship, the *White Star*. He always hated sitting in one place for too long, though, and the chance to demat with an inspector drone was an opportunity any operator would treasure for the rest of his life, especially when it was a personal request from the Lady. But in this maze of thousands upon thousands of dangerous humans, Betsy hoped that the rest of his life would last longer than the next few minutes.

“Targets descending. Approaching ground level.”

Betsy squinted at the video feed in front of his eye. The two teenagers and Sunflower scrambled down a stepped series of roofs and landed safely on the street.

“They need to go west,” murmured Betsy. “Rotate one-eighty. Target that human structure.”

The video from the inspector’s camera blurred. Red lines in the screen highlighted a brick building with the sign, “Wilson’s Chemical Supply.”

“Confirm structure?” asked the monotone voice of the inspector drone.

"Yes."

"Nitrates detected. Confirm structure?"

Betsy groaned. "Confirm structure! Ten second blast!"

The tiny screen flashed white and the street shook with a mighty boom. A hot, sulfurous breeze ruffled Betsy's fur. Beams of charred wood and chunks of brick thumped on the cart and the street outside.

"Good gravy," barked Betsy. "Switch to starlight mode!"

A wobbling green and yellow fire covered the screen. The supply building was now a deep pit of smoke and flame.

"I didn't mean to do that! Is Sunflower okay? I mean ... switch back to the target."

The camera rotated to the image of two humans and a cat lying prone on the cobblestone.

Betsy squeezed his eyes shut and shook his head violently.

"Oh no! I've done it, I've done it! I've killed them."

"Targets are not damaged. Proceeding northwest on Middlesex."

On the video feed, Philip and Amy picked up Sunflower and slowly shrank as they ran down the street and away from the camera.

"Thank the Lady," breathed Betsy.

"The Lady is great and glorious and I am grateful for every second she lives."

Betsy growled. "Not you! I was talking to myself."

"I have received damage to my servo casings and now operate at ninety percent efficiency, if you are done taking a doggie break," said the metallic voice of the drone.

"Disable snark mode," barked Betsy. "Follow the targets on a thirty-meter leash!"

Feet ran past the cart. Betsy tensed his muscles, hesitating on whether to leave. The drone would soon fly out of range if he didn't run after it, and even if it didn't, he might lose track of Sunflower.

"Blast and double blast," he said, crawling out into the street.

The street shivered from a pair of detonations and a fiery mushroom cloud turned the night orange.

"Double blast confirmed," said the drone.

Betsy rolled his eyes and ran toward the fire. "This thing is just making fun of me."

"Hey," yelled a boy. "That mutt's got something on his back!"

Betsy ran as fast as he could from the rapid footsteps, but the heavy transceiver on his back slowed him down. The terrier felt himself lifted from the cobblestone by three giggling children.

"What's it got on? Is it a messenger or something?"

"Good doggie!"

"What's it running from?"

"The fire, stupid. Just like us!"

"Nah. He was running to the fire!"

Betsy barked and snapped at the young children, but they held him tight in their grip and pulled off the silver headset. In desperation, Betsy swiped the quick-release buckle at his chest and squirmed down to the street and away from the gang of kids.

"He's getting away!" yelled a boy.

"It don't matter," said another, and held up the pack. "Here's a few crowns, I warrant!"

Betsy scampered toward the flames and the last position of the drone, wondering what he was going to do now.

=====INSPECTOR 047 LOG TRAFFIC=====
013209 SNARK MODE DISABLED
013209 PURSUE TARGET@BEARING 301 ALLOW 30M DO NOT ENGAGE
013327 FIRING DOUBLE SHOT@BEARING 93 CONTACT POSITIVE
013401 QUERY OPERATOR, NO RESPONSE
013431 QUERY OPERATOR, NO RESPONSE
013501 QUERY OPERATOR, NO RESPONSE
013531 QUERY OPERATOR, NO RESPONSE
013615 TARGET ENTERING SUBSTRUCTURE THOR SIGNAL OBSCURED
013716 QUERY OPERATOR, NO RESPONSE
013746 QUERY OPERATOR, NO RESPONSE
013816 QUERY OPERATOR, NO RESPONSE
013846 QUERY OPERATOR, NO RESPONSE
013903 REVERTING TO SYSTEM DEFAULTS, TRANSFER POWER TO RECEIVER
013904 TRACE SIGNAL ACQUIRED@BEARING 279, PURSUIT ENGAGED
013905 SNARK MODE ENABLED
013905 STUPID DOG
=====END TRAFFIC=====

AMY SLID DOWN the almost-vertical stone wall, picking up speed as she neared the bottom. Philip caught her in his arms before she hit the gravel.

“Thanks.” Amy brushed the soot from the back of her skirt. “That could have been a bad case of road rash.”

“What’s road rash?”

Sunflower fell to earth with a spray of tiny gray stones and glared at the teenagers.

"I didn't see anyone rushing catch ME," he growled.

Philip shrugged. "Cats always land on their feet. Isn't that right?"

"The next place I'll land will be your face. I don't have to sleep, unlike you monkeys."

Amy exhaled a long white stream in the cold air, and pulled the sides of her wool jacket tighter.

"Stop fighting, both of you, and run!"

"Wait!" Philip stepped out of his floppy leather boots. "Take them. I insist."

Amy shook her head. "Your feet are more delicate than mine, I guarantee it."

She ran after the orange streak of Sunflower, wincing with pain as her feet struck the sharp gravel, but turning her head to hide it. Did they have tetanus in 1889? A more important question--did they have tetanus shots?

This section of the London Underground wasn't really underground, but a walled ditch thirty feet deep with four railway tracks and gravel at the bottom. The backs of tenement buildings rose several stories above the top, giving anyone standing at the bottom the feeling of being in a brick canyon that smelled of coal and oil.

Amy ran after the cat, giving lots of space to a handful of shadowy figures in filthy rags who tottered along the tracks and stared at the orange glow in the sky.

"Should we watch for a train?" Amy asked Philip, who jogged beside her.

"Why?"

"Um ... so we don't get squashed."

"Don't worry. The lines don't run at night."

"Why not?"

Philip grinned. "Because nothing good happens after dark. You know that!"

"The story of my life," said Amy.

The concrete arch of a tunnel curved high above the four railway tracks. Amy slowed to a walk as she entered the shadows and lost the benefit of starlight and the illuminating glow of the fires.

Philip squinted in the darkness. "Where's that cat?"

"Keep going!" came Sunflower's voice.

"But we can't see anything!" yelled Amy.

She heard a feline grumbling. A pair of tiny red circles jiggled left and right in the darkness ahead of them, and Sunflower's orange-striped head appeared.

"I thought the two of you had your sight back," he said. "You know, that funny blindness thing."

Amy rubbed the sole of her foot. "It wasn't funny! We can see now, just not in the dark."

"Ra-ther!" said Philip. "We're not cats."

"That's obvious. Well, there's nothing in this tunnel to see anyway. Keep a hand on the wall to the left, if you have to. If you need foot coverings, Amy, there's a dead human up ahead."

"I'm not wearing a dead man's shoes."

"Good, because I'm not one hundred percent on whether he's dead or not. Maybe by the time we get there."

"This is a barrel of bad pickles if I've ever heard of one," muttered Philip.

Amy followed Sunflower into the darkness, keeping her left hand on the greasy stone wall and wincing with every step. Behind her, the crunch of Philip's boots on the gravel echoed through the tunnel. After fifty feet the pain was so great that she was forced to stop.

"What is it?" asked Philip.

"Nothing," said Amy through clenched teeth. "Nothing to worry about."

"Now look here, Miss Armstrong, I insist that you take my boots. It's not going to help our cause if you become lame and I have to carry you over my shoulder, is it?"

"I'm not lame. Wait––what's that? Do you see it?"

An orange-red dot glowed in the darkness, but low to the ground like the end of a burning cigarette held by a chain-smoking rabbit. Amy pulled the metal pigtail from her pocket and crept forward.

"Put that thing away," said Sunflower's voice. "It's me."

He walked forward and Amy noticed a dim red light coming from a point just above the cat's eyes.

She giggled. "A glow in the dark cat? What else are you hiding under that skin of yours? Nail file? Bottle opener?"

"Why would I need any of those? That's what dogs are for. This is an emergency beacon in my forehead, not a party trick for your amusement."

Philip grabbed Amy's arm. "A body!"

Sunflower swiveled his head. The crimson light glowed on the worn soles of a pair of shoes and legs in rumpled trousers.

"He's not dead," said Amy. "Can't you hear the snoring?"

"Of course I can," said Sunflower. "But that doesn't mean he's alive."

"People don't make sounds when they're dead!"

The cat sniffed and paused for a moment. "How about, 'Gurgle, gurgle, why did you land on my head?' That's a sound."

"He's sleeping, okay?"

Philip helped Amy untie the brown leather shoes and pull them off. A powerful stench boiled from the man's feet, forcing Amy to cover her nose and mouth.

"Great fishcakes, they stink!"

"My word, you're right," said Philip. "Keep in mind this man isn't the cream of English society. They wouldn't be caught dead on these tracks, and in such a state."

"Hey! I thought of a riddle," said Sunflower. "What's creamy and English and standing right next to me? You!"

Philip shook his head at the giggling cat. "Perhaps, but I'm not lying by the tracks. Or dead, for that matter."

"Should we just leave him here? It can't be safe."

"I'd say it's a frequent resting spot for a drunk like him," said Philip. "And safe as houses."

The boots were slick inside and may have smelled like rotten fish guts, but they protected Amy's feet from the gravel. She and Philip ran into the darkness after Sunflower's bouncing emergency dot.

After a few minutes of jogging a slice of starlight glowed ahead––the other end of the railway tunnel. Beyond lay another canyon of track exposed to the sky and thirty feet below street level.

Amy stopped and caught her breath, her hands on her bare knees.

"What's the plan here?" she gasped. "Do we have a plan?"

Sunflower's red dot gleamed up at her. "Of course I have a plan. The plan was to lose the inspector by obscuring my Thor signal. Now that I've done that, Philip can run back to his mommy and daddy, and you and I can start walking to Egypt."

Amy put a hand on her hip. "Seriously?"

"Which part of what I just said is a problem?"

"I thought all three of us would help Phil get back home. It sounds like they'd be very grateful people." Amy cleared her throat. "With lots of valuable ... 'emotions' ... locked up in safe places and ready for us to liberate."

Philip pouted. "The emotions of those who live at Clarence House aren't buried deep within a vault-- they simply don't exist."

Sunflower sighed. "Amy wasn't talking about feelings, you boob. She was talking about gold coins and jewelry."

"My family does have more money than God, and glittering piles of gems."

Amy shrugged. "Not important. Don't really care."

"Miss Armstrong, I know you and Sunflower are thieves. Don't look at me like that! It doesn't bother me in the slightest. I'm on your side."

The opening of the tunnel behind them glowed sapphire.

"Oh, no," whispered Sunflower.

Amy sighed. "More running?"

"There's always running," said the cat. "Don't you know anything about operations? Running, running, and more running. Hey, lover boy! You said your parents have a house in London. Where is it?"

"In Kensington. I'll take us there."

"No, no. I'm the one it's tracking, so we have to split up. I'll get rid of the inspector drone or get rid of the dope controlling it while the two of you go to Kensington."

"Don't go to the house directly," said Philip. "We'll meet in Hyde Park at the north end of the Serpentine. That's the largest body of water in the park."

A gout of orange flame burst from the darkness with an ear-piercing roar. The steel rails of the underground line shrieked and the gravel below Amy's feet shook like flour in a sifter.

"Later, gator!" yelled Sunflower.

The cat raced down the tracks like a streak of orange lightning and disappeared into the dark mouth of the railway tunnel.

Amy and Philip jumped to the wall of the underground trench and began to climb a vertical line of narrow stones that seemed designed for the purpose. Amy moved faster than she thought possible up the stone ladder, and her limbs burned with effort. She rolled over the top ledge and pulled Philip up only a second before the tentacled silver ball of the inspector floated out of the tunnel and into the night air.

The pair lay on their bellies as flat as lizards, wide-eyed and with cheeks pressed to the greasy dirt. The electric hum of the inspector grew louder and louder, and the evil sapphire beam flashed over the top of the wall.

Amy watched the blue light cast shadows over Philip's face. The whites of his eyes were showing. He must have been scared, but his jaw was clenched and his mouth pressed into a thin line.

The look reminded Amy of Lucia and her face on the hospital bed. It was also the same expression of grim determination the first time Amy had made her foster mother angry, years ago, when they'd all gone to the Monterey aquarium. Amy had ducked out a side door and spent a few hours wandering around Cannery Row stealing purses from careless tourists. Tony had found her and dragged her back to the shark display at the aquarium. Lucia had stood in front of the huge glass window, the blue light playing over her face as she stared at Amy, her jaw set.

Amy closed her eyes and bit her lower lip, but the wooly ball of emotion had already started to unwind inside her chest. She burst into tears and rolled onto her back in the blue aquarium light, her hands over her face.

"Miss Armstrong, please be quiet," whispered Philip.

"I can't! It's absolutely horrible!"

Philip touched her shoulder. "Steady on there. We'll get through this."

Amy wiped her eyes. "I'll never see my mother again," she whispered. "I thought this was a dream or a nightmare or whatever, but it's not. This is real and I'll never see her again."

The hum grew louder and the inspector's scanning beam flicked back and forth like a blue flashlight in the hands of a child. Philip ignored this and slid closer to Amy, his face only inches away.

"Miss Armstrong," he said quietly, "you're the bravest and smartest girl I've ever met. If anyone can cross space and time to find her mother, it's you."

Amy sniffed. "You haven't met that many girls, have you?"

"Perhaps not. I don't think my female relatives should count as human. Having been to the future, I'd have to say they have more in common with sauropods."

Amy held a hand over her mouth to stifle the giggles. It didn't work, and she shook with laughter.

"Here we go," sighed Philip. "Hysterics of a different sort."

Amy wiped her eyes after a moment and sighed. Stars sparkled in the night sky, and the buildings around her had returned to inky darkness. The electric hum had faded.

"It's leaving," she whispered.

Philip lifted his head and peered down to the tracks.

"It's gone! We did it!"

Amy looked down to the other railway tunnel, where a faint sapphire beacon flashed back and forth.

"You mean Sunflower did it."

"No matter." Philip stood and helped Amy to her feet. "To the Kensington house!"

10

The conflagration caused by the inspector had shaken the East End and the entire city of London from their beds. This was not surprising, given the ever-present rumble of fire engines through the streets, with the clang of their brass alarm bells and the clatter of teams of iron-shod horses.

Amy and Philip fled west away from the fire and smoke. They had escaped the crush of people fleeing the monstrous robot, but now faced crowds of excited Londoners running toward the disaster, each one eager for a bit of news and excitement. Amy's injured feet were needled with pain, but she kept up with Philip's rapid jog.

"I'm sorry I gave away all that money!" she yelled.

Philip grinned. "Don't be. Those urchins needed it more."

"That's not what I meant. I think I cut my feet on the rocks. A cab would be great right now."

Philip slowed to a walk and watched her carefully. "I doubt we could find one now, even if we had money. It's far too early in the morning and we're dressed like a pair of workhouse tots."

An orange tabby crossed the street. Amy thought for half a second that it was Sunflower, but the cat had a crooked tail.

"London sure has a lot of cats," she said.

Philip nodded. "In greater number perhaps than people. They're very useful in keeping the rat population down."

"Yuck. I didn't even think about that."

"One tries not to."

"How far is it to Hyde Park?"

Philip thought for a moment. "I haven't spent much time on this side of London, so I can't say precisely. It's at the very least a few miles, straight as the sparrow flies."

"A few miles?!!"

"Don't worry, I'll carry you if necessary. You can't weigh more than a few stone."

"How much does a stone weigh?"

Philip laughed. "More than a feather."

The teenagers plodded southwest out of the slums and into a different world. The sidewalks were swept clean and not a scrap of rubbish blew under the light of the hissing, gas-powered street lamps. On stout granite and brick facades were fixed the shiny brass nameplates of respectable-sounding companies such as "Bishopsgate Brokerage," "Lee & Wilson Solicitors," and "Oriental Trading and Investments."

The pair walked a dozen blocks to a star-shaped intersection of five avenues. Philip stopped and pointed at a massive edifice of classical granite columns.

"There she is. The woman my father loves more than anything else. He's probably spent half his life with her and the other half at the Royal Exchange behind us."

Amy squinted up at the building. "I don't see anyone. It looks like a library."

"It's not a library, it's the Bank of England. Haven't you heard of the Old Lady of Threadneedle Street?"

"Does she sell sodas? I'd kill for a Diet Pepsi right now."

Philip shook his head. "The Old Lady is the Bank of England. It's the center of finance for the entire British Empire. The world turns not by the minute but by the pound, as my father says."

"I've never heard of a bank with a nickname."

"It's an old story."

"Let me guess: a poor old woman didn't pay her bills, so they locked her in the basement until she died, blah, blah, blah. Now she haunts little children who don't shove their tuppence in a piggy bank or something silly like that."

Philip held a finger over his lips and shushed her. "A ghost is involved, Miss Armstrong, but it's not silly at all. A clerk at the bank was caught forging banknotes and hanged for the crime. For the next twenty-five years his sister came to the front desk and asked for her brother. When she died, she was buried in the old churchyard behind the Bank. The Bank was extensively remodeled years later, and the churchyard was purchased for use as a garden. The Lady's ghost appeared soon after, wandering along the shrubbery and asking any unlucky souls the fateful question."

"What question?"

"Where her brother was, of course!"

"I still think it's silly to believe in ghosts."

Philip shrugged. "Life is full of oddities we don't understand. I'll wager that until yesterday you probably didn't believe in space travel or machines that could fly through the air."

Amy took a sip from a bubbling public drinking fountain and wiped her mouth.

"Um, no. You're getting your centuries mixed up, Phil. I've been to Houston and seen the moon rockets."

"In any case, you've seen the amazing machines on the Lady's ship; creations that would be magical to normal people. London is two thousand years old and absolutely chock full of ghosts. You can't say that a thousand stories about the spirit world aren't true simply because we don't have the right spectacles."

Amy pointed at her eyes. "Oh, I've got the spectacles to see them, Phil, and the talk-talk box is right below that. Let's go see this ghost."

"That's perfectly absurd! We're on our way to Hyde Park."

Amy grabbed the teenager's arm and pulled him down the sidewalk. "I think we can afford a tiny little detour."

A thick fog had swept in from the south while they had been talking, covering the Old Lady in a gown of opaque white and transforming the street lights into a fantastical string of bluish-white moons. The giant columns of the Royal Exchange disappeared, along with the bronze statue of a man on a horse. Even the orange glow and distant clamor of the East End fires was silenced. The world had been rubbed away by nature's foggy brush, and only the gray stone below their feet was left.

Philip let Amy pull him along the pavement with a sort of half-smile on his face, but when she turned the corner and strode along the west face of the massive, fort-like building, he let go of her hand.

"Miss Armstrong! I can't believe you're serious."

"I'm always serious."

"But it's the Bank of England, not someone's back garden! To get to the center we'd have to climb five floors and cross the roof. Not to mention the guard regiment!"

Amy locked her arm with Philip's and strode forward into the fog.

"I've done worse."

A moan sounded over the shuffle of their steps.

"Don't whine," said Amy. "It's childish."

"I didn't say anything."

The pair of teenagers stopped and stared at each other.

An inhuman sound pealed in the fog behind them; the gurgling, desperate wail of an animal who'd suffered a fatal, horrible wound and now sobbed in pain.

"Sounds like a goat," said Amy. "Do you have goats in London?"

Philip's face drained of all color, and he covered Amy's mouth with his hand.

"Please," he whispered. "Don't speak."

Amy brushed the boy's fingers away. "You think it's the Old Lady, don't you? I bet it's just a poor animal that's been run over."

"No! We must flee!"

The sickening howl of grief came again, louder this time and definitely closer. Amy squinted but couldn't see a thing through the white fog.

"I'm sorry, Amy!"

Philip jerked his arm out of her grasp and sprinted away from the gurgling moan. He quickly disappeared into the fog and the slap of his boots faded away.

Amy shook her head and watched the direction he'd gone.

"I'll be a monkey's uncle," she muttered. "What was all that crap about the bravest and smartest girl he'd ever met?"

She sighed and pulled the pigtail from her back pocket.

"I'll put this poor animal out of its misery," she said, slapping the tiny crowbar in her palm. "Then I'll catch up to that posh twerp and do the same to him."

Amy crept forward, hand with the pigtail raised and the fog dotting her face and neck in cold pinpoints of moisture. The mist gradually revealed the shape of a brown and white terrier plodding along slowly, his head drooping almost to the pavement.

"Betsy?"

The dog raised his head and scampered up to Amy, his tail wagging furiously.

"Amy! I thought I'd lost you!"

Amy bent down and hugged the terrier. "What are you doing here? How is that even possible?"

"Well ... I ... uh ... the Lady caught us," said Betsy. "She sent me here to find you and Sunflower and Philip and trick you into coming back, but I tricked her instead! I found you but I'm not going to trick you into going back! Or am I? I'm so confused!"

"So you're going to stay here forever?"

"Of course not! Old Earth smells bad and the food is awful."

"You'll have to go back to the Lady at some point. She's going to be mad because you didn't do what she said."

Betsy jumped in the air and barked. "Right, but the Lady is great and I love her!"

Amy sighed and patted the terrier on the head. "I don't think you're very good at making plans, Betsy."

"Not really. Hey, can I ask you something? You haven't seen three humans running around with a video headset and a little backpack, have you?"

"No, why?"

"Just asking. Absolutely no reason at all. I don't even know why that question popped into my head. Forget I asked. Please don't tell Sunflower."

Amy straightened up. "Speaking of the devil, we'd better get moving. We're supposed to meet the cat in Hyde Park."

Betsy gaped at her. "Sunflower's not with you? Is he okay?"

"I hope so. He's trying to get rid of an inspector drone that's on his tail. It's tracking him, and not us, so we split up."

"That's smart," said Betsy. "I didn't think about that."

"What?"

"Nothing," said the dog. "Well, let's get a trot on. Hyde Park is miles away."

"How do you know?"

"I've got a map in my knowledge implant. I can find pretty much any place with an address. Just don't ask me to deliver pizza."

"Why not?"

Betsy stared at her. "Because I really hate pizza!"

The Jack Russell terrier crossed the street, tail wagging, and headed west. Amy jogged after him.

"Where's your friend, Philly?"

"He's not my friend."

"Really? I think he liked you. I'm friends with anyone who likes me."

Amy sniffed. "My friends don't run away."

AMY AND THE TERRIER kept walking west along the wide, fog-covered Cheapside Street, keeping a close eye on early-morning strangers and hiding in dark corners from the occasional policeman in brass-buttoned uniforms. The few officers they met were more interested in running to the conflagration at the East End than harassing a dog and a teenage vagrant in a brown skirt and wool jacket five sizes too big.

Jewelry shops dominated the ground floors of the five-story brick and granite buildings on Cheapside, selling the type of jewelry men either bought for themselves or received as gifts. Watches, tie chains, masculine rings, and cuff links dominated the goods on offer, along with men's tailors, shirt and sock makers, and tobacconists.

A limestone church spire broke the mercantile parade of buildings, proudly standing on a street corner like a white rook. A rectangular black clock with roman numerals and golden hands projected from the tower over the sidewalk, where a group of a dozen men stood around in conversation. A sign next to the door said "St. Mary-le-Bow."

Amy covered her face with the lapel of her jacket as she passed the arched stone entrance of the church.

"Oy, lass!" yelled one of the men. "Did you hear about the Jeremiah?"

Amy turned and spread her hands. "The what?"

"The fire, you moppet!"

"Hear about it? My dog started it!"

Betsy watched the group of men point at him and laugh wildly. The terrier scampered after Amy.

"The fire wasn't my fault! That thing has a mind of its own."

"Don't get excited; it was just a joke." Amy stopped walking. "What 'thing' are you talking about?"

Betsy pointed his nose to the sky and trotted away.

"Nothing. I said nothing!"

The fog brightened as they continued their trek through the city. Men in tan or brown trousers with the determined, head-down attitude of early risers walked briskly along the sidewalks to their shops. Carriages full of fresh produce rattled over the cobblestone, followed by long horse-drawn omnibuses full of working men. Two-wheeled hansom cabs pulled by a single horse snapped and clopped toward the railway heads at Waterloo, Broad Street, or London Bridge to catch the morning rush of City workers. Gulls screamed and spiraled above the fog, waking gray pigeons in the eaves of the great basilica of Saint Paul's, who fluttered down to the wet streets and waited patiently for a dropped biscuit.

Amy sat on the eastern steps of Saint Paul's, chewing on an apple that had fallen from a passing cart. Patches of blue sky showed through the fog and the city hummed with activity. The bells of St. Paul's tolled for morning worship and parishioners walked up the steps with bowed heads and the scrape of shoes. A constant stream of men in smart bowler hats and black wool suits poured from the Underground exits and stepped down from omnibuses, adding the squeak of thousands of leather shoes to the slam of greengrocers opening their shops. Old women and girls wandered through the crowds with pails of quick breakfast for sale: meat pies, roasted potatoes, or coffee. Public transport omnibuses, heavily loaded carts, and all manner of horse-drawn wagonry filled the streets, adding the slap of reins and crack of horse shoes to the touts of tobacconists and boys standing beside huge stacks of newspaper. These young drummers beat the air with the morning papers and screamed themselves hoarse on last night's horrible events in Aldgate.

Amy swallowed the last of the apple core and wiped her mouth on her sleeve.

"Never thought I'd be that hungry," she said.

Claws scraped the steps beside her and Betsy appeared with a golden loaf of bread in his mouth.

"Mmm hmm mmm mmm," said the terrier.

"Is that for me? Thanks!"

Amy pulled the loaf from Betsy's mouth and bit into the fresh bread. She swallowed and sighed.

"That's the best. Nothing makes food taste better than starving to death."

"I know what you mean," said Betsy. "There was this one time when I didn't eat for two weeks. That first plate of ReCarb was the best!"

"Why couldn't you eat? Were you stuck on a job?"

"No, I was at home," said Betsy. "I just forgot to eat for two weeks."

A priest climbed the steps and passed them, his eyes boggling. He kept watching the pair and stumbled straight into a marble column.

"Too many people around," whispered Amy. "Keep your voice down. I don't want to be on the cover of the evening papers with a picture of a talking dog."

Betsy wagged his tail. "A talking dog? Who is it? I might know him!"

"It's you. People are going to get suspicious if we keep talking to each other."

"But how am I supposed to tell you stuff?"

"What stuff? I'm following you to Hyde Park. If there's any problem, I'll ask. You answer by wagging your tail for 'yes' and barking for 'no.' "

"That's confusing," said Betsy. "I pretty much wag my tail and bark all the time."

"Here's a test--want to visit the glue factory?"

Betsy barked and wagged his tail.

Amy sighed. "Somehow, I think we'll survive."

She finished the loaf of bread and drank cold, clear water from a public fountain in a nearby park, then followed the brown and white terrier west through the city.

Betsy stopped under the marble lions of Nelson's column in Trafalgar Square and let Amy's feet have another break. Amy pulled off her boots and wished she had normal shoes or a pair of thick socks. This would have been a fun hike across the city if she weren't wearing boots that weighed a ton and smelled like rotten fish guts.

"Who's this Nelson guy on the column?" whispered Betsy.

Amy touched the soles of her feet and hissed at the pain.

"Nelson? He saved England from the French or something like that."

"Why do they make him stand up there all day?"

"That's a statue, you silly dog!"

More horse-drawn carriages and wagons than Amy had ever seen in her life clopped along the wide boulevard that circled the square. Streams of pedestrians from all walks of life crossed the open plaza or gathered in thick clusters at the edges, some waving hand-painted signs. A building faced in Grecian columns with a small dome stood at the north side, next to a church of white limestone. Amy watched a man in a top hat stroll through a cloud of gray pigeons. He dodged a group of construction workers in leather aprons and hopped into a hansom cab.

The uniformity of broadcloth and black wool suits was a source of amazement for Amy, and made the city seem like a disturbed mound of black ants. The exceptions were the working class, who wore uniforms appropriate to their job, whether it was a white apron for milkmen, red coat for the shoe-shiners, or long coat and bare, shaven faces for hansom drivers.

"There's a water fountain," whispered Betsy. "Why don't you wash your feet?"

"Okay, but only if you play lookout. It's probably illegal."

Amy walked over to one of the two public fountains and dipped her feet in the wide pond below the splashing column. The freezing water quickly numbed her feet.

Betsy hopped onto the brown stone at the edge.

"Do you like this place?"

Amy shrugged. "It's all right. The city smells like a horse sandwich with cabbage and coal on the side, but I don't mind."

"If you want to go back to the ship, I can take you," said Betsy. "We can go right now."

"Did you forget what I said about tail wagging and barking? Why should I go back to the ship?"

The voice of a young boy spoke behind Amy.

"Who's it you're talking to?"

The child looked about eight and carried a stack of newspapers tied in brown string in his thin arms. A floppy brown cap sat backwards on his head and he wore a filthy gray shirt, suspenders, and dark green trousers with shiny knees.

"I was talking to myself," said Amy. "Don't you ever do that?"

The boy shook his head and turned away. "Only when I'm drunk."

"Wait! Can I have a paper?"

"That depends," said the boy. "Can I have a ha'penny?"

"Sorry, I don't have any money."

The boy shook his head. "A Yankee pearl with no bangers? Never heard that one before. Massive Jeremiah in Aldgate and Spitalfields last night. Still burning, I hear. Everybody what's anybody says gyppos started it."

"That's ridiculous."

"You bet your brass tacks! My brother was there last night, never you might what he was doing, and he says it's a Kraut war machine."

"You mean German? Why would Germany attack London?"

The boy turned up his nose. "Don't you know anything? The Kaiser is one crazy geezer. If anyone loves to read and write, it's him!"

"Read and write? Do you mean, 'fight?' "

"Of course, you nonce!"

The boy skipped across the crowded square with his newspapers.

Betsy looked up at Amy. "Was he speaking French? I can't speak French."

"No, it was cockney."

"Oh, wow. Now I also can't speak cockney!"

Amy dried her feet and wrapped them as best she could with strips of cotton torn from the lining of her jacket.

"Is Hyde Park that far away? I don't know how much walking I can do."

Betsy wagged his tail and trotted across the square. He came back a moment later with a sturdy black umbrella in his mouth. Amy took it from the terrier and used it to support some of her weight.

"Thanks! I'm not going to ask where you got this."

Betsy barked. "Good, because I forgot already!"

The strange pair left Trafalgar Square and walked along a street lined with white marble buildings, each one guarded by a doorman in a crimson jacket. The trees and green space of a park glowed in the sunshine at the end of the street beyond a two-story Roman arch. The manicured lawns and well-kept greenery of the park were a welcome sight to Amy and she hobbled on her umbrella cane with renewed vigor after the brown and white terrier.

Outside the clatter of the streets and early-morning hustle, leisure was the focus. Women in bright pastel dresses and hats walked along the dirt paths of the park, admiring the equally bright flowers on display. Tall maple and oak trees stood on the clipped lawns, too far apart to call them a forest and too close to call it a field. Pairs of riders bounced on the backs of chestnut horses, their silhouettes framed against a lake that rippled in the morning breeze. Mallards swam through cat-tail reeds at the edge of the lake, and the white triangles of sailboats flapped in the distance. At a cafe on the water, a black-uniformed waiter made the same sound as the sails as he unfurled and tossed white cloth over the wrought-iron tables.

"Finally," sighed Amy. "We made it. Now where's that cat?"

"This is the south end of the Serpentine," said Betsy. "You said that Sunflower would be at the north."

"Good gravy, not more walking!"

Amy and the terrier joined a line of well-dressed Londoners following the trail along the eastern shore of the lake, which curved like a new moon for at least half a mile before it tapered to an end.

Amy stopped in the middle of the path and leaned on her umbrella. "Here we are! I'm not moving another step."

Betsy snuffled the ground with his nose and ran a circle around Amy.

"I don't smell Sunflower anywhere!"

Amy sighed and pushed into a thick stand of mulberry bushes.

"Come and get me if you find him. I'm taking a nap."

She found a little hollow inside the mulberry and curled up on the dry leaves. The chatter of squirrels and swish of branches tossed by the wind quickly put her to sleep.

SHE WALKED on a beach. The bitter froth of the ocean constantly washed the wet sand from her feet, and a north wind brought the familiar smell of salt, fish, and rotting kelp.

Wake up

Amy spun on the wet sand, but she was alone.

"Who's there?"

Get up stupid

Amy balled her fists.

"Who said that?"

She must be dead. Humans. Turn your back and they die faster than a poona jumping off a cliff.

A matted pile of olive-green kelp flew up from the sand and covered Amy's face. She fell down and rolled on the beach, struggling to pull the soft mess with her fingers.

Amy opened her eyes. The kelp changed to yellow and orange fur in her hands, and the beach to mulberry bushes.

"Stop!" yelled Sunflower, and jumped down to the leaves. "I get it. You were just sleeping."

Amy brushed cat hair from her cheeks. "Sunflower! You're alive!"

"Did you expect something different?"

"I thought the inspector might catch you."

The orange cat narrowed his green eyes. "Catch me? That's a riot. I had to squeeze through some extremely disgusting tunnels, but no way in the seven lives of Saint Fluffy was I going to be found by that flying garbage can."

"Where's it now?"

"Where's what? Identify your pronouns, girl."

"The flying garbage can!"

"Who cares? As long as it doesn't blow up the little part of England that I'm standing on, we're golden."

Amy frowned. "Speaking of that, were you sitting on my face just now?"

Sunflower blinked. "I thought you were dead."

"How does covering my face in cat fur solve that problem?"

"It's an old tradition," said Sunflower sheepishly. "When a cat dies, his closest friends have to spend the night sitting on his head. It's an old cat remedy to see if he's trying to fake it or not. Quite effective, actually. No living creature can stand eight hours of cat butt in the face."

Amy held up her hands. "That's it--you cats are weird."

"Don't blame me! I didn't start the stupid tradition."

"Does this mean we're friends now?"

Sunflower shrugged. "I'm here and not in Egypt, aren't I? What happened to your boyfriend?"

"He's not my boyfriend! The idiot saw a ghost and ran off. I haven't seen him since last night."

"Good riddance. Now we don't have to bother with his silly family."

Betsy's voice came from outside the mulberry bushes. "Hello? Are you in there, Amy?"

Sunflower's green eyes popped wide. "What the devil?" The orange cat crawled outside to the manicured lawn. "Betsy!"

The brown and white terrier barked and wagged his tail. "Sunnie!"

"Where did you come from?"

Betsy shook his furry head. "You'll have to ask my parents. They won't tell me!"

"You imbecile," hissed Sunflower. "I mean this dimension. How did you get here? There wasn't enough power for another transport."

"I don't know," whined Betsy. "Don't ask me science stuff."

Amy crawled out of the mulberry bushes and stood up. "The Lady sent him to catch us and bring us back."

"Right," said the terrier. "But I'm not doing that anymore."

"Ixnay on the alkingtay," hissed Sunflower.

A pair of ladies in lace dresses and parasols strolled by. When they walked a hundred feet down the path, Sunflower stuck his furry face close to Betsy's nose.

"I don't believe a word of it," he spat. "You're the worst operator alive. You couldn't catch a cold!"

"That's not very nice," said Amy.

"Of course. That's why I said it."

"It's not true!" blurted Betsy. "I've stolen many props for the Lady."

"But––"

Amy knelt down to Sunflower and spoke in a whisper. "Listen––Betsy's here now so stop arguing about it, especially in a public place where people aren't used to cats and dogs arguing about it!"

"I don't like it," said the cat. "I still think it's fishy."

"Cats think everything smells like fish," whispered Betsy. "Something's wrong with their noses. Don't growl at me like that, Sunnie. It was just a joke. Oh, I almost forgot, Amy! I found your boyfriend."

Sunflower stuck his tail in the air. "See? Even the dog knows."

Amy waved her arms like a windmill. "Listen, you four-legged nincompoops, he's not my boyfriend. The next one who says that is going to learn how to fly with my foot shoved up his butt."

"Why would you do that?" yelped Betsy. "It sounds painful."

"Of course. That's why I said it."

"Fine, whatever," said Sunflower, his tail twitching. "Take us to the boy––um, the thing."

Amy and the cat followed Betsy along a dirt trail that crossed the tip of the lake to the west side. Philip sat on a wooden bench, elbows on his knees and head bowed as he stared at the ground. He looked up at the sound of their footsteps and the anxious expression on his face changed to a smile.

"There you are! I didn't––"

Amy cut him off with a chop of her hand. "Don't say a word, you coward. Why did you run away? Don't answer that! Friends don't leave friends in the middle of a strange city in another dimension!"

"I agree," said Sunflower. "What a human thing to do. Let's stuff his clothes full of leaves and throw him in the lake."

"No, no! I've got it," said Betsy, tail wagging. "Let's throw his clothes in the lake and stuff HIM full of leaves!"

Sunflower nodded. "That's probably worse."

Philip sighed and stood from the bench. He dusted off his filthy jacket and glanced around the park for a moment. At last he turned to Amy.

"I'm sorry that I ran away, and I feel perfectly beastly about the whole thing. The thing is, I'm terribly afraid of ghosts! I know that's not likely to make you feel better, Miss Armstrong, but––"

"It certainly doesn't make me feel better."

"I'm sorry. I'm certainly not worthy of your forgiveness. I sincerely apologize and I'll try to make it up to you. On my word, I promise it will never happen again. I've been feeling like a terrible coward the entire morning."

Amy frowned. "I don't like it when people run out on me."

Philip held a hand over his heart and bowed his head. "I think you're a superb and bricky girl, but I understand completely if you want me to leave. Let's shake hands and part ways in good humor."

"I'm not done with you just yet, Phil. But if your parents aren't loaded, we'll have a huge problem."

"Two problems," said Sunflower.

Betsy barked. "I hate you, too!"

"If it's gold and jewelry you're after," said Philip quietly, "I promise you'll find more than your cold little hearts can imagine."

Sunflower laughed. "I can imagine quite a bit, thank you very much."

11

3317 A.D.
Penal station in the former orbit of Kepler Prime

Recruit Officer Flistra sat down at a monitoring station full of blinking green lights and tiny round display screens. Detention Officer First Class Nistra stood with arms crossed behind the recruit, as the sauropod nervously flicked a dozen toggle switches on the console with his sharp claws.

"I'm waiting," growled Officer Nistra.

"Yes, sir! Sorry, sir!"

Flistra blew into a silver microphone and tapped it with a claw.

"Prisoner Armstrong, Amy returned to 'status temporalis.' Testing 1, 2, 3. Can you hear me?"

"Of course she can hear you," hissed Officer Nistra. He bared rows of needle-sharp teeth. "Use your eyes, poona-breath."

Flistra glanced up at the holographic image floating just inches from his yellow eyes. At the bottom of a mostly-transparent sphere, a blonde girl in an orange jumpsuit sat up, her eyes squeezed shut and hands over her ears.

"Sorry. Reducing levels."

Flistra twisted a knob. The holographic girl got to her feet and silently banged her clenched fists on the side of the sphere.

"You forgot to turn on the sphere volume," said Nistra. "Holy cat vomit, Flistra––is this your first interrogation?"

Flistra bowed his scaly green head. "I ... uh, I was sssick that day of training, sssir."

"You'd better look sharp, egg breath. I've got so many people breathing down my neck to find Kepler Prime that the people breathing down their necks have people breathing down the necks of the people breathing down their necks!"

"Yesss sir. Sorry sssir."

Flistra searched the hundreds of buttons on the console and flipped a toggle. The girl's voice crackled through the air.

"--green-skinned, motherless piles of goose poop don't let me out of here, I swear to God--"

Flistra cleared his throat. "Stardate ... um, what day--"

"Shut up and get to the real business," said Nistra.

"Yessir. Stardate eleven-thirty-four and something. Interrogation start point for Prisoner Armstrong, Amy."

Inside the spherical prison Amy glanced left and right. "Who's talking? Show yourself."

"This is Recruit Officer Flistra. Question: what happened to Kepler Prime?"

Amy shrugged. "How would I know?"

Flistra looked at Officer Nistra. "She said she doesn't know."

"I heard it speak, dill brain," snarled Nistra. He pushed the recruit out of the way and leaned close to the microphone. "You stupid monkey! Where's our homeworld?"

"Oh! You mean Kepler PRIME," said Amy. She patted the chest and legs of her jumpsuit. "It's probably with my keys. Do you guys have my keys?"

"Do we have her keys?" asked Flistra.

Nistra snapped his sharp teeth and clicked the speaking toggle. "This is no joke. Your ship was in asynchronous orbit around Kepler Prime when the planet disappeared. Your ship emitted a surge of power greater than 2.3 BEU a nanosecond before Kepler Prime disappeared. Your ship was the only thing left in orbit! Not even a scrap of dirt or metal anywhere for a distance of two light seconds!"

"There was that shuttle of cat hippies on landing approach," said Flistra. "Talk about a bunch of confused moggies."

"I don't know anything about any planet disappearing," said Amy. "Maybe you guys should check with LoJack. Do they have one for planets?"

"Five billion souls gone in a blink of an eye, including my entire family," fumed Nistra. "You think it's funny?"

"I wouldn't say five billion, sssir," whispered Flistra. "At least a billion of those have got to be atheist. They don't have souls, do they sssir?"

The scales on Nistra's face turned bright green. "Recruit Officer Flistra, get me a cup of slurm," he said. "From the B dispensary."

"But that's across the station! Sir."

"I know that!"

"Of course, sssir. Leaving now, sssir."

The automatic door swished and Nistra settled his bulk in the chair behind the console. He bared a grin full of sharp teeth at Amy's holographic image.

"Human, you will tell me what happened to my planet, to my life mate, and to my hatchlings. We sauros are the greatest civilization in the galaxy, with the greatest star fleet and most Galactic Cups to our name, and it's all due to the fact that we know how to make people talk. I don't mean the coffee and cakes kind of talk, I mean the screaming in horrible pain kind of talk!"

Amy spread her hands and shrugged. “It was an accident, okay? Some kind of gravity rift thing! Honestly, I had nothing to do with it.”

Nistra’s slimy black lips curled into a grimace. “That’s not what the Lady said, and she never lies! Prepare yourself, Armstrong, Amy, for the most horrible torture in the entire galaxy.”

The sauropod reached under the console and flicked several hidden switches. Soft violin music began to play inside the sphere and invisible projectors covered the walls of Amy’s prison with images of a soft green lawn. A black and white tuxedo kitten tottered across the grass, his head bobbing around in wonder.

“Gaze upon the filthy cat larva,” whispered Nistra. “Its tiny skull and disgusting eyes filled with hate and evil. Look at those horrible ears and the stomach-churning mat of fur! How does such a foul, nasty creature even draw breath? I can’t even look at it or I’ll spew chunks of my breakfast all over this console. Do you know how many sauro prisoners have gone mad after ten seconds of these images? Do you?!!!”

The kitten batted a yellow dandelion flower with its paws, and Amy pressed her hands on the wall to cover the image.

“Please don’t,” she moaned in mock horror. “It’s so awful!”

Nistra smiled. “If you think that’s bad, cast your gaze upon an even more repellent beast! I’m going to press the button and look away, because this one gives nightmares to even a hard-skinned veteran like me.”

A furry gray Yorkshire puppy walked up to the kitten, his pink tongue lolling. He sniffed the kitten and the two animals cuddled on the grass.

"Nooo," wailed Amy, trying to keep from laughing. "I can't take this torture! Where did you find these nightmares! There is no god ... there is ... no god!"

Nistra nodded, his scaly claws covering his eyes. "That's exactly what I said."

London, 1889

Philip led the small group west through the park and past a wide, three-story mansion of red brick circled by a black, wrought-iron fence. He waved at the mansion and grounds lazily.

"That's Kensington Palace."

Amy squinted at the dozens of paned windows. "Where the Queen lives?"

Philip shook his head. "Buckingham is the official residence of Queen Mary."

"Mary? That's not right. Victoria was Queen in the 1890s."

"You're American," said Philip. "You obviously don't pay attention to these things." The teenager pulled a wet newspaper from a trash can. "See?"

An illustration of the East End fire stood out from the front page, and below that a caption: "Queen Mary Consults On Blaze."

"It still doesn't sound right," said Amy. "I think this is one of those differences between our dimensions. Victoria was definitely queen on my Earth in 1889."

Philip shrugged. "That's as may be, but everything seems in order to me."

The teenagers and pair of animals strolled from the west end of the park and into Kensington proper.

Three-story buildings of rust-colored brick and paned windows framed in white stood behind the wide limbs of old-growth oaks. Heavy entrance doors with polished brass fittings waited for their owners to alight from black hansom cabs and stride up to them with a polite knock. Even more upper class were the pedestrians strolling on either side of the shade-covered lane. The men dressed in tails and top hats, and the ladies wore gigantic hats, dresses with tight bodices, and full skirts as if they were on their way to a garden wedding.

Amy felt embarrassed at her shabby men's jacket and boots. It wasn't that she wanted the approval of these posh fat cats; she just wanted to be invisible.

"Are we almost there?"

Betsy barked. "Yeah, Phillie! I'm starving!"

"Keep your voice down, please," said Philip. "We've arrived."

The dark-haired teenager removed his cloth cap and bowed as he gestured with one arm to a three-story brick mansion on the left. The paned windows of each story jutted out like tiny bay windows in painted white wood. A cleanly swept brick sidewalk led to the front steps and a dark blue door with a brass knocker and handle.

Sunflower looked up at the top windows. "So how do we break in? Top floor? Attic window?"

"I'm not a good climber," said Betsy.

Philip shook his head. "No need. Anthony should be in the garden, and he'll let us in that way."

"I hope he doesn't have a problem with cats or dogs," said Sunflower.

"As long as you keep quiet, I don't think he will."

Amy followed the teenager down a narrow, paved path between the brick buildings, her shoulders brushing the walls on either side. She passed through a wooden gate and walked into a walled garden filled with carefully tended roses, cherry trees, and a small, raised pond. Smoke curled from a white shack in the corner, next to an ivy-covered rear fence.

"This is more like a park than a garden," said Amy. "I don't see a tomato plant anywhere. I smell something weird––is that pine tar?"

The paved brick led to the rear entrance of the house, where several windows were open and a white-painted door gaped wide. A man's deep hum and a scraping sound came from inside.

Philip walked up to the back door and knocked. "Good morning!"

Steps pattered inside the house and a middle-aged man with graying black hair rushed forward. He was in shirtsleeves and held a scrubbing brush.

"Goodness, you're early." His eyes narrowed when he saw Philip and Amy. "You're not the linen boy. Trying to nick the silverware when the family's not about? Get away from here, you scroungers."

"Mark, it's me," said Philip. "Have you gone blind?"

The man peered at Philip's face and his expression slowly changed to wide-eyed shock. "Master Philip? But you're so tall! What are you doing in London? Why are you dressed like a chimney sweep?"

Philip laughed. "A thousand questions! It's a long story, Mark, but we're absolutely starving and need a proper bath."

"Certainly, certainly," said Mark, his eyes flitting over Amy's equally filthy rags. "Might I have the pleasure of this young lady's name?"

"My apologies. This is Miss Amy Armstrong, a friend of mine from America."

Amy stepped back with her left foot and curtsied.

"Yes, I see," said Mark, a pout of disapproval on his face. "I'll have Anthony fetch his cousins. Both are lady's maids and will help Miss Armstrong change into clothing that is ... less covered in filth, if I may be so bold."

"Thank you, Mister ...?"

"Mister Leonard."

"Thank you, Mister Leonard," said Amy.

"Mark's the finest butler in all England," said Philip. "By the way, what's all this fuss about cleaning?"

"Your family is coming down to London at the end of the week," said Mark. "May I assume your appearance is a sudden harbinger of that visit? Or rather, is it a matter that requires an urgent telegram to Clarence House?"

"Thank you, Mark, but there's no need for that." Philip paused for a moment. "No one's said anything about me being missing, have they?"

"I haven't heard a whisper," said Mark, and winked. "If you've been missing like that time in Calais, then we've nothing to worry about. All's well that ends well. Isn't that so, Master Philip?"

"That's the spirit!"

A PAIR of teenage girls in black cotton dresses and white aprons arrived at the back door of the house. Both girls were out of breath, with flushed faces and locks of brown hair flying from beneath their white cotton caps.

"Good morning, Mister Leonard," said the tallest one.

The butler nodded. “Good morning, Jane. Good morning, Nellie.” He waved at the kitchen table where Amy sipped a cup of tea. “This is Miss Armstrong from America. Please draw a bath and find suitable attire for the young lady. We’ve been cleaning, so the copper is full of hot water.”

“Very good, Mister Leonard.”

“Lady Gloria left a few trunks of clothing from her last visit, and Miss Armstrong may be able to wear them. However, the particulars of that delicate assessment are best left to your judgment, not mine.”

The girls curtsied. “Yes, Mister Leonard.”

Amy followed the pair up two flights of stairs made from dark, polished wood and along a hallway lined with doors and patterned maroon wallpaper.

“I’m Nellie,” said the shortest and youngest maid. “Are you really from America?”

“Don’t be nosy,” said the taller maid, Jane. “Miss Armstrong is too tired to be bothered with your questions.”

“It’s fine,” said Amy. “Yes, Nellie. I’m from California.”

“That’s so far!”

“Farther than you think,” said Amy wistfully.

“Are you running away?”

“Nellie! Mind your manners and bring the tub.”

The younger girl bowed from the waist and sped away.

Amy stared at Jane. “She’s going to carry the bath tub?”

“Yes, of course, Miss Armstrong.”

Jane led her down the hallway and into a small room with a mahogany wardrobe and a small bed with no sheets or blankets. A blue trunk with brass fittings and leather straps stood in one corner. Jane opened the trunk and pulled out stacks of folded white cotton and lace.

Amy sat on the bed. "I'm not running away."

"It's not my place to ask. Or to wonder how a young lady like yourself could walk about the city in a ragged old coat and man's shoes without even a scrap to cover her legs. Were you and Master Philip robbed?"

"This skirt is more than a scrap! You should see the things girls wear at the Del Monte Center."

Jane thumbed through the folded cotton and held up a white chemise. "Yes, I've heard about America. This looks about your size."

"It's true. Philip and I were attacked last night. The thieves stole our clothing and we had to walk across London."

Jane held a hand over her mouth and gasped. "You had to flee through the fire! That's why both of you are covered in soot and smell of smoke. It must have been horrible!"

"You don't have to be Sherlock Holmes to figure that out."

"Who?"

Amy sighed. "Never mind. It wasn't any walk in the park. Apart from the walking in the park."

The door squeaked and Nellie walked in with a large, oddly-shaped basin in her hands. Three feet long and two high, the white-painted, metal container looked more like a giant egg cup or a tub for infants than anything meant for adults. One side was higher than the other like a seat back, and the edges were smooth and rounded. The base was flared and the sides were decorated with hand-painted flowers.

"I'm supposed to take a bath in that?"

"Yes, Miss Armstrong," said Jane. "Pardon me for asking, but you don't have these in America?"

"Not that tiny! Our tubs are five times that size. This one doesn't look big enough to drown a cat."

Nellie's eyes popped. "Good golly! Sorry, Miss Armstrong."

"Very good," said Jane. "But a tub that large would grow tepid even before it was full. I expect the servants would also be worn to death carrying it through the rooms and running up and down the stairs with that much hot water."

"But how do I take a bath in this?"

Jane nodded. "Nellie, go check on the copper. Miss Armstrong, the lady wishing to take a bath sits down with her back against the raised edge."

"So my arms and legs don't get wet?"

"The lady taking a bath may use a washcloth to wet her arms and legs. Those parts normally stick out of the basin. The lady may also kneel in the tub and hold the sides, and a servant may douse her with warm water."

"Sounds like a lot of work, carrying water and tossing around basins."

Jane curtsied. "We are here at your pleasure, Miss Armstrong. This is how the finest English ladies bathe."

"Okay. I'll try it."

"Very good, Miss Armstrong," said Jane. "Oh-- did you wish to send a message to your family? Would they be worried at your absence?"

"My family is back in America. I'm visiting London with friends of mine."

Jane shook her head. "I've heard that American girls are independent, but it's still hard to understand.

I'd be frightened to death if I traveled by myself, worrying about strange men and all the dangers of travel."

"Indigestion is the most dangerous part of travel." Amy pulled the metal pigtail out of her pocket. "Everything else can be solved with the careful application of violence."

"From what I hear of California girls riding horses and shooting guns, I wouldn't expect any less!"

The maid opened the wardrobe and pulled out a long dress of dark red velvet. She motioned for Amy to stand up, then held the dress up to Amy's neck.

"How do you fancy this, Miss Armstrong?"

"I'd prefer to wear something less formal. How about a pair of Levi's?"

"Levi's? Is that a dressmaker?"

"Jeans. American trousers made of blue cotton."

Jane frowned. "Please forgive me for speaking bluntly, Miss Armstrong, but this is London, not California. A young lady of society can't wear trousers unless she wants to be laughed at by every Tom, Dick, and Harry."

"But that dress looks so uncomfortable!"

Jane bowed her head. "Please look through the rest of the outfits, and see if another is suitable. I must check on Nellie and the copper."

The maid left, and Amy searched through the dresses hanging in the wooden wardrobe. She considered climbing out a window and fleeing for her life instead of having to wear one of the heavy things, but found a pale yellow dress made of cotton and embroidered in tiny roses. Stiff white lace bordered the high neck and cuffs of the long sleeves.

"Very nice," she murmured.

"Who are you talking to?"

Amy spun around. “Don’t scare me like that, Sunflower!”

The orange tabby glided into the room and sat on a circular brown rug next to the tub.

“Your stupid human boyfriend and the other human tried to give me a bowl of milk. Do you know what could happen if I drank that? This entire house would be matchsticks!”

Amy spread her arms. “I’m sorry, Sunflower. What about Betsy?”

“He’s hiding somewhere and whining that the humans won’t let him in the house. I’ve looked all over this place but I haven’t seen anything worth stealing. They probably have the valuables hidden inside an invisible parallax field, but I’m not detecting any power source.”

“I don’t think they had invisible parallax fields in 1889. This is only one of their houses and the jewelry is probably at the country estate.”

“Who are you talking to?”

Jane stood at the door, her blue eyes wide.

Amy cleared her throat and laughed nervously. “Just the cat. I like talking to myself.”

“I could have sworn that I heard a man’s voice,” said Jane. She bent over Sunflower and stroked his head. “Is this your moggie?”

“My what?”

“Your cat.”

“Oh, yes. He’s a bad kitty who doesn’t like people. Be careful.”

Sunflower hissed with appropriate timing and Jane yanked her hand away.

“Saints preserve us! My apologies, Miss Armstrong––the hot water is ready.”

Nellie huffed and puffed behind her, a bucket of steaming water in each hand.

"Thank you," said Amy. She wagged a finger at Sunflower. "Now go play somewhere else, kitty. Mommy has to take a bath."

Sunflower growled and slunk out of the room.

Nellie set the buckets next to the tub. "Is that a trained cat, Miss Armstrong? I've never heard of a cat that takes orders."

"He used to belong to a circus, but don't ever say that in front of him," said Amy. "He's very sensitive."

The two maids glanced at each other.

"Very good, Miss Armstrong," said Jane. "Do you need help taking off your clothes? What little there is of them?"

"I think I can manage."

Amy waited for the maids to leave, but the girls stood patiently and watched her.

"I said, I think I can manage."

"Very good, Miss Armstrong," said Jane. "The soap and brushes are on that tray, and the towels and robe are there. You may speak out if you need anything. We'll be outside the door."

"You don't have to do that. Take a break or have a rest or something."

"Not at all. It's our pleasure."

Both maids curtsied and left the room.

Amy stepped out of the nasty boots and dropped her hat, jacket, and the rest of her filthy clothes onto the rug.

"This is going to be messy, I bet."

Amy poured both buckets of hot water into the tub, and sat in the tiny basin with her legs sticking over the sides. She scrubbed the fascinating collection of soot and grime from her face and body, washed her hair, and then lay back in the steaming water with her eyes closed. It wasn't the same as a full bath, but still relaxing enough to make her sleepy.

"This is the life," she murmured.

The door vibrated with a loud knock, and Amy startled awake, spilling water onto the bedroom rug.

"Miss Armstrong, do you need assistance?" asked Nellie through the door.

"I'm fine. Out in a second."

Amy climbed out of the small tub, toweled off, and wrapped a thick white robe around herself. She stuck her toes into a pair of white slippers and opened the door.

Nellie smiled. "I hope you're feeling better, Miss Armstrong. Did you find a suitable dress?"

"Yes, this one."

Jane examined the yellow embroidered dress in the wardrobe.

"I had a feeling you would like this more than the others," said Jane. "Nellie, help dry Miss Armstrong's hair."

"I like it very much," said Amy. "Does it have any pockets?"

"I certainly hope not!" Jane laughed, and cleared her throat. "I mean, I'm certain we can find a handbag or something in which you may carry your ... weaponry."

"Super."

Jane patted a stack of white cotton. "Please drop your robe, Miss Armstrong, and we'll help with your undergarments."

"What? I'm not wearing those things! Where are my other clothes and underwear?"

"Soaking in lye," said Jane. "If you ask me, we should have burned the things. Those were scraps of bearskin compared to this fine French cotton."

"I'd rather wear bearskin than dress like a clown!"

Jane held up the cotton undergarments. "Miss Armstrong, there is nothing clownish about wearing a chemise, three petticoats, bloomers, garters, and stockings. You're not old enough for a corset, but that's something to look forward to, as my mother says."

Amy shook her head. "I've never worn anything this silly in my life!"

"I agree that it must be difficult to ride a bronco and shoot a buffalo while dressed as a proper young lady," said Jane. "But there aren't any broncos or buffaloes around here, Miss Armstrong."

"All the better for it," said Nellie.

Jane curtsied with the yellow dress in her arms. "Trust me, Miss Armstrong--don't taste the pudding 'til it's done. You'll be very pleased with the result."

Amy sighed. "Fine, fine."

Instead of arguing with the maids about it, she decided to think of the dress and supporting garments as something she had to wear for a fancy Halloween party. After drying Amy's hair, the maids helped her to dress in the knee-length bloomers and chemise, white stockings, and several petticoats. The yellow dress went over her head and covered Amy like the brass shell casing of a bullet. The upper half above her waist--the bodice--was tight and the skirt was long and full.

"I feel like a battleship," said Amy. "A battleship with legs."

Nellie clapped her hands. "You look absolutely precious!"

Jane handed her a mirror, and Amy admired the styling to her blonde hair. The girls had curled her bangs and Amy's blonde locks were piled on top of her head.

"Why does it have to be so foofy-doofy? Can't I just wear a pony tail?"

"Foofy-doofy?" Nellie tilted her head. "Is that a New York word?"

"Miss Armstrong is from California," hissed Jane.

Amy pursed her lips. "Does pink lipstick go with this outfit?"

"I should think not," said Jane. "Proper English ladies don't wear rouge or any makeup at all. It's very low class, Miss Armstrong."

"Really?"

"Pardon me for saying so, but yes."

Amy pulled at the material around her ribs. "Is it supposed to be so tight? I can't even see my feet. How am I supposed to climb a tree or run in this thing?"

Nellie giggled. "She's joking! I told you, Americans are funny."

"Unfortunately, I believe Miss Armstrong is quite serious," said Jane.

AMY LIFTED one side of her skirt as she descended the stairs one step at a time. If she had had a choice of footwear, it wouldn't have been these high-heeled leather boots. Catch a toe on her hem or miss a step and she'd tumble down the stairwell like a bag of potatoes, but these were the best shoes that Nellie and Jane could find. It wasn't like they could pop down to Payless Shoes and buy another pair of sneakers.

Mark waited at the foot of the stairs for Amy. He opened a door and preceded her into the parlor.

"Miss Amy Armstrong, my lord."

Philip had been sitting in the parlor watching the carriages rattle past the window. The teenager had changed into a jacket and trousers of light gray wool with a white collared shirt and pink bow tie. He looked up at Amy's entrance and almost stumbled over his own feet in the sudden effort to get up from his chair.

"Great Scott!"

"I know, right? I look ridiculous."

Philip shook his head. "That's not it at all. This is the first time since I've known you that you actually looked like a young lady."

Amy wanted to cross her arms, but halfway through the motion realized she'd probably rip something. She settled for sneering at Philip.

"Is that supposed to be a compliment?"

Philip bowed from the waist. "Please take it no other way."

"Well, don't get used to it. I'm only wearing this costume because your maids pinched all of my clothes and won't give them back. Also, I don't want anyone staring at me on the street."

Philip adjusted the neck of his tie. "You may not want to hear this, Miss Armstrong, but a young woman with such a striking countenance may find that unavoidable."

"What? Speak English!"

Jane giggled. "Master Philip means that everyone stares at a pretty girl."

"That's enough, you two," said Mark, and pushed the teenage maids out of the room.

Amy held up a small purse of yellow silk. "Anyone who looks at me too long gets a countenance full of what's in this. I promise they'll need a dentist."

"I hope doesn't come to that," said Philip. "Would you like some tea? After that, perhaps we could take a walk to the park."

"Did you forget what happened last night? I think I've done enough walking for the rest of my life."

"I promise we'll have a better time."

"Not if you see a ghost, you won't."

Philip grinned. "They don't come out in the day-time. I know that much!"

Mark brought out tea, cheese, and sandwiches on a silver tray. Amy drank a cup of strong tea and ate a marmalade sandwich. She dropped several hunks of yellow cheese into her purse when nobody was looking.

"Just a short walk," said Philip. "To the palace and down to Rotten Row."

"That doesn't sound like a good time."

"Oh, don't let the name fool you. It's where anyone who's anyone goes to see everyone."

Amy sighed but didn't protest when the maids reappeared with a pair of lace gloves, a white shawl, and a broad-brimmed straw hat. Jane secured it to Amy's hair using a handful of long and dangerous-looking pins.

Philip pressed a floppy gray cap over his dark hair--a style that Amy associated with golfers and old Greek men--and offered his arm to Amy.

"Shall we?"

"Do I have to?"

"I'm simply being polite. When strolling with a lady, a gentleman must always offer his arm, whether the lady is a friend, relative, or otherwise. To act in any other way is the mark of a boor, or a cad."

"You act like you're fifty, not fifteen!"

Philip dropped his elbow and looked down. "I'm sorry. I'm just trying to explain how we're supposed to act. This is the modern world, you know, and not some ridiculous, far-flung future with talking cats."

Amy sighed. She pushed Philip's elbow up and linked their arms together. This caused a broad smile to spread across the teenager's face.

"That's the spirit!"

Amy stuck out her tongue and didn't look at him.

The pair walked along the boulevard, Philip tipping his hat to passing couples and Amy admiring the exquisite brick mansions.

"Not a security system in sight," she murmured.

"Excuse me?"

"Nothing. So Phil, have you met the Queen?"

"Once, but it was many years ago. Her Majesty came to visit Clarence House for a few days. Honestly, I don't remember much about it, apart from the mean German guards who wouldn't let me play in the garden."

"I thought your family was loaded. You should be hanging around the palace day and night."

"By 'loaded,' do you mean my family is wealthy? That's certainly true. But wealth and favor at court don't necessarily go hand in hand. Also, these aren't the days of Henry the Eighth, with massive banquets, construction of palaces, and celebration of excess. Her Majesty is quite reserved and studious."

They crossed into the green swath of Kensington and strolled leisurely along a path of hard dirt lined with trimmed rosebushes. Other couples walked arm-in-arm along the straight paths. Although every man, woman, and child wore a hat, some of the ladies carried a parasol as shade from the afternoon sun. These happy people were a long way from the grinding poverty of the East End, thought Amy, and might as well have been on the Moon.

With its equestrian character and faint smell of coal, London was certainly different from Pacific Grove, but what struck Amy was the lack of an electrical hum, the faint fluorescent buzz of transformers and store signs and street lamps that formed the background noise of a modern city. London had a buzz––steel on cobblestone, pubs roaring with laughter, the puffing screech of steam engines––but it was a buzz that felt better in Amy's ears. It was the difference between sheepskin and polyester, natural and unnatural, music and noise.

Philip pointed to a broad dirt track along the southern edge of Hyde. "There's Rotten Row."

Hundreds of horses covered the long track, cantering singly or stopped in small groups, ridden by elegant men in short black jackets, white trousers, and top hats. The gentlemen chatted with each other as they rode, tipping their hats to any ladies nearby. A long line of carriages and their drivers waited on a parallel street. The crowds, the riders, the equestrian path all seemed to go on forever, and to Amy seemed like a mile-long summer party.

"Is this a special day?"

Philip shook his head. "Not really."

"Then why is everyone dressed up?"

"It's warm today, and the beginning of the season. This is how gentlemen and ladies meet their friends and social acquaintances in public, at least during this part of the day. Don't you have this sort of thing in your time, Miss Armstrong?"

"I don't think cruising downtown on a Friday night is the same kind of thing. Also, you can drop the 'Miss Armstrong' crap. Call me Amy."

"It wouldn't be polite."

"Geez, Phil! Why are you so prim and proper?"

Philip turned red.

"I know that you're from a different time, Miss Armstrong, where these sorts of things don't matter. In England when a man and woman call each other by their Christian names, it's a very personal matter. It signifies a bond that cannot be broken."

Amy giggled. "You mean, like 'sweetie' or 'honey'? No wonder you always look so embarrassed when I call you 'Phil.' "

"I suppose I've become used to it, although I wish you would try to avoid calling me that in public. Among unmarried men and women, speaking that way means we're engaged."

"Hey! Don't get your hopes up, Phil. This girl isn't getting married anytime soon."

Philip touched the brim of his hat as they passed other couples. Amy watched the pale ladies and the men with mutton-chop beards and wondered what kind of life were they going to have in the years ahead. Only a generation separated these elegant couples from a bloody and devastating world war. Would there even be a war in this parallel dimension, this 'snapshot' of Earth? The ladies to whom Amy gave a polite smile, would they spend two decades raising a happy family, only to lose their children in the fields of France? Amy wondered if she could make a difference. Where would you start, and would it even matter?

"What's going to happen?" she murmured.

"Don't worry, I'm sure dinner will be grand," said Philip. "Mark's sister will cook us fantastic dishes with heaps of potatoes and lashings of cream. We'll take the early train from King's Cross and arrive in Yorkshire tomorrow afternoon."

"I was just talking to myself. I meant, life in general."

They separated from the other couples and followed a path deeper into the trees of Hyde Park. Philip didn't say anything for a long moment and Amy wondered if she'd upset him somehow.

"It's a good question," he said. "I'm looking forward to seeing my family tomorrow, but honestly, I never liked them a bit."

"That's a horrible thing to say about the people who raised you."

"If you mean the nursemaids and governesses that actually spent time with me, then you'd be right. I never saw my father or mother unless it was to be whipped with a willow branch for something I had no idea I'd done, or to be yelled at and locked in the cellar. Just because my father was rich doesn't mean that my childhood was bliss."

Amy looked across the wide lawn of the park. "At least you had a family to yell at you. Some children aren't so lucky."

"Luck doesn't enter into it. Trust me, my father won't have noticed I've been gone. I spent two years in that smelly Junktown apartment, and that annoying little bug Nick is missing me more than anyone, I wager."

"You want to go back after all the crap I suffered to get you here? That's rich, buddy."

Philip sighed. "I didn't mean that. I'm indebted to you and Sunflower for what you've done, and quite appreciate the sacrifice you've made. But you asked about life in general and that's the whole problem. I don't know what to do about the future or my family. Knowing too much about history and what can happen is just the icing on the cake, as you Americans say."

"Because something can happen, doesn't mean it will."

Philip tipped his hat to a passing couple. "Yes, and in the opinion of my father, I'm one of those somethings that never will."

"He's just a man," said Amy, and swung her handbag in a sudden burst of energy. "Remember what I said about the careful application of violence?"

Philip smiled. "I know I must have said this before, but you're the most interesting and yet most frightening girl I've ever met."

"You haven't met that many. I know I've said that before."

Philip cleared his throat. "You're welcome to stay at Clarence House in Yorkshire as long as you like, but I'm afraid the fabricated story about you being a traveling American isn't going to hold water, even if we increase your age to sixteen or seventeen. Young women don't travel without a servant or a relative. It's positively peculiar and definitely not done, and my mother and father will see through it after a few days. They might be forced to contact the authorities."

"Do I look sixteen?"

Philip turned red. "Absolutely. I thought you were older than me at first. Are all the girls so tall in America?"

"Only the ones that eat Wheaties."

"Is that a medicine? Some sort of fortified tonic?"

“Could be,” said Amy. “I won’t be sticking around, Phil, so it doesn’t matter if your parents don’t believe my story. Good gravy, look at your face! Don’t say you’ll miss me.”

“Well ... I ... uh ... I’d be happier if you could stay longer. You’re the only person with whom I can talk about traveling to the future. Once I mention talking cats and dogs, anyone else in England is going to think I’m crazy.”

Amy put both hands on Philip’s arm and squeezed. “I don’t know about that, Phil. Someday you’ll find a girl just as scared of ghosts as you are.”

Philip burst out laughing and Amy joined him in a loud giggle, giving quite a start to an elderly, well-dressed couple and a Pomeranian.

THE DINNER was exactly as Philip described, and Amy went to bed stuffed with roast beef, boiled carrots, celery, roasted potatoes, buttered bread, and raspberry and currant tart. Compared to the mattress back home, the downy feather bed was like sleeping on a cloud, and she drifted off to sleep almost as soon as she closed her eyes.

A weight landed near her feet and Amy blinked at the gray light of morning that streamed from the window. The weight climbed along the quilt, passing her knees and waist, testing each step as carefully as a soldier in a minefield.

Sunflower stuck his whiskers into Amy’s face and sniffed with his tiny pink nose.

“I’m not dead,” murmured Amy. “You need to write these things down.”

“How? Where am I going to keep a pen?”

Amy sighed and closed her eyes. "I can think of a few places."

"How crude." Sunflower curled up on Amy's pillow. "I hid on top of a cupboard all night, and thank you for asking. The sacrifices I make for you ..."

"Why didn't you sleep in here?"

"I wasn't sleeping. I already told you that operators don't have to do that. The real reason is there are too many humans around, doing this or doing that. Luckily you hairless monkeys never look up, so it's easy to hide on top of things."

"We still have hair, there's just not enough to keep us warm," said Amy. "That's why we have to wear silly things like blue jeans and smelly wool jackets."

"Yes! Why do you have to smell so bad all the time? Take for example the bath yesterday. You came downstairs covered in a gassy cloud of roses, like you'd been doused with an entire planet's worth of the disgusting stuff. Only a homeless cat addicted to poona juice would do something that crazy. I'm beginning to think you humans don't even like your natural scent!"

Amy chuckled. "At least we don't sniff each other's butts."

"Of course not! You don't do anything right."

"Speaking of doing things right, don't think I haven't forgotten about that gold Super Nintendo," said Amy. "You still owe me."

"That old thing? We're in the wrong century and wrong continent."

"It's still mine."

"What about the jewelry we're going to liberate from your human friend? That should be enough to make you forget about that stupid gold prop from the future."

"I don't know," said Amy. "Maybe we don't have to steal anything from his family. Maybe I want to stop taking things that aren't mine, period. Too much stress and too many problems."

"Don't get soft on me now! With the Lady after us, we'll need to bring something back to her as a peace offering. Preferably many valuable somethings."

"But what if I want to stay here?"

Sunflower blinked his green eyes. "I give up my Egypt plans and you're the one who wants to stay?"

"I've got a right to change my mind."

"It's your boyfriend, isn't it? You don't want to leave him!"

"He's not my boyfriend and stop repeating yourself, Sunflower. You sound like a broken record."

The orange cat sighed. "So what was all that stuff about the gold Super Nintendo? And don't forget, if you stay here you'll never see your family again."

"I don't know what I'm doing, does that help? I want to go back, but I don't want to go back. I know what I want but not how to get it. Half my brain is saying one thing, and half another thing."

"Too much rose gas is what my brain says," murmured Sunflower. "You should really look into that."

Amy turned onto her stomach and jammed her face into the pillow.

"Thanks for the advice," came her muffled reply.

12

Philip had suggested leaving for Yorkshire as early as possible, so the morning turned busy far faster than Amy would have liked. Jane brought her a tray with a cup of strong tea and a plate of two fried eggs, sausage, sliced tomatoes, and a scoop of something Jane called "bubble and squeak," which looked and tasted like a mix of refried vegetables and potatoes from yesterday's dinner. After Amy finished breakfast, the maids brushed and re-braided her blonde hair and helped her wear the yellow dress from the day before.

Farewells were polite and reserved. Mark pulled away slightly and his face turned red after Amy squeezed him in a tight embrace.

"Thanks for letting me keep the clothes," said Amy.

The butler bowed his head. "Considering the situation, I'm certain Her Ladyship would want you to have them."

The two teenage maids grinned after Amy hugged them.

"Don't be bothered by it, Miss Armstrong," said Jane. "She never liked that dress anyway."

Mark sent one of the girls out to the cab stand. A few minutes later, a two-wheeled black hansom pulled by a chestnut mare stopped in front of the house. The driver climbed down from his perch at the back of the cab and held out a hand to assist Amy into the small box of a compartment that was covered on all sides but the front. She and Philip took up both seats while Betsy and Sunflower sat on their laps. The driver stepped up behind them, took the reins in his hands, and clicked his mouth, causing the chestnut mare to snort and trot away. Amy waved at Mark and the young maids as the hansom bounced along the cobblestones.

Betsy looked up at Philip. "Can I talk now?"

"Please, don't. The driver might hear you." He turned to Amy. "How was breakfast?"

"It was great, thank you, although I could die for a glass of orange juice."

Philip squinted at her. "Does that you mean you want orange juice, or not?"

"Thanks for asking how I'm feeling," said Sunflower. "Which is awful, by the way."

"It means I'd like a glass. But don't worry about it."

Philip nodded. "Tropical fruits aren't as common in London as they are in California. My family has an orangerie––they were all the rage years ago––but it's May and I'm afraid nothing will be ripe."

The cab rattled over the streets and through intersections packed with horse-drawn transport of all shapes and sizes, directed by policemen on raised stands in the center of traffic, arms waving like marionettes and high-pitched silver whistles between their teeth. The traffic was far more furious than Amy expected, with pedestrians dodging between carriages and few laws apparently governing the speed and passing behavior of the equestrian mob. Steel-shod wheels rattled, horses in blinders stamped their hooves and whinnied, and drivers snapped whips and shouted all manner of epithets at all manner of people under the gray morning sky. Guards in red jackets and black bearskin hats stood at the front entrances of official-looking limestone buildings. Shopkeepers in black ties and white aprons swept the sidewalks. Schoolboys in blue caps and coats stampeded by, carrying stacks of books tied with rope over a shoulder. Children dressed in ragged clothing stood at busy corners with brooms in hand, waiting to sweep horse manure out of the path of well-dressed men in exchange for a farthing or two.

"It's almost like Junktown," said Amy. "Apart from all the people, the buildings, and not being inside an asteroid slash spaceship. In space."

Philip laughed. "You must be joking, because that's everything."

"Not exactly," said Sunflower. "I've seen hundreds of cats in London, and not one of them is smarter than a hair on the tip of my tail."

"I met one!" barked Betsy. "His name is Mr. Bismarck and he lives in a box!"

"I don't believe that for a second."

"Shush, both of you," whispered Philip.

The crenelated spires of a four-story Italianate structure of red brick rose on the north side of the street to Amy's left. A square tower with large clock faces stood on the far corner, its roof covered in gray-blue tiles that matched the color of the overcast sky.

Amy pointed at the tower. "Is that King's Cross Station?"

"Not quite," said Philip. "It's a hotel that fronts St. Pancras. King's Cross adjoins it."

They passed an intersection staffed by an energetic traffic constable and pulled to the curb behind a long line of horse-drawn cabs, each emptying a load of passengers. Beyond an open-air cement plaza stood a more modest building with a plain rectangular facade of beige limestone. Two huge half circles of paned glass bracketed a clock tower, and made Amy think of a nose separating massive eyes. Through the half-moon "eyes" she saw the glass-covered galleries over the railway platforms and clouds of white steam.

Philip paid the cab driver. He escorted Amy and their two animal companions––who for the sake of appearance wore a collar and leash––into the station and purchased a pair of first-class tickets.

Instead of sitting in the stuffy and tiny first class waiting room, Amy went out to the platform to watch the monstrous black engines roll into the station, wheezing and puffing like asthmatic iron beasts. After a final screech of brakes, the polished wooden doors of the carriages swung open and freed a swarm of determined, briskly walking travelers.

"Strange to see so many doors," said Amy. "One for every compartment."

Philip laughed. "Those are the first class carriages. The second class are more closely packed together, with only one entrance at each end of the carriage. We won't have to worry about that, thank goodness, because we've got proper seats."

"Can I ride with you, Philip?" whispered Betsy. "Or do I have to wait in a hole like last night?"

"Of course you can stay with us. There isn't anything like a hole when it comes to a train."

"You obviously don't know Betsy," murmured Sunflower. "I think the Lady gave him a special 'hole-finding radar.' "

Amy pointed up at the curved steel beams and glass panes above. "It seems like a waste to have such a huge roof covering the whole station."

"Not with our English weather it isn't," said Philip. "It's much safer and convenient to embark out of the pouring rain, especially for the ladies who travel."

Their train arrived a quarter-hour before departure, hissing with steam and shaking the concrete platform below Amy's feet. Porters in dark green jackets and brimmed caps arrived and helped the arriving passengers exit the carriages and to cart away the substantial amount of luggage on metal dollies.

Unlike the silver Amtrak trains that Amy had seen streaking through the Salinas Valley, the carriages were all wood. Each compartment was separate from the others, and had no interior hallway. A door on either side of the compartment served as entrance and exit.

Philip found the appropriate carriage and held Amy's hand as she lifted her skirt and stepped carefully up and through the high door. The interior of the compartment was lined in polished walnut and the seats were heavily padded chestnut leather.

Amy sat down and sighed.

"Good gravy! I hate long skirts, especially with these boots."

Philip grinned. "Please don't say that, Miss Armstrong. You look absolutely beautiful."

"You'll sing a different tune if I slip and fall on my face. There's a high chance of that happening, since this outfit is basically made for two things: sitting and standing."

Betsy jumped into the carriage, followed by Sunflower.

"Are you two lovebirds arguing?" asked the orange cat. "I love watching humans yell at each other."

Betsy barked. "Yeah! It's like a weird little show!"

"Keep quiet, you two," whispered Amy. "People can see through the windows, and someone else might sit next to you."

Philip held up a hand. "No, it's fine. Mark gave me enough money to purchase four tickets. The animals can talk freely once we leave the station."

"I'm glad at least one of you humans knows what he's doing," said Sunflower. "Such a bright thing he is."

"Too bad you two will have to split up," said Betsy. "It's like a movie!"

Amy sighed. "I'd like another seat. Preferably at the other end of the train from these two."

"I'll join you," said Philip.

"When are you getting married?" asked Betsy.

Sunflower licked an orange paw. "Today, I bet. That's why they want to get away from us."

"I'll tell you when," said Amy. "Right after cats fly."

"Impossible."

"Maybe. Just don't go near open windows. Or be on a speeding train." Amy held a finger to her lips. "Wait a sec––there's a window ... and you're on a train. That's too much of a coincidence."

Sunflower curled up on the seat. "Yeah, yeah. I get the point. You don't have to rub it in."

Betsy scrambled over to the window and put his paws on the glass. "Did you guys hear that?"

"Was it the sound of my life slipping through my paws?" murmured Sunflower through his tail. "Because that's definitely happening."

"No, it was more of a pew-pew, boom-boom, oh-god-help-me kind of sound."

Philip shook his head. "I didn't hear anything strange. One of the porters must have dropped a package."

"Maybe," said Betsy. "It must have really hurt, though, because he wasn't happy. Not even a little bit."

"Welcome to the club," murmured Sunflower.

Doors slammed, conductors shouted warnings, and the whistle blew. The train shuddered forward with a wheeze and slowly pulled out of the covered glass tunnel of the station. Amy waved at a pair of young girls standing outside the station with an older woman, but they were pointing at something behind the train.

"Does anyone smell a fire?" asked Philip.

"Even I know this is a steam train," said Amy. "It basically runs on fire."

"Not that kind of smell. This is a heavier kind of smoke."

A red flash lit the sky. A half-second later, a roll of thunder vibrated the compartment windows.

Sunflower opened his eyes. "Uh, oh."

"I thought you got rid of that thing!" yelled Amy.

"I did!"

A pair of windows bracketed each door to the compartment. Philip jerked up the sash of the nearest and stuck his head out. Amy tossed her wide-brimmed hat onto a seat and opened the other window.

A breeze tossed strands of her hair as the train clanked along the rails at little more than a horse trot. A column of black smoke rose from the railway station behind them.

A window in the next compartment slid up and a gray-haired man in a bowler hat leaned out, just in time to see another red flash. Glass panes fell from the roof of the station and shattered on the platforms. Another stream of smoke rose into the sky, boiling orange with heat and flame.

"It's on fire, by Jove," said the man in the bowler hat. "Look there!"

A tiny silver octopus floated through the fiery cloud, linked to the station by a crimson ray of light.

Steel beams turned yellow and white and twisted into ghastly curls under the crimson ray, and the pair of curved gallery roofs collapsed in an explosion of glass and smoke.

"Come and have a look," said Amy. She grabbed Sunflower and held him halfway out the window.

The man in the bowler hat pointed at the inspector. "That's the Aldgate demon! The German scourge!"

"It's not from Germany and it's definitely not a demon, I can tell you that," yelled Sunflower.

"Thanks for that, Kitten Obvious," said Amy. "But if this train doesn't move any faster, we're all going to that great big recycling bin in the sky."

The bowler-hatted man looked back at Philip and Amy, and the orange tabby clinging to the window frame.

"Great what in the sky?"

Sunflower sniffed. "You heard what she said, buster."

"She said recycling!" barked Betsy from inside the compartment.

The man pointed a trembling finger at Amy. "Am I going mad, young miss, or did your cat just speak?!!"

Philip cleared his throat. "Sir, a killer robot from the future is pursuing this train. Talking pets are the least of your problems."

THE TRAIN rapidly increased speed, either through luck or the actions of a quick-thinking engineer. The inspector dwindled into a silver dot against the columns of smoke and finally disappeared as the train thundered north at maximum velocity.

Philip and Amy closed the two windows of the compartment and returned to their seats.

"This is going to put a crimp in your plans of staying here," said Sunflower, and jumped up to the leather cushion across from Amy.

Betsy wagged his tail. "A big, inspector-sized crimp!"

"What plans are you talking about?" asked Philip.

"It's not important," said Amy. "It's a moot point if the inspector catches us."

"An inspector-sized moot!" barked Betsy.

Philip rubbed his forehead. "Steady on, you two. It's a machine. There must be a way to disable and destroy it."

"There is," said Sunflower. "But the cat who designed the tools to make the weapon that can destroy it hasn't been born yet. You don't want to wait around for that."

"You lost it by going underground," said Amy. "Can't you do that again?"

"Sure, but I'm not a cave troll so don't expect me to stay in a hole for more than half an hour at a time. My name is Sunflower, after all."

Philip sighed. "We either think of a plan, or we're done for."

"If you only had a portable voice controller backpack," murmured Betsy, glancing back and forth. "I heard those work really well on inspectors."

"Right," said Sunflower. "And if monkeys fly out of my butt, we'll all go to heaven."

"Just saying."

Amy looked down at the handbag in her lap. "The three of us will leave at the next station and Philip will continue to Yorkshire. There's no reason he can't go home."

"There is too a reason! I'm not leaving you to the mercy of that inhuman machine!"

"Don't be stupid! The entire point of this trip was to take you home."

"I might jolly well be stupid, Miss Armstrong, but I won't save myself at the cost of anyone's life, especially yours. How could I stand to look at myself, knowing that you had perished or suffered imprisonment by the Lady on my account? That's a dog's life, and I'd rather not live it."

"What a silly thing to say."

"Exactly!" growled Betsy.

"It's not! It's what I believe, and I won't be sorry."

Betsy lay on the seat next to Sunflower. "I think they're arguing again," the terrier whispered.

"Shut up, dog," hissed Sunflower. "You're ruining the tender moment."

"Sorry. Continue!"

Amy shook her head and moved to the far side of the compartment, where she focused on the tall smokestacks and telegraph poles whistling past the window. Philip grumbled to himself for a bit and then pretended to take a nap, his feet on the opposite seat and trilby hat over his face.

Sunflower sighed. "Thanks, dog. You definitely ruined it."

"You're welcome," said Betsy. "Hey! This reminds me of that time we took a vacation to Alpha Centauri."

"What vacation? The flight was cancelled. We sat in the spaceport twelve hours staring at each other and eating from the vending machine!"

"Right! It was awesome!"

Sunflower growled and turned away from the terrier. Both animals soon fell asleep on the cushioned leather.

The smoking factories and signs of busy industry were soon replaced by gentle waves of countryside. Stone walls separated harvested fields, and men strolled about in waist-length tunics and floppy hats. Cinnamon-colored brick houses with peaked slate roofs clustered around the Gothic spires of village churches like chicks at the feet of a gray-feathered hen. The train passed stone and cement bridges, muddy rivers, and wagons loaded down with tall piles of hay.

The train whipped through the countryside for at least half an hour before squealing to a stop at a long platform covered by a narrow wooden roof.

Sunflower opened his eyes. "Are we there yet?"

"Not quite," murmured Philip, hat still over his face. "Ask me in four hours."

"What if the inspector catches up to us?" asked Betsy.

"I share in your concern," said Philip. "But the train halts only momentarily at these stations, and is quite punctual. This is England, after all."

The whistle blew as a full stop to Philip's statement and the train crept out of the station. Amy felt better once they started to move, and rested her head against the corner of the compartment, hat in her lap.

The train stopped several times each hour. A visit from the conductor at one station and a girl in white selling cheese sandwiches were the only other disturbances to their naps and quiet, uneasy thoughts.

"We'll change trains at the next station," said Philip, after he purchased sandwiches from the girl. "A few stops after that, we'll exit and hire a carriage to Catcliffe."

Amy turned and stared at the dark-haired teenager. "That can't be a real place."

"I'm being perfectly honest, Miss Armstrong. Why would I lie about such a thing?"

Sunflower blinked his green eyes sleepily. "Are there lots of cats in Catcliffe?"

"Only the normal amount, more or less," said Philip. "In ancient times there was a cliff inhabited by cats. That's where the village received the name."

Amy snorted. "I never would have guessed."

"It's just as well that it's not a real city of cats," said Sunflower. "Old Earth animals are about as interesting as a cup of dried mud."

"I like mud!" barked Betsy.

"You would, wouldn't you?"

Amy smiled. "This is all fine and dandy, but has anyone come up with a plan yet? Other than dying under the claws of an insane robot from the future."

Betsy wagged his tail. "Don't worry, it won't kill you. The inspector will just take you back to the Lady."

"Who will banish us to a random dimension full of insane clawed robots or where apes evolved from men," said Sunflower. "That's assuming the inspector hasn't been damaged in some way and reverted to its original programming. Humans like to shoot everything that moves, and they've probably hit something important by accident."

"Let me guess," said Amy. "It's not just a killer robot from the future, now it's an insane killer robot from the future."

Sunflower blinked. "Mabily."

"That's not a word!"

"I promise you it is," said the cat. "It means something we don't want to happen but probably will, like trying to escape from a titanium-armored cato-cidal reject from the dog special forces."

"Dog special forces?"

"The Lady bought a whole bunch of our robots after the last war," said Betsy. "You wouldn't believe the money she saved!"

Philip rubbed his chin. "If it can't be defeated in direct combat, perhaps it can be trapped. After all, it's better to catch a tiger in a pit than fight it."

Amy stared at him. "A pit? You've seen it fly, right?"

"I didn't mean a literal tiger pit. I meant a kind of trap designed for the inspector."

"It's going to break out of any feeble rope or cable you try to wind around it," said Sunflower. "We've got a better chance running from it until the batteries run out."

"How long will that take?" asked Amy.

Sunflower stared out at the speeding countryside.

"Depending on how much energy is used on weapons, about a thousand hours."

Amy played with a strand of her blond hair, rolling it between her fingers as she thought over the problem.

"Six weeks? Are serious, cat?!!"

Philip nodded. "Good show. That was my calculation."

"Hey, don't get mad at me," said Sunflower. "I didn't make the silly thing. In case you forgot, I'm the one with a target painted on his fur."

Philip sat up straight. "I've got it! We can go on a voyage around the world. As long as we don't dawdle for too long in one place, the devilish machine would never catch up. After six weeks it would finally lose power."

"Hopefully in the middle of the Pacific Ocean," said Amy.

"It's a good plan," said Sunflower. "Especially since Laughing Boy here has got more money than God."

Philip frowned. "I see that phrase has come back to haunt me. But with any luck, I'll be able to give my parents persuasive reasons for the trip, secure the necessary bank notes, and set off almost as quickly as we arrive. Given my father's eagerness to be rid of me, I doubt we'll have a problem."

Betsy wagged his brown and white tail. "If he's Laughing Boy, can I be Laughing Dog?"

Amy realized that she'd absent-mindedly been biting a lock of her own hair while watching Philip. She pulled it out of her mouth and sat up straight.

"What happens if you can't persuade them?"

Philip smiled. "In that case, Miss Armstrong, we'll steal every gem in sight."

13

The train halted at a covered railway platform and Philip gave Amy a hand in stepping out of the compartment. While their animal companions fidgeted on a bench, the teenagers purchased cups of coffee and oranges from a stand on the platform manned by a toothless old woman with a red kerchief around her white hair.

"You've come from London?" she asked. "People say the devil is roaming the East End, killing, burning, and cursing all the poor souls what live there. It's the end times, I warrant."

Philip tipped his cap. "My apologies. We haven't heard anything of the sort."

After a short wait on another platform they boarded a local train. Huge clouds of smoke poured from the engine and the wooden seats were hard and uncomfortable. After a handful of stops they arrived at the bare platform and simple hut of Treeton station.

"Not far now," said Philip cheerily.

The teenager hired a two-horse brougham outside the station. This took longer than it would have in London, as Treeton was a small village and the driver had to fetch and harness the horses. The carriage had no roof and the driver sat in front, snapping the reins at a pair of black mares. The road of hard-packed dirt wove through a cluster of shops and small houses with pale plaster walls and exposed timber crossbeams into a pleasant country lane lined with sturdy oak and maple trees. Black-and-white Holstein cattle wandered in meadows surrounded by damp stone walls. A collie chased a herd of sheep toward a barn roofed in brown thatch.

Amy breathed in deep lungfuls of the fresh air and felt stress leaving her body like water wrung from a dishrag.

"I should change when we get there," she said to Philip.

"There's really no need. You look absolutely perfect and they won't suspect a thing."

"That's not what I mean. If the inspector is still after us there's a good chance we'll be hoofing it at some point, and I'd rather be wearing pants. That, or a shorter skirt."

Philip squinted at her. "Hoofing it?"

"Running. You know, that thing you do with your feet."

"I see. I'm not sure how to arrange that. As I said before, young women––especially respectable young women––don't wear trousers. It's simply not done."

Sunflower raised his head. "Even if she's being chased by an insane killer robot from the future?"

Philip sighed. "I'll do my best to find some trousers. If I do lend you boy's clothes, Miss Armstrong, please keep them hidden, especially from the maids. My family must believe your story of a wealthy American traveler until the last moment."

The cab bounced and rattled along the road, leaving a cloud of dust. A gentle valley curved up to a line of hills, the individual fields broken into green and brown puzzle pieces. The slowly passing scenery didn't seem to interest Philip. With a pale face, the teenager stared blankly at the horses pulling the carriage.

"Penny for your thoughts," said Amy.

Philip shook his head. "What will happen, must happen."

"You're still worried about your father?"

"In a way. I was reminded of what happened the last time I traveled this road. It was the beginning of summer hols. I was happy to be away from school, and my sister had written to tell me father was to be appointed Viceroy of India. I was positively bonkers at the news, you see, because he would be away from England for years."

"I guess it didn't turn out so great," said Amy.

"A fabulous understatement. My sister had lied in her letters as a sort of prank. My father was in an even worse mood over the holidays, having just enough work as Home Secretary to make him bitterly angry, and take that anger out on his children."

"Sounds like he should meet our new friend, the ex-army robot from the future."

Philip laughed. "He'd probably scare it into the next dimension!"

"I don't think that's possible," Betsy piped up from the floor. "He'd be shot with lasers and fall down and die. Or maybe get strangled and fall down and die."

Philip rubbed the terrier's furry head. "We can only hope, Betsy."

"Do any of these farms belong to your family?" asked Amy.

"See that hill topped by a red farmhouse?"

Amy pulled down the brim of her hat to shade her eyes. "Past the lake? Yes, I think so."

"That farm is the only plot of land in five miles that isn't part of the Marlborough estate."

"Good gravy!" Amy half-stood from her seat to get a better view. "Even the forests and lakes?"

"That's certainly part of the land, isn't it? Along with the river and a stone quarry. But I'd trade it all for a family who could eat dinner without throwing silverware at each other."

"You don't mean that."

"I'd certainly trade a hectare or two."

The driver snapped the reins left and turned onto an arrow-straight gravel road lined with cedar trees. At the end of the long path stood a four-story mansion of beige limestone. Hundreds of walnut-framed windows flashed in the sun. Past a series of barns, a dozen horses trotted in a fenced pasture.

Philip squinted through the cedar trees at the horses. "I don't see Ellie anywhere ..."

"Good gravy," whispered Amy. "That's not a house. It's a palace!"

"The old place puts on a good show, doesn't it? You'd be shocked to find out how much cash mother wastes on frippery and public display. She likes having more servants than furniture."

As the carriage approached the mansion, the double oak doors of the entrance swung open. A pair of young men emerged in black trousers, jackets with tails, and brilliant white shirts and gloves.

The carriage halted at the entrance with a froth and pop of gravel. The tallest of the footmen, a strikingly tall character with cropped ginger hair and acne scars, opened the door on Amy's side. His mouth was pressed into a round pout and his eyes wide.

"You've returned early, Master Philip. I hope nothing unpleasant happened with the fishing?"

Philip paid the driver and glanced at the footman. "Uh ... no, Tommy. I'm simply not feeling well."

"Very sorry to hear that, Master Philip."

The footman offered a hand to Amy and she stepped out of the carriage, followed by Philip and the two animals. The cab driver tipped his hat, snapped the reins, and the carriage rolled away, leaving Philip awkwardly shifting his weight back and forth in front of the two servants.

"This is Miss Amy Armstrong," he said. "An acquaintance of mine from London. I happened by chance to meet her at the station."

Tommy looked puzzled. "At Treeton, sir? Forgive me, but I thought you and the other masters had gone salmon fishing."

"You're certainly right, Tommy, but as I mentioned, I ate something awful for lunch and felt absolutely green to the gills. It just so happened that I ended up at Treeton." Philip leaned close and held a hand to the side of his mouth. "Let's be honest--I drank far too much claret last night and was absolutely legless. I have no idea how I ended up in Treeton."

Tommy bowed his head. "Say no more, Master Philip. May we take your bags? Thank you, sir."

A happy squeal erupted from the doorway of the mansion, and a short and stout woman in a peacock-blue dress ran out. She crushed her brunette bun of hair against Philip's chest and wrapped her arms around his waist.

"My boy! It's so lovely to see you!"

Philip stood stiff and straight, his arms away from the woman, but her outburst of affection caused him to bite his lower lip.

"Yes, mother. I'm glad to be home."

She looked up at him. "You scamp. What are you doing home a day early? Don't tell me you missed your old mother!"

"That's exactly it," said Philip, his voice strained. "I missed you. It feels like I haven't seen you for years."

Philip's mother let go of her son. She looked Amy up and down and smiled.

"This beautiful young lady has something to do with your change of plans, I think. I hope you didn't pull her out of the river!"

"Mother, please," said Philip, with a strange waver in his voice. "This is Miss Amy Armstrong from America. Miss Armstrong, this is my mother, Lady Marlborough."

"Good afternoon, your Ladyship."

Amy intended to curtsy and stepped back with her right foot, but her boot caught on the inside hem of a petticoat and caused her to stumble backwards. She would have fallen flat on her bottom in a very unladylike fashion if Tommy hadn't caught her.

"Dear, oh dear," said Philip's mother. "Are you not well?"

"I'm afraid she's exhausted from the travel," said Philip. "Miss Armstrong is a cousin of a friend of mine at Eton, and I invited her to take the train from London and stay with us a few days. The surprise is completely my fault. I simply forgot to tell you, mother."

Philip's mother gasped and held Amy's hand. "Did you travel all the way by yourself?"

"Not exactly. I came over with my aunt and cousin."

"Still, you poor darling! The hordes of people in London and the crowds on the platform can be absolutely debilitating for a young lady. Come in and we'll have some tea."

"May my pets come inside also?"

"Certainly, dear."

The short, ebullient woman charged through the doorway of the mansion like a cavalry officer at Waterloo, belting out cheery orders to the footmen to bring tea and the maids to prepare rooms for the new guest.

The scarlet foyer opened to a two-story entrance hall with high columns of dark walnut and a two-story split staircase. Dozens of heavily framed paintings covered the deep green wallpaper. The slowly vaporizing oil of the artwork hung in the air and mixed with the smells of wood polish and rosewater.

Soft Arabian rugs muffled their footsteps as Philip's mother gently pulled Amy through a doorway into a long parlor. She gestured to a collection of pale yellow couches and chairs in French provincial style, with ornate wood accents.

"Please. Have a seat and rest for a moment, won't you?"

The teenagers sat on a sofa across from Philip's mother, and the animals took position beside the furniture.

Amy slipped off her white gloves and held them in her lap. She didn't know if she should remove her hat or not, but Philip's mother gave her a strange look, so she carefully pulled out the long pins and lifted it off her head.

"One of the servants will take that for you, dear," said Philip's mother. "Please leave it on the table."

Philip cleared his throat. "It's rather good to see you again, mother. How are you?"

She tutted at him. "What a strange thing to say! You act as if you haven't seen me for two years." She waved a hand at Amy. "Miss Armstrong, are you part of the Boston Armstrongs?"

"Not quite, Lady Marlborough. I'm from California."

"How delightful! I did hear about an Armstrong that traveled out there to seek his fortune in gold. Instead, he became quite successful in the mercantile trade. That wouldn't be one of your relatives, would it?"

"He ... um, that would be my grandfather."

"I thought as much. He must have had a horrible time of it, what with all of the Indians and Spaniards. If there's one thing more dangerous and untrustworthy than a native, it's a Spaniard."

Amy frowned. "I don't think that's very--" Philip kicked her foot. "--I mean, I wouldn't know anything about that."

"I certainly hope not," said Philip's mother. "The Times said there are barely any natives left in California, but even so it must be an exciting place for a young lady."

A footman brought a silver tea setting and porcelain cups and plates along with a selection of small cookies. Amy took a small sip. The tea wasn't as strong or bitter as the cup she'd had on the station.

"I didn't see Ellie in the pasture," said Philip. "Is she on the eastern grounds?"

"There's the Philip I know," said Lady Marlborough with a laugh. "Always making jokes, especially about horses that we sold years ago!"

"Sold Ellie? I don't understand."

Lady Marlborough turned to Amy. "Your dress is perfectly adorable, Miss Armstrong, and yet very familiar at the same time."

"I won it in a card game," said Amy.

Philip sprayed a mouthful of tea into the air and coughed violently for a long moment.

"Miss Armstrong ... American ... humor," he finally wheezed.

"I'm not surprised," said Lady Marlborough. "She seems a very jolly and pleasant young lady. Your sisters will be very put out not to meet her. They left for London this morning."

"I assume father is in the study?"

Lady Marlborough's eyes bulged and her face lost all color. She covered her mouth with a handkerchief.

"Philip! How dare you utter such a horrible thing."

"What's wrong?"

"Don't make light of what happened, especially when we have a guest."

"Mother! I don't know what you're talking about!"

Lady Marlborough peered at Philip's face and looked him up and down.

"There's something different about you, son. I swear you've grown since I saw you two days ago."

"It must be his new shoes," said Amy. "Philip was telling me about them on the train. They make him look taller."

Lady Marlborough shook her head. "Your face is different; pale but stronger, like your father's. Even worse, you've asked about him as if you had no memory of the accident."

A distant thud rattled the windows and shook the china cups. Lady Marlborough stood up from the sofa as quickly as if the Queen Herself had strolled into the parlor.

"Heavens! That must be the boiler again," she said. Her face relaxed into a gentle smile. "Please excuse me, I must find Mark. Oh, he's down in London! Never mind, I'll find someone."

As soon as the door had shut behind his mother, Philip turned to Amy and grabbed her hand.

"Something horrible is going on!"

"I know what you mean," came Sunflower's voice beneath the sofa. "I found a dead bee. Wait––a family of dead bees."

Amy frowned. "You mean the thing about your father? Or your horse being sold?"

"Yes and no," said Philip. "I mean, yes. But that's not the worst of it. Mother is never this nice to anyone, especially me!"

"Maybe she's just being polite because I'm here."

"She's never polite to anyone, not even the Crown Prince! He came here to hunt one year and mother closed up all the windows and pretended we all had typhus. There's a reason she's called the Marlborough Monster, and I've got the scars on my legs to prove it!"

Amy bit into a cookie. "I don't know what to tell you. This is your dimension, this is England, and according to Sunflower it's the right year."

"Don't start questioning my work," came the cat's voice from under the sofa. "I pass my operator tests every year."

"That's because the cat that runs the test is sweet on you every year," said Betsy.

"Don't tell them that," whispered Sunflower. "Besides, it's not always a female cat running the test."

"It's not? Also, why am I whispering?"

A peal of thunder shook the windows and vibrated the floor. Everything in the room rocked back and forth, from the fringed lampshades to the oil paintings on the walls.

"Felt like an earthquake," said Amy. "Do you have earthquakes in England?"

Philip ran to the nearest window and pushed aside the drapes. "Look!"

Amy jumped up from the sofa and peered over Philip's shoulder. Above the trees a black question mark of smoke curled into the blue sky.

Amy sighed. "Let me guess––that's the railway station and the flying killer inspector robot."

"It's not the inspector," said Betsy, putting his paws on the lowest pane of the window. "It's just the smoke from where it's blowing up things and shooting lasers."

"Thanks for clearing that up, Betsy."

Philip clenched a fist. "We must flee immediately! Clarence House may have protected my family from the Roundheads, but it won't save us from an inspector. Follow me!"

Amy held up the skirt of her yellow dress. "You expect me to run in this? I have to change."

"I'm sorry, Miss Armstrong, but there's no time!"

The teenage boy sprinted out of the room and through the stately halls of the mansion. Amy had to gather up the delicately embroidered fabric of her skirt and petticoats and run with it balled at her chest, her long white bloomers exposed for all the servants to see. She might have felt embarrassed if she'd actually been a rich girl from the nineteenth century instead of a teenage burglar from the future.

Philip dashed through a kitchen area, dodged the astounded cook and her scullery maids, and burst out a rear door of the mansion. Amy, Sunflower, and Betsy ran after the boy as he jumped a fence and ran through a field of damp, knee-high alfalfa.

Amy cupped one hand around her mouth as she ran. "Where are we going?"

"A safe place!" Philip yelled over his shoulder.

A brilliant flash lit the sky behind them, and a second later a deep, crackling boom rolled over the grassy fields.

"How did it catch up so fast?" asked Betsy, his pink tongue lolling as he galloped as fast as he could.

"Don't ask me," gasped Sunflower as he ran beside the dog. "Maybe it took the train!"

Philip stopped at a wall of flat gray stones. He held Amy's hand as she clambered over one leg at a time, her knee-length bloomers in full view.

"Such a gentleman," said Amy. "Why is your face red? Are you embarrassed?"

Philip looked away. "Uh ... no! It's the exercise."

They sprinted across green meadows dotted with sheep, along the bank of a lake, and into a forest of tall oak and maple trees. The thudding booms of the inspector's weapons came at irregular intervals, but each time closer and closer.

The ground began to rise and the trees were spaced farther apart. At a wide clearing in the forest, Philip climbed to the top of a grassy bank and pointed at his feet.

"There!"

Amy climbed to the top and gasped at the sight. Below lay a deep rock quarry, three hundred feet wide and almost as deep. Water collected in a small pond at the bottom of the rectangular pit, and the sides were cut sheer and vertical, revealing multiple layers of earth and rock. Trees hung over the edges and a vast network of ivy grew on the south face of the pit. The gray timbers of the opening to a mine shaft protruded from the base of another wall.

Sunflower peered over the edge and quickly backed away.

"Are you two lovebirds going to jump? Keep me out of it," he said.

Betsy wagged his tail. "Hey! I just realized. That's what 'lover's leap' means!"

"I'm not jumping and neither is he," said Amy. "Are you?"

"Of course not," said Philip. "We're going to lose the inspector in the mine shaft."

Amy crossed her arms. "Excuse me?"

"Jumping is a better plan," said Betsy. "You'll thank me!"

"They wouldn't survive it like we would," said Sunflower. "These are Old Earth humans, remember? They can't walk two feet without breaking a bone or having a stroke."

The terrier wagged his tail. "Sorry! I forgot. Do that other thing, the one Philip said."

"How are we going to 'lose' it without getting lost ourselves?" asked Amy.

"My brothers and I have played in this old quarry since we could walk," said Philip. "One benefit of having uncaring parents and a nanny we could boss around. With the light provided by Sunflower and Betsy's emergency lamps, we won't have a problem navigating the tunnels and confusing that bloody machine. Pardon my language."

Sunflower nodded. "The electronics on board the inspector will be useless once we go underground. That's how I escaped from it last time."

The earth trembled from a massive blast. An orange fireball of smoke and flame boiled up from the trees behind them.

Amy shaded her eyes. "What's it shooting at? It's not even close to hitting us."

"Squirrels," whispered Sunflower. "It's came from the dog army surplus, remember?"

"Squirrels?!! Where?" yelped Betsy, and chased his tail.

Philip hurried Amy, Sunflower, and the tree-rodent-hating terrier down a narrow path that had been cut along the inside wall of the deep quarry.

As she descended lower and lower, holding her skirt up and trying not to stumble, Amy felt as if she were leaving the world of light and passing into a realm of death and decay. The air was cold without the sun to warm it and full of the smell of moldering earth. The sounds of birds and insects, of leaves whispering in the breeze and branches knocking against each other, were all sucked up and silenced at the bottom of the pit as if it were the crypt of an ancient, malevolent queen.

Philip stopped at the timbered entrance to the mine shaft and held up a hand in front of Amy.

"Miss Armstrong, you must stay here. I know the tunnels well, and there's no need to put you in further danger."

"You want me to wait outside for that crazy robot? No, thanks. It's all for one and one for all, like the Three Musketeers. Stop talking and get inside."

Philip shook his head. "We have to lure the machine into the tunnel. That means staying outside until it sees us."

"Sees us and blasts us!" growled Sunflower.

A mechanical voice boomed from above their heads.

"Halt! Operator SF063, you are ordered to return to synch point for debriefing and de-operation. Do you comply?"

The metal sphere and claw-tipped tentacles of the inspector floated above the rocky lip at the top of the quarry. The surface of the orb was covered with dozens of tiny dimples and stripes of carbon scoring marred the silver skin.

Sunflower looked up and laughed. “What if I don’t?”

The inspector made a sound like hundreds of ball bearings inside a tumble dryer.

“If you refuse to comply, I have the Lady’s authority to bring you back, squirrel or non-squirrel. Sorry–—dead or alive.”

Sunflower bared his teeth. “You know what I say to that, you outdated pile of scrap?”

The inspector whirred and hovered high in the air. “Um ... you say ‘I give up?’ ”

“No. I say, nuts!”

The orange tabby dashed into the black hole of the mine shaft, his tail straight up and Philip, Amy, and Betsy scrambling after him. The two animals switched on their emergency beacons, and bouncing red light from their foreheads lit the earthen walls and old supporting timbers of the mine shaft.

“Left here,” shouted Philip, and sprang to the head of the party.

He led them on a wild, twisting sprint through the black tunnels, dodging rusted mine carts and deep cracks in the earth. Amy ran as fast as she could, trying her best not to become separated from the group or fall and break her neck in a vertical shaft. The blue light of the inspector’s scanning beam flashed behind them at times, blasting warnings and the occasional thunderous laser at something in the darkness shaped like a squirrel.

One explosion cracked the stone ceiling and covered everyone in black dust.

"The tunnels won't survive another one of those," Philip yelled.

Amy wiped her eyes with a sleeve. "Well? Get us out of here! Now!"

After another five minutes of twists and turns, climbing up and climbing down, running through cross shafts and squeezing through narrow gaps, a square of light glowed ahead. All four burst out of the mine shaft and stood in the sunlight, coughing and leaning over the broken shale at their feet.

Amy let go of her heavy skirts and plopped onto the rocky ground.

"I'm not doing that again," she gasped. "Need a costume change."

Sunflower cleaned his blackened face and ears with a paw. "Bath time for me."

"Now the inspector will take us back to the Lady," barked Betsy. "Or he'll murder us all. That's life for you!"

Philip wheezed and coughed, his face and clothes covered in black dust. "I thought we'd find something to block the entrance, but there's nothing."

Amy lay on her back and stared at the sky far above the quarry. "Good gravy, that was a stupid plan. Now I'm going to die tired."

"And filthy," murmured Sunflower. "Sister, you do NOT want a mirror."

"I know, and I'm sorry," said Philip. "If we had dynamite, I could close the entrance. I might as well wish for a regiment of Life Guards, as much chance we have of finding explosives."

Amy sat up. "Explosives?"

Sunflower stopped licking himself and stared at her with his wide green eyes. "Don't even think about it, you backwoods, undeveloped orangutan!"

"Tell me what's worse, Sunflower. Eating cheese or letting that robot turn you into a cheese toastie?"

Philip helped Amy to her feet. "Cheese! That's a perfectly wizard idea, Amy! I mean, Miss Armstrong."

"You pair of low-tech jungle-dwellers don't know what it does to my system. I'll be sick for weeks!"

Betsy jumped in the air. "He'll be sick for weeks!"

Amy fished around her tiny handbag and pulled out a hunk of yellow cheese. "Take your pick: feeling sick, or feeling a laser blast?"

Philip clenched his fists. "Dash it all! Hurry up before the machine comes out!"

"All right, all right," said Sunflower, with an exasperated growl. "But I don't need that much. We don't want to turn this place into the Crescent Canyon on Tau Ceti. Scrape off a tiny ball about the size of a mouse eye. Smaller! Also, one of you has to stay here and hold me tight, unless you want to see a cat fly through the air."

"Miss Armstrong, I must insist––"

Amy shook her head. "Don't even start with the knight in shining armor crap, Philip. Take Betsy and climb out of here."

"Don't be absurd."

"Go on, you stupid boy! Leave!"

Philip stamped his foot. "Miss Armstrong! I deserted you once and I won't do it again. I am not a coward!"

"I am!" barked Betsy, and scrambled up the narrow path to the top.

Amy held the tiny ball of cheese over Sunflower's head.

"What now?"

The cat blinked with quiet disdain. "This is going to kill all three of us. Are humans born without brains or do they leak out of your heads naturally?"

"I live dangerously and die the same way," said Amy. "Tell me what to do before I forget how much I like cats."

"Fine, fine. Pick up your skirts and hold them in a ball at your chest, just like you were doing when we ran."

"Why?"

"It'll protect your monkey organs from the blast. Don't ask questions, okay? Sit down inside the entrance to the mine and face the tunnel."

"What about me?" asked Philip.

"Sit behind the girl and hold her, lover boy."

"I really, really hate cats," muttered Philip.

Amy sat cross-legged under the timbers, her embroidered skirt and petticoats a large ball of fabric in front of her chest. Philip's legs kicked up dust as they slid to the left and right of her hips, and his arms wrapped around her waist.

"Now what?"

Sunflower trotted up. "Grab me and hold on tight. No! That's the business end!"

The orange cat turned his rear to the black hole of the mine shaft. A blue light flickered faintly in the tunnel.

"I see the inspector coming," hissed Amy.

"Don't panic," said Sunflower. "Keep your mouth open and don't hold your breath."

"Why not?" asked Philip.

"Because the explosion will pop your stupid monkey lungs! No more questions!"

"Sorry."

"Put the cheese in my mouth, point my rear at the tunnel, and hold on tight."

Amy dropped the ball of cheese onto Sunflower's pink tongue. The cat swallowed painfully and the orange fur on his back shivered.

"Aw, poopie," he said.

A force like a sledgehammer hit Amy's stomach and tumbled her backwards. The world exploded into a cloud of broken rocks and pain, where every breath was a jagged knife in her ribs, until black spots covered her eyes in complete and utter darkness.

14

3317 A.D.
Penal station in the former orbit of Kepler Prime

The curved walls of her prison and the images of the puppy and kitten disappeared and were replaced by a room with four equal walls and a tan carpet that smelled of mold. Amy looked down and found herself in a metal chair with her wrists and ankles fastened to the sides. No door, window, or opening broke the symmetry of the square room and the pale green walls.

A battered aluminum table flashed into existence.

"Surprissse!" hissed the disembodied voice of Officer Nistra. "Wait ... that's not the right button. Where's the stupid manual ... cheap, dog-designed poona crap ... here we go!"

The giant lizard appeared behind the table in a long white coat and puffy chef's hat. He slammed both fists on the table.

"Surprise!"

Amy sniffed. "Oh no. I just crapped myself in terror."

"Ha! As you should do!"

"Did you teleport here? Because that's pretty cool."

"If I said that I did, would you tell me the location of Kepler Prime?"

"Probably not."

"In that case it was just a simulation," said Nistra. "Your body is still in the confinement chamber."

"Why are you dressed like Chef Boyardee?"

The sauro frowned. "Who?"

"Like a cook in a restaurant!"

"I don't know what lonely farm or backwater planet you come from, human, but this hat and coat strike fear into a hundred billion life forms across the galaxy."

"Because you'll eat them?"

"Don't be silly; we haven't done that for ages." The sauro scraped a sharp talon across the aluminum table, causing a horrendous metallic shriek. "You said you would tell me where my home world is. Don't make me show the kitten again."

"I'll tell you what I know and we'll go from there. Is that okay?"

The lizard man growled. "There is nothing reasonable about me at this point!"

"I'll take that as a yes. Anyway, I was in California, trying to steal a gold Super Nintendo from this rich kid––"

A clipboard and pen snapped into existence in Nistra's hands and he began to write.

"California? Is that in the Orion sector? I'll have to check SpaceBook."

"It's on Earth. Hello?"

"Hello," said Nistra, confused.

"Old Earth," said Amy. "In 1995."

Nistra sighed. "Tell me the year in P.E. numbers. What star date?"

"Star date? I don't know."

Nistra crossed out a few lines. "Never mind, I'll just make something up. Continue."

"So I almost had the thing, when this orange cat shows up and teleports me into the future. Here. Well, not HERE here, but the Lady's spaceship. The hollowed-out asteroid one?"

"What's the name of the orange cat?"

"Sunflower."

"Ugh. Cat hipsters," growled the sauro. "Continue."

"So I skulked around the inside of the ship for a bit, met another human, and we helped him go back to his time. His dimension, I mean. Turns out it wasn't even the right dimension. We got chased by a flying robot and I broke my arm and foot, so we came back to the future. To now. To whatever. The Lady said Kepler Prime was missing because of some gravity rift, and then you lizard psychos showed up and took me away in handcuffs. Can I get a drink of water or a Fanta or something?"

Nistra continued to write for a moment. When he finished, the lizard man squinted hard at Amy.

"This is a simulation! Why would you need to drink anything?"

Amy nodded. "I guess you can't do it. Hey, no problem. I mean, we do hologram drinks where I'm from all the time, but we're just backwoods farmers. You lizards are much more advanced."

Nistra gave her a black look. The sauro pulled a dog-eared manual from his white coat, flipped through it for a moment, then snapped his claw-like fingers. A can of grape Fanta appeared on the desk.

Amy popped the tab and took a swig.

"Good gravy," she said. "This is warm. Your dumb computer couldn't program a cold can of Fanta?"

Nistra waved his clipboard wildly. "The silly fantastical story you've just told me doesn't have any mention of where my planet is!"

"That's because it isn't anywhere at all. We linked all the dimensional teleporters on the Dream Tiger into one circuit." Amy thought back to all the sci-fi clichés she'd heard. "The planet was the largest mass nearby, and the energy surge from the dimensional jump must have reversed its polarity. It's right in front of you, but a second behind the universe!"

Nistra screamed and swatted the air around his head. "In front of me?!!"

"Not you. Out in space, where it's supposed to be."

"Yes, of course. That makes more sense."

A pair of heavy thumps shook the room and Amy glanced at the ceiling.

"That sounded like an asteroid strike," she said. "Maybe a space toilet. Do space toilets make that much noise when you flush?"

Nistra glowered at her. "There's no such thing as a space toilet. Is this what you stupid humans call a joke?"

"No toilets? Is everyone wearing space diapers?"

A series of heavy vibrations rattled the room and a high-pitched alarm began to warble. The table and chairs, Nistra, the entire room disappeared. Amy found herself back in the spherical womb of her prison cell.

She sighed. "At least you still like me, Mister Space Egg Prison."

The curved floor bounced violently and the lights clicked off, throwing the room into complete darkness.

"Aw, nuts."

Amy felt all the weight leave her body, as if she were in a roller coaster that had just crested a hill and now hurtled down the other side. She spun slowly through the air for a few seconds, arms outstretched, and then a gentle force pressed her against a wall and kept her there.

Yorkshire, 1889

The faint ticking of a clock and the earthy smell of fresh cotton were the first things she noticed. Then pain flashed through her numb consciousness, and Amy groaned.

"She's waking up! Get the doctor," hissed the voice of Lady Marlborough.

Footsteps padded on carpet and door hinges squealed.

The pain in her left side made it difficult to breathe, and Amy barely felt the quilt covering her and the soft mattress of the bed below. The back of her head throbbed with a strange numbness, and she reached back to touch it. A sting of terrible, white-hot pain shot through her right arm and Amy yelled.

"Ow ow ow ow!"

"Please don't move, Miss Armstrong," said the voice of Lady Marlborough. "You've broken an arm and possibly your foot."

Amy blinked through tears of pain and opened her eyes. Overhead waved the pale fabric of a bedroom canopy, and flowered yellow wallpaper covered the walls. The bed shivered as Philip's mother moved to Amy's side and gently moved Amy's splinted and gauzed-wrapped arm down to her side.

"What happened?" Amy whispered.

Lady Marlborough smiled sympathetically. "A wall of that old quarry collapsed in an avalanche of rock. Philip led you there and put your life at risk like the silly, irresponsible child he is. Poor dear! How were you supposed to know the danger in that old mine? At least Philip had enough sense to dig through the stone and carry you and the cat home."

"How is he?"

"Philip? He's as fit as houses. I wish those rocks had knocked a bit of sense into the boy. Imagine taking a delicate flower like yourself into that filthy, perilous quarry!"

Amy coughed. "No, I mean my cat."

"He's right at your feet. You know what they say about cats and their nine lives."

Amy lifted her head slightly and looked down to the foot of the bed. Sunflower lay curled up with his tail around his nose, and blinked his green eyes lazily.

"He's used up two or three today," whispered Amy, and lay back on the pillow.

"You mean yesterday," said Lady Marlborough. "You've slept through an entire day, dear girl."

"I feel like an elephant sat on me."

"What a colorful metaphor," said Lady Marlborough. "If you don't mind, I'd like to telegraph your parents. I assume the San Francisco office? What is your father's name?"

"I don't remember."

Lady Marlborough dabbed at Amy's forehead with a damp cloth.

"Poor Miss Armstrong. You've hit your head worse than we thought. But never mind! I'm certain Philip will remember your father's name, or we can look him up in the book. There can't be that many wealthy Armstrongs in California!"

"You'd be surprised," said Amy weakly. "We made it to the Moon."

"Oh, dear. That must be the laudanum he gave you."

The door opened and a bald, white-bearded gentleman in a black three-piece suit walked in. He held a leather satchel in one hand.

"Pardon me, Lady Marlborough," he said with a Scottish accent. "I wonder if I might ask the wee lass a few questions."

"By all means, Doctor Miller," said Lady Marlborough. "I'll leave you to it."

"Och, there's no need to leave, your ladyship. No need at all."

"Quite the opposite. I need to find out where Philip has scampered off to. If you'll excuse me, please."

Lady Marlborough closed the door as she left, and Amy and Sunflower were alone with the doctor. He smiled in a grandfatherly manner and stepped to the foot of the bed.

"You've been in a terrible accident, Miss Armstrong, but quite fortuitously I happened to be at a nearby farm yesterday and was here within minutes. How are you feeling today?"

"Like I was hit by a ton of bricks."

The doctor nodded and rummaged in his bag. "That proves your head's no mince, lassie. Now, I'll perform an examination if you've no objection. Can you point to where it aches?"

Amy winced. "It hurts to point."

"Och, no. I meant on this wee doll."

The doctor held a figurine of a nude woman, as featureless as a Barbie dipped in nail polish remover and hit with a belt sander a few times. The model seemed to be carved from pale ivory and reclined on a small strip of darkly stained and lacquered wood.

The doctor touched the head of the figurine. "Is this where it aches?"

"It hurts everywhere. You're a doctor, right? Pull down the blanket and look yourself."

"I've no mind to offend you, lassie, especially with Lady Marlborough here and gone. It's the old ways that have stood me tried and true, and I'll protect the modesty of a young lass when I can."

"After what's happened the last few days I don't think I have any modesty left. The last scrap flew away when I was unconscious and someone changed me into this nightgown. Where's my dress?"

"Aye, it was a bonnie dress," said the doctor. "You'll be no happy to hear it was torn to ribbons and stained with blood. Now tell me, do you remember anything before the rocks came down on top of ye?"

Amy closed her eyes for a moment. "Something was chasing us, that's I can say. Then I woke up in this bed, my head throbbing, arm broken, and knives stabbing my sides. Breathing in and out feels like hard work."

"There's a poultice on your ribs," said the doctor. "We splinted your arm and foot yesterday, and time will sort out the rest. Enough time in bed, of course."

"How much exactly? When can I leave?"

"You have a well-meaning heart, lassie, I know you're thinking on the burden ye might have to Lady Marlborough and Clarence House. But it's no good worrying on it; you're to lay in bed another week and not leave this room for another two. Longer in bed is better than the grave."

Amy gasped. "Impossible! I can't stay here."

"Your body needs to recover from several great blows, and I'm not spinning a yarn when I say you can't leave this bed and not risk dying. Don't worry about putting Lady Marlborough out by tarrying in bed. The grand lady has a great feeling of guilt on the matter, seeing as it was her son that led you down the primrose path to the quarry."

A knock sounded at the door.

"Enter!"

Philip eased into the room, his face pale and jaw slack.

"Speak of the devil," said the doctor. "I can see you're still worried about the bonnie lass, but don't go on about it any longer. As long as she rests in bed, Miss Armstrong will be as fit as a fiddle."

Philip blinked at the doctor with glazed eyes, then stared at Amy.

"That's not the problem," he whispered.

A woman's scream echoed through the mansion.

"Och, there's my call," said Doctor Miller, and sprinted out of the room with his bag.

Amy sighed and winced at the pain in her ribs. "What's the real problem? Did you see another ghost?"

Philip licked his lips and stared at a spot on the wall above Amy's head.

"Do you remember what I said yesterday? About mother being too nice, and father strangely being dead?"

"From what you said about your family, both of those sounded like improvements."

Philip twitched his head left and right in tiny, shivering movements.

"That's just it. They're not my family at all."

The thump of footsteps on carpet came from the hallway, and Lady Marlborough burst into the room, face red and teeth clenched. She stood in front of Philip with her fists balled at her waist.

"Who are you?!!"

Philip bowed his head. "Lady Marlborough, I'm your son. Whatever happens, that is still the truth."

"How dare you invade my house and family! I knew something was wrong the moment I laid eyes on you. You and this odd American girl."

"Don't pull me into this," groaned Amy, and lay back on the pillow.

"A pair of swindlers," hissed Lady Marlborough. "A pair of burglars!"

A murmur of male voices came from the hallway and three young men walked into the room.

All three wore jackets, trousers, and soft caps of light brown tweed. Amy glanced between Lady Marlborough, the three young men, and Philip. A strong family resemblance lay in the eyes, nose, and deep black hair of all five. Two of the young men were taller and muscular, but the other was a shorter and younger version of--

"Philip!" shouted Amy, causing Sunflower to spring several feet in the air.

Both the new boy and Philip stared at her and spoke in unison.

"Yes?"

Amy lay back on the pillow. "Check, please," she whispered.

The new Philip turned to Lady Marlborough. "Mother! Is this some kind of joke?"

"It's not a joke," said Philip. "And especially unfunny."

One of the older boys burst out laughing. "Oh, I think it is. What a great trick, Mummy! I don't know how but you've found a perfectly wizard doppelganger of Phil. We'll bring him to parties and have a smashing good time! Is he a traveling apprentice? A cousin of one of the servants?"

Lady Marlborough stamped her foot and startled everyone in the room.

"He's nothing of the sort! He came here pretending to be you. If it weren't for the accident at the quarry, I expect these two would have scampered off with the silverware and every scrap of jewelry I own!"

"Not true," murmured Philip. "I just wanted to come home. I'm really your son."

"It is kind of true, the part about the jewels," said Amy.

"I don't see how you mistook him for me, mother," said doppelganger Philip. "He's got such a beastly, common face!"

The tallest brother giggled and pointed at Amy. "She was with him? You should have known it wasn't Philip, mother. He's absolutely the worst with the female sex."

Doppelganger Philip turned red. "Shut up, you troll!"

"What? I'll box your little ears!"

"Quiet, both of you," said Lady Marlborough. "Doctor Miller, would you do me a favor? Please ride into the village and fetch the constable."

"Aye, my lady, but the poor lassie––"

"Doctor Miller!"

"Of course, my lady, of course."

The grandfatherly figure left the crowd of servants at the door, his bulky footsteps noisily creaking over the hallway floor.

Lady Marlborough jabbed her finger at Philip's nose. "And you, miscreant. I'll have you locked up for the rest of your life!"

Philip bowed his head. "Do you remember when I was three? I shucked off all of my clothes and ran to the village, completely naked."

"Everyone knows that story," said one of the older brothers.

Doppelganger Philip sniffed. "Unfortunately, that's true."

"My actual son is right," said Lady Marlborough. "You could have heard that from any milkmaid in the village."

"How about the January you fell ill, right before the trip to France? When you couldn't bear to be alone and forced me to stay here with you?"

"Common knowledge," said Lady Marlborough. "Come on, out with it. Any other tales you've stolen from my real son?"

Philip turned red and straightened up. "Only one. I'm certain you remember the mishap with father's hunting rifle? There wasn't any 'accidental discharge' in the library. I know, because I was hiding there. You confronted father about the woman he'd been seeing in London, and fired it point-blank at his chest. Luckily, the shot missed its mark, or––"

Lady Marlborough's face turned purple and she slapped Philip across the cheek. "Who told you that horrible lie?"

"Finally, the dear mother I know," said Philip, rubbing his face. "All of these pleasantries were simply an act. Your heart is as black and uncaring as ever."

"I refuse to be pulled into an argument with a common thief. You and this American trollop will be thrown in prison for so long, you'll forget what the sun looks like!"

Doppelganger Philip and his two brothers pulled Lady Marlborough away, and then crowded around Philip.

"Don't worry, mummy," said the doppelganger, and poked a finger in Philip's chest. "We'll teach this pilfering layabout a thing or two before the constable arrives."

Amy lifted her left hand and waved. "Hello? Can the trollop on the bed get more painkillers before you do that?"

The three boys stared at her. This was Amy's intention and gave Philip a slight opening. He pushed new Philip away and pulled a black revolver from his jacket pocket.

"Back, you monsters! Get back!"

Philip pointed the revolver at the boys and waved them toward the door.

"You're a mad one," murmured doppelganger Philip, his hands in the air.

"This is such a dastardly waste," said the tallest brother. "He would have been a grand trick."

The third brother laughed. "I bet it's not even loaded!"

Philip pointed the revolver at the ceiling and pulled the trigger. A deafening crack burst from the revolver and filled the room with the sulfur and carbon smell of gunpowder. Philip extended his arm and aimed the revolver at the three boys.

"Please leave," he said, his jaw clenched. "I'll die before I go to prison."

The boys barreled out of the room. Philip slammed the door behind them and pulled a heavy cabinet across it to block the door from opening.

"Talk about dramatic tension," Amy said. "Where in the name of tube socks did you get a gun?"

"This thing?" Philip held up the revolver. "I borrowed it from Mark in London. He was very sympathetic after hearing about the troubles we had in the East End. I never intended to use it, especially against myself."

Amy coughed. "I guess it's pretty obvious that we're in the wrong dimension. Sorry about that."

Philip sat on the bed next to her. “No great loss. I’m more worried about your condition.”

“It’s weird; I’m usually fine after getting buried under a bone-crushing pile of rocks, but not this time.”

Philip smiled. “I’m glad to see you’ve still got that beautiful sense of humor. You’re going to need it when I have to move you.”

“No bueno. That Scottish grandpa said I have to stay in bed for a week.”

“I know, but I don’t think I’ll be able to hold off the constable and an army of farmers with only five rounds in the revolver.” Philip stared at Amy and said nothing for a long moment. “Miss Armstrong ... the state you were in after I dug you from the rocks ... all the blood and dust ... I don’t know what I would have done if you hadn’t lived.”

Amy laughed and immediately winced in pain. “The jury’s still out on that, Phil, but I promise I won’t become a ghost and haunt you. And ... you can call me Amy now.”

Philip touched her hand. “Are you sure? Do you know what that means?”

Amy nodded and looked into his eyes. “Yes, I do.”

“Are they going to kiss now?” Betsy whispered from beneath the bed. “I want to see humans kiss.”

“You idiot,” hissed Sunflower. “They’ve heard you already. Why do you always have to ruin everything?”

The bed shivered as the two animals squeezed from beneath it and jumped up to Amy’s quilt.

“I’m only being polite, because I know you two humans don’t have a clue,” said Sunflower. “But what’s the plan now?”

“Marriage!” barked Betsy.

"I hardly think so," said Philip. "That joke is getting a bit old, if you ask me."

Sunflower blinked. "Nobody did."

"How are you still alive after that monstrous explosion? From your ... you know."

"I don't have time to answer questions like that," said the orange tabby. "It involves physics, molecular nanoscience, and other quiz-show topics that your monkey brain couldn't understand."

"Back to the real world," murmured Amy.

"Exactly," said Sunflower. "In the real world, your girlfriend here––"

"I'm NOT his girlfriend!"

Sunflower blinked. "My apologies. Your 'special' friend here can't be moved. I know enough of human biology to agree with that ignorant tribal doctor. She won't survive rapid movement, especially not the kind we'll need to flee this place. Any jarring and several bones in her chest will enter her lungs and stop the breathing."

"I don't believe it," said Amy. "You don't know human biology. You can't even tell when I'm sleeping!"

"Maybe not, but I can tell not sick from bad sick, and you're bad sick."

"What are we supposed to do, then?"

Betsy wagged his brown and white tail. "Back to the future!"

Amy groaned. "Why did you have to say that? That's so corny. Of all the things you could have said, that's the worst."

"What? What did I say?"

Philip shook his head. "You're suggesting that we leap from the frying pan into the fire. By traveling to this dimension and destroying the inspector, we've escaped the Lady. We'd be trading one execution for another."

"Possibly," said Sunflower. "It's a bad idea."

"It's not," barked Betsy. "The Lady won't hurt us. She wants us back home, safe and sound!"

Sunflower blinked at the terrier. "How do you know that, dog?"

"I just do," said Betsy, glancing around frantically. "Trust me! I vote we go back."

"This isn't a democracy," said the cat. "But in case it is, I vote we stay. With enough cheese I can blow this whole joint sky-high."

Philip raised a hand. "Let's keep a lid on the cheese for now." He looked down at Amy. "I trust your opinion, Amy. What do you think? Risk our lives here, or a thousand years in the future?"

Amy frowned. "This isn't my time, Phil. It's not even yours. We're not supposed to be a part of this dimension."

Philip nodded. "That settles it––we're going back."

Betsy tried to chase his tail and succeeded in falling off the bed. "Hooray!"

"Fine," said Sunflower. "Don't blame me when the Lady banishes all four of us to a dimension of ice and snow and we have to work in a hot fish shop. FOREVER."

"It's better than having a broken arm," said Amy.

Sunflower tilted his furry head. "You'd think so, wouldn't you? Everyone get on top of the bed. Amy needs to move right. Laughing Boy, you can help with that. Lay down next to her. Betsy, sit next to me. Nobody move, unless you want to lose one or two body parts. In my experience, humans have a problem with that."

"Where's my purse? The embroidered one."

Philip reached over to a night stand. "Here it is!" He lay the yellow cloth pouch in Amy's hands.

Sunflower shook his head. "Females and their bags."

"Quiet, cat, or you'll find out what's in it," said Amy.

Philip lay on the bed next to her and looked over at Sunflower. "You can teleport us back to the ship by yourself? No engineering or power or anything?"

"Yes, if the Lady isn't blocking my Thor ID," said the cat. "I'm pretty awesome."

"I can do it, too!" barked Betsy.

"Ignore the dog," said Sunflower. "He only got into operator school because of his dad."

The air crackled with lightning and filled with the smell of burnt toast. A sphere of blue energy surrounded the bed and everyone on it, burning an orange line of fire through the walls and floor. The world beyond the blue sphere exploded into a spinning panorama of stars and planets, lavender and oily smoke, and disappeared in a brilliant flash.

15

Amy woke with her head on Philip's shoulder, the quilt piled at her feet, and the bed tilted down sharply. On the floor was the edge of a red circle, but the rest of the room was impossibly, brilliantly white.

Something pinched her arm. Amy yelped and swatted at a silver claw that hung from the ceiling, then stared bewildered at her bandage-covered hand.

"What? This was broken a second ago."

Amy sat up and flexed the fingers of both hands and rotated her elbows and shoulders. She ripped away the bloody cotton and wooden splint around her arm and inspected the pale skin.

"I don't even have a scar. The pain went away from my ribs and foot. What's going on?"

Sunflower walked lazily around the side of the bed and began cleaning himself.

"Medical science," he said. "The transport system detects incoming operators and heals any injuries they've sustained while hunting down a prop."

"Why didn't you tell me that before? That's a pretty important fact for a girl with broken bones."

"Because it's classified. You're not an operator, so I didn't know if it would work. Also, it could have moved around some of your important bits. You might want to check that."

"Gee, thanks."

Philip groaned on the bed next to Amy. "My head ... ugh."

"I know I'm not an operator," said Amy. "The stupid inspector tried to kill me the first time I came here because I wasn't an operator. Why did it heal me this time?"

Sunflower stopped in the midst of licking his paw. "That's a good question."

Betsy scampered up to Philip and licked his face with a long pink tongue. "Wake up!"

"I'm awake, I'm awake!"

"Luckily, the Lady also didn't program the transmat to look for our incoming teleport signal and keep it from materializing," said Sunflower. "Condemning us to perpetual non-existence. The electronic version of a hot fish shop, if you will."

"It's not luck," barked Betsy. "She likes us!"

"Another thing you didn't tell us about," said Amy. "For your sake, cat, let's hope that's the last surprise we get today."

"I doubt it," said Philip, pointing up at the ceiling.

Amy followed the line of his finger to the silver spheres and waving metal tentacles of a dozen inspectors overhead.

THE INSPECTORS marched the four dangerous criminals through the shambles of Junktown, clearing the streets with loud warnings from their built-in loudspeakers. Without shoes and wearing a long white nightgown, Amy felt less like a prisoner in space and more like Wendy Darling on her way to Neverland. The surreal architecture around her and the cats and dogs cheering her from the windows added to the atmosphere of unreality.

"Let's make a break for it," she whispered to Sunflower, who trotted beside her with his orange tail held low.

"Impossible," said the cat. "But keep your eyes open and purse handy. I've got a plan."

The ring of flying metal octopi prodded them forward to a bright, needle-like tower at the center of the vast urban mess of Junktown. Amy's eyes followed the white thread of the tower until it disappeared into the mist-covered rafters of the dome far above, and she almost fell backwards with the effort.

A pair of doors opened at the base of the needle and the inspectors pushed Amy, Philip, Sunflower, and Betsy inside.

"This is where the Lady lives!" barked the terrier.

Amy waved a hand at the walls. "Here? She must be smaller than I thought."

"Silly! Not here here. This is just a movie-movie thing."

"You mean a lift," said Philip.

Amy giggled. "No, YOU mean an elevator."

Sunflower yawned and showed his sharp white fangs. "All three of you are right, but you'd better talk about something less boring. Maybe our impending death or banishment at the hands of the Lady?"

"Have you met her before?" asked Amy.

The orange tabby shivered. "Never!"

"I have," said Betsy. "She's great."

"I wonder about you sometimes, dog," said Sunflower. "If the transmat replaced your brain with a walnut, we'd never know the difference."

"I like walnuts," said Philip. "Walnuts are perfectly wizard!"

Sunflower blinked. "True, but you wouldn't give them a 401k and a health savings plan, now would you?"

The elevator doors whisked open and all four walked into a small, steel-walled compartment. Large wire grates covered the floor and ceiling.

"Hold your breath!" said Betsy.

"Why?"

Amy yelped as a cold shower of disinfectant fluid covered her from head to toe, then held down the hem of her nightgown as a hurricane-strong torrent of air blew up from the floor and exited through the ceiling. The whole process was over in ten seconds.

Amy straightened her messy hair with her fingers. "That'll wake you up in the morning."

"Quite," said Philip, and retrieved his cap from the grated floor.

A door in the wall of the disinfection chamber swished open, and Amy followed Philip and the two animals into the next room. Her toes sank into the white carpet and she gasped––partly from the gentle fibers caressing her feet, but mostly because of the apparition clicking and whirring in front of them.

Half human and half mechanical spider, the thing sat surrounded by keyboards and floating holographic displays in a pit in the center of the curved room. Thick cables hung down from the ceiling and spread across the carpet like a black webbing, linking the pit with other displays on the curved walls that showed the red-dot interiors of transmat chambers or the carefully curated warehouses of valuables stolen from other dimensions. A green and gray striped sweater hung loosely over the upper limbs of the creature like cloth on a scarecrow.

The end of a sharp metal leg tapped on a keyboard. The apparition spun around, flinging a white braid across its shoulder, and Amy realized it was female. The tightly pulled hair, the sunken eyes, and the hollow cheeks covered in liver spots made Amy feel cold inside. She felt as if she was looking at a thing that should have been dead long ago, but continued only by force of will, a will transmitted through the bright blue eyes. Those orbs were liquid and large like the blinking eyes of a kewpie doll, but unmistakably human.

"Hello, Amy Armstrong," said the Lady. Her voice was warm and grandmotherly, like fresh apple pie in the afternoon.

Sunflower grabbed the strap of Amy's handbag with his teeth and leaped in front of the group.

"Don't move, you monster!" he snarled. "I'm going to make you pay for what you did!"

The Lady nodded solemnly. "Yes, of course. Are you planning on beating me to death with that purse?"

"No. I'm going to eat the five grams of cheese inside and blow us all into space!"

"That sounds less like a plan, and more like suicide," murmured the Lady.

"I don't have a choice. If we try to escape, you'll track us down and send us to another dimension like you did my wife!"

The Lady reached into a pocket of her green-striped sweater and pulled out a thumb-sized silver disc.

"Sunflower, I knew that someday you would come to me and ask about her disappearance. Andy was one of my best operators, and her loss affected me deeply. All the data that I have on her last mission is on this disc."

"You expect me to believe that? Why didn't you tell me this a year ago?"

"Andy's final mission had to remain confidential. If it weren't for that, I certainly would have revealed everything, my dear cat. Have you ever known me to lie?"

Sunflower stared at the white carpet for a long moment. He dropped Amy's purse and walked up to the Lady. She clipped the disc to the orange tabby's ear, and he returned to Amy.

"Is that some kind of futuristic memory device?" asked Amy. "Are you going to read it with your mind or wait for it to dissolve into your bloodstream or something?"

"Don't be silly," said the cat. "It goes in my CD player back at the apartment."

"Oh."

Philip clapped his palms together. "Well! Now that we're out of that spot of trouble, I believe it's time to ask the Lady her intentions. It's rather apparent, from my point of view, that she's been manipulating Amy into a certain course of action."

Betsy looked up from his kneeling position on the carpet. "She's the Lady," barked the terrier. "She just wants to help us!"

The Lady shook her head. "Now Betsy--I told you no groveling, and no bowing. Raise your head."

"Sorry, Lady! It's because I love you so much!"

"Still groveling."

"Philip's right," said Amy. "Why have you ... wait a sec. Is that outer space?"

She walked around the perimeter of the circular room to the segmented window. Beyond lay a vast field of stars, where a swarm of silver craft inched and wriggled like miniature neon tetras.

"Amazing," she whispered. "It's more beautiful that I ever imagined." She squinted and leaned closer to the window. "Where's the Big Dipper?"

"You viewed that constellation from Earth, and we're in a different part of the galaxy now," said the Lady. "To be specific, we're in the exact spot where Kepler Prime floated several days ago."

Amy shrugged. "So we moved. This is a spaceship, and spaceships move."

"We have not deviated significantly from our galactic coordinates. Kepler Prime has disappeared."

Sunflower's jaw dropped. "An entire planet? That's impossible!"

"It's entirely possible. I watched it happen."

Amy pointed to a video feed of Junktown. "That's the problem! You've been watching me since I came to this crazy place. That's how you know my name. That's why I can open all the doors. You're the one behind it!"

"It's true I have followed your progress, but that's not why you have free access to the ship," said the Lady. "The systems are coded for a very specific pattern of DNA, one that you happen to have."

"Then I don't understand the point of all this. Why did you let me wander around?"

The Lady bowed her head. "You're a very special person, Amelia Earhart Armstrong. It wouldn't have been right to interfere with your visit to the *Dream Tiger*. I gave dear Philip the same treatment, because he is also a special person."

"Pardon me, your ladyship," said Philip. "But your proclaimed non-involvement in our affairs is rather unbelievable. What about the murderous inspector you sent to England? Burning down the East End is a nasty bit of interference."

The Lady smiled with ancient yellow teeth. "The road to Hell is paved with the best intentions. I sent Betsy after you with a special backpack to control the inspector and prod you gently toward returning to the *Dream Tiger*."

Sunflower flattened his ears and growled. "Betsy!"

"Don't get mad, you guys! I was always on your side! Remember?"

"Betsy has a true and honest heart," said the Lady. "But without, perhaps, the highest skill. Please do not blame him for what happened. The responsibility is all mine."

Amy waved her hand through a holographic yellow triangle. It passed through effortlessly.

"Why'd you let us leave in the first place, then? Just stop us in the transmat room."

"Your departure gave me time to prepare a certain project. Also, both of you needed to learn an important lesson."

"Which was?"

The Lady rotated on her spider legs to face Philip, and the teenage boy stared at the carpet.

"That we can't go home," he whispered. "That was the lesson."

"Ridiculous. Sunflower said we could link the power of all the transmat chambers and get to the dimension we wanted."

Philip shook his head. "You saw the results of that experiment."

"I did the best I could," said Sunflower. "It's not the kind of thing you can look up on SpaceBook, you know!"

"Returning home is incredibly difficult," said the Lady. "It was important for both of your futures that you understood that in the strictest of terms. Billions upon billions upon billions of dimensions exist. The transmat chambers can narrow the range of general time periods, but returning to the same dimension is like finding a needle in a haystack the size of the Milky Way."

Amy rubbed her nose and thought for a moment. “But ... you’re saying that needle is still out there.”

“Yes,” said the Lady. “For your sake, I hope that it exists.”

A beam of jade flashed across the blackness outside the window and the floor vibrated. The displays in the room changed to red triangles and a beeping cacophony filled the air.

The silver legs of the Lady whirred into action, spiking on keyboards with a rapid blur.

“The problem, Amy Armstrong, is that by connecting all the transmat power sources and activating a linked dimensional demat, you caused a gravity rift. Kepler Prime was the largest mass within a light-second, so Kepler Prime was absorbed in the rift.”

“Great poona droppings,” whispered Sunflower. “I’ll be known as the cat who stole a planet.”

Betsy jumped in the air. “Chicks will love it!” he barked.

Amy shook her head. “A planet can’t disappear! A Twinkie or a Super Nintendo, sure, but not a planet!”

“In the case of a linked transmat, mass on a planetary scale is no different from the mass of a high-calorie snack,” said the Lady. “The immediate problem of recovering Kepler Prime, if that is even possible, is of less importance than dealing with the incoming battle fleet.”

“Of Kepler Prime?”

“Sauros,” barked Betsy. “Smelliest bunch of space lizards in the galaxy!”

Sunflower sighed. “Actually, the only space lizards in the galaxy.”

“No! My cousin went to Cassiopeia and saw pink lizards.”

"Those were humans, you moron. Your cousin is the dumbest dog I've ever met, and that's saying a lot."

Multiple beams flashed the window and the room vibrated again. The scaly green face of a sauro appeared on one of the Lady's holographic displays.

"*Dream Tiger*, this is Admiral Sistra of the L.S.S. *Deathspar*. Energy traces link your ship to the disappearance of Kepler Prime. Respond immediately or prepare to be boarded. Spoiler: we need killing practice and will probably board you anyway. *Dream Tiger*, do you copy? Is this thing even on?"

The Lady tapped a keyboard. "*Deathspar*, this is *Dream Tiger* actual. We copy your boarding request. We have the individual responsible for stealing your planet. Opening hangar bay one; please follow the beacon."

"This is turning out to be a perfectly horrible day," said Philip.

Amy steadied herself against the wall. "We can't just give up! Is there some way to fight back?"

"Certainly, there is," said the Lady. "This ship has enough radiologic missiles to turn half the Sauro fleet into space dust, and hundreds of snub fighters and bombers manned by the best cat and dog pilots. I am the captain, owner, and spiritual leader of this ship, and I would sacrifice hundreds of pilots and kill thousands of Sauros if that was the only option left."

Amy shook her head. "You're looking at me like I'm the other option."

"Very smart," said the Lady. "But you always were a quick-witted girl, Amy Armstrong. Simply put, to meet the Sauro force directly will cost hundreds, perhaps thousands of lives. If I yield to their demands to turn over the criminal responsible for making their homeworld disappear, along with the incriminating evidence, then no one will suffer."

"Apart from Amy!" yelled Philip. "I won't allow it!"

"Better to go out with a bang," said Sunflower. "Send a few radiological missiles up those Sauro tail-pipes."

"The Sauros will take you to a prison station in this sector," said the Lady. "This will give me and my crew valuable time to prepare a rescue and investigate methods of pulling Kepler Prime from the gravity rift. If we can return their homeworld, the sauros will look upon your disappearance from their custody as a sort of *fait accompli*. I promise, Amy––you won't be in the sauro prison for very long."

"That's the worst plan I've ever heard!" said Philip. "We can't throw her to those beasts without a fight."

"Every man must choose his battles, or have them chosen for him," said the Lady. "Amy, what do you think? I will accept either course of action you choose. The pilots are already suiting up, and can launch in seconds."

Philip glanced around. "Where did Sunflower and Betsy go?"

Hundreds of holographic screens flashed to life around the Lady, each with a cat or dog wearing a protective EVA helmet.

"Commander SF063 finishing initial check," said a flickering image of Sunflower in a helmet. "Red Squadron tubes are green."

"Ensign BL8519 here," growled a helmeted Betsy. "Blue Squadron tubes green."

Amy gaped at the floating displays. "They were just here. How did you––"

"It's not important," said the Lady. "We have seconds before we lose tactical advantage. Do you want to make the smart choice, Amy, and give yourself up for a short time? Or do you choose to sacrifice your friends?"

Philip grabbed Amy's hand. "Don't listen, Amy. It's a trap!"

Amy squeezed back. "I still have to do it." She faced the Lady. "The smart way."

The Lady bowed her gray head. "I will escort you to the hangar and transfer you to the sauro representatives myself."

16

Fangs bared, Sunflower watched the platoon of sauro troopers in gleaming black armor march Amy into the docking tube that linked the hangar bay with their transport. After all hatches were sealed the bulbous, frog-like craft jetted away and quickly shrank to an emerald dot on the display screens.

The orange tabby sprinted through the corridors of the hangar bay and out to the streets of Junktown, at last arriving panting and out of breath at his apartment. He dug into piles of neckties on the floor and raced around the room, flinging combs and brushes behind him.

"Where is it? Can't find anything when you need to ... a-ha!"

Sunflower pulled a black box about the size of a pack of playing cards out of the mess and shoved the silver disc the Lady had given him into a slot on the side. A speaker on the flat side crackled and a female voice began to speak.

"Stardate eleven-thirty-three point seven one. Personal journal of Operator AN015, Andy Nakamura. The Lady has given me another sealed order for the same prop on Old Earth. What's so special about a gold video game console from 1995? I've already brought back twelve of the useless things. Why would the sauros want any in the first place? Had a physical check and Thor calibration this morning. Some slight frequency variations in the Thor beacon, but the medic said it won't cause any problems. Wish I could tell Sunnie about it, but everything's top secret and hush-hush. Andy signing off."

Sunflower sighed and rested his head on his paws.

Twelve hours later, after quite a bit of waiting in the waiting room and very little torture in the torture room

The penal station turned slowly in the vast emptiness of space like a wagon wheel tossed into the night sky by a lonely cowboy. Constructed in high orbit around Kepler Prime and designed to hold the most dangerous criminals in the galaxy, the fact that Kepler Prime no longer existed to be in orbit around caused quite a commotion among the sauro staff. However, the administration of the "High-security Anti-recidivist Long-term Penitentiary" were less concerned about the lack of a home planet than lack of quality, lizard-friendly television programming. At last the commander of H.A.L.P. ordered the staff to "stop whining about gravity and rogue moons and crap" and promptly went back to sleep. He'd had quite an exhausting morning filling out the forms on the new prisoner. She was apparently the mastermind behind the disappearance of Kepler Prime, but the commander couldn't believe such a pale and unimpressive human female––one that lacked armor or natural weapons of any kind––could steal a newspaper, much less a planet.

A thousand kilometers from the station a strange craft approached, its wide metal branches shining in the light of Kepler 22 like a silver tree. A dozen black knobby globes––each about the size of an Old Earth trash can––hung from the titanium branches. A long silver spear formed a central axis for the supports, had a small cockpit at the tip, and a cluster of powerful intersystem engines at the rear. A pair of large winged craft were attached to the silver trunk directly above the engines. The craft were ten meters wide and flat, like interstellar manta rays the color of asphalt.

Sunflower's voice crackled over the inter-ship radio. "Red and Blue Squadrons, prepare for detach. Mother One, detach."

"Copy, Red Leader," said a perky female voice.

The black spheres separated from the long stalks of their moorings, followed by the gray manta bombers. The tree-like carrier reduced speed and curved back the way it had come, while the fighters hurtled forward through space like a swarm of buckshot.

Inside the lead fighter, faint crimson light reflected on the glassy surface of Sunflower's helmet as he stared at the spinning wheel of the prison. The orange cat bared his teeth inside the pressure suit as he thought of the horrible tortures Amy was almost definitely experiencing at the hands of those degenerate sauros.

The tiny fighters were designed for short-range defense, not assault, necessitating the use of a transport for anything over a few thousand kilometers. The latest in military design from Tau Ceti, the ball-shaped fighters had thrusters mounted at sixteen different points around the fuselage, allowing it to instantly change direction. A cocoon of anti-accelerant gel surrounded the cat pilot, who operated the fighter by sticking his paws into control pits on either side of the main display. The minuscule radar profile of these tiny and nimble craft made a swarm deadly for even a sauro cruiser.

"Target in sight at Zebra 15," Sunflower whispered into the comm. "Red Two and Red Three, take the CAP at Zebra three zero zero. Two sauro bandits on my screen."

"Copy, Red Leader."

No wind resistance or sound traveled in the vast emptiness of space. The only frame of reference for speed––apart from the digital numbers on the readouts––was the slowly increasing size of the space station on Sunflower's display. The anti-radar coating on the fuselage of the twelve fighters and the fact that they were almost completely powered down––having used the inertia of the fighter carrier to continue forward––meant that they could approach the station undetected.

Sunflower hummed a tune to himself as he watched the closing distance spin down on the digital readout.

I come in last night about half past ten
That baby of mine wouldn't let me in
So move it on over. Rock it on over
Move over little cat, a mean old cat is movin' in.

Betsy's voice crackled over the inter-ship radio. "Red Leader, your mike is open. Also, you got the words wrong."

"Shut your trap, Blue Two," hissed Sunflower. "Keep that bomber on target."

"Okay, okay! Don't be so mean."

Sunflower wished he could scratch his nose. That was the worst thing about a pressure suit.

The wheel of the station grew larger and larger in the display. When the closing distance dropped below one hundred kilometers, Sunflower touched the mike button with his chin.

"Red Squadron, charge reactor and power on. I'm marking the target on my display. Red Two and Three head for vector zebra-niner, guns free. Repeat, guns free."

Radioactive energy spurted from two of the black spheres and they darted below the pack to intercept a pair of arrow-shaped sauro fighters. The rest of the spheres and the two gray bombers continued toward the silently turning wheel of the station.

"Red squadron, retro burn," murmured Sunflower as the station filled his screen. "Alpha Wing follow me. Bravo take the far section. Blue team, start your op."

Bright jets flashed at the front of the black spheres as they slowed and matched the rotational speed of the station. The fighters separated into two teams thirty meters apart and arranged themselves around the tubular fuselage. A clawed silver arm emerged from the knobby front of each fighter and snapped into the metal like a hungry alligator.

"Red Four has contact," crackled the inter-ship radio.

Sunflower nodded at the stream of radio chatter.

"Start cutting," he ordered.

He toggled a switch inside the control pit and the viewscreen automatically darkened as a brilliant aquamarine laser began to burn through the skin of the station along a pre-programmed line. On either side of the tubular section the ten fighters followed his example, cutting through the curved steel of the fuselage like blades through cooked macaroni. The blue lasers were normally for anti-missile point defense, but cat engineers had modified the powerful equipment for close-range work after a few hours of tinkering.

Sunflower's fighter rocked from a series of vibrations. He twisted his arm and deployed another claw for stability as the laser at the front of his fighter continued to burn a black line through the skin of the station. Both teams of fighters had almost finished the work of cutting through the left and right sides of the thirty-meter-long tube.

The inter-ship comm crackled with a female voice. "Red Leader, this is Red Three. Bandits are down, repeat bandits are down. Red Two is disabled, not responding."

Sunflower touched the talk button with his chin. "Red Three, grab Red Two and exfil to Mother One."

"Copy."

The station shuddered as the gray manta bombers settled onto the center of the curved section, one to each side, and fired spiked landing gear into the metal.

"Red Leader, Blue One is attached."

"Me, too!" crackled Betsy's voice.

Sunflower winced. "Turn your volume down, Blue Two."

The control panel beeped and the laser on Sunflower's fighter shut off automatically. He double-checked the readings and clicked his talk button.

"Structural integrity zero percent," he said. "Blue One and Two, you are go for departure. Repeat, go for departure. Red Squadron, dig in those claws and hang on!"

White streams of radioactive energy poured from the large engines at the rear of the manta bombers. The curved section that the bombers and fighters were hanging on to ripped away from the space station in a spray of gas and plastic and insulation, and accelerated away rapidly from the giant wheel.

***

COMPLETE DARKNESS covered Amy, but she could feel irregular vibrations and hear strange creaks and popping sounds from outside her prison cell. She tried to push away and stand up, but a strange and powerful force kept her pinned to the wall.

"Is this some kind of stupid trick?" she yelled. "I don't know what happened to your planet, you big, ugly crocodile!"

No response came. After a few minutes, Amy wondered if this truly was another strange torture or if something had happened to the space station. Were those lizards just going to leave her to die while the station broke apart? Was it a simulation of a slightly disconcerting ride at a theme park, intended to make her spill the beans? Maybe sauros were afraid of the dark. Or roller coasters.

The force pinning her to the wall gradually softened and Amy floated weightless into the center of the prison cell.

"Hello? Anybody there?"

Lucia had always said the only thing doctors couldn't replace was your brain, so Amy kept her arms up in case the gravity came back and she was upside down. She bounced gently from wall to wall, gradually feeling numb, cold, and sleepy.

After a series of loud bumps and clanks, a moderate gravity returned. Amy slid to the concave floor of the cell, blinking drowsily with her arms over her face. She didn't stir when the door broke open and lights waved into the cell, nor when a pair of cats in white spacesuits and bubble helmets expertly wrapped a rope under her shoulders and pulled her rapidly along the corridor toward a blinding white light.

"Not the light," Amy murmured and closed her eyes. "Not ... die ... in space."

She heard a door click and a warm breeze that smelled of new plastic and rubber tossed her hair. Something hard covered Amy's mouth and nose and she inhaled cold, dry oxygen.

Amy opened her eyes and saw a black cat in a space helmet. Above the cat spread the segmented white ceiling of a small compartment.

"Where am I?"

The cat reached up with thick gloves and twisted his helmet ninety degrees. He pulled off the helmet and blinked yellow eyes at Amy.

"You're on the *Dream Tiger*, Miss Armstrong."

Amy groaned and tried to sit up, but the cat's gloved paw held her down.

"Please wait for a moment, Miss Armstrong. The atmospheric adjustment needs a moment."

Amy looked around the small compartment. From the warning diagrams and cat-sized spacesuits hanging on the walls, she guessed it was an airlock. The other spacesuited cat in the room was a gray tabby, but neither he nor the black cat were very talkative as they took turns unzipping each other and pulling off sections of the white spacesuits. When the gray tabby pulled the gloves from the black cat's suit, Amy saw skeletal metal hands wrapped around the cat's paws, like a bracelet with long fingers.

"Looks like she's never seen a manos before," whispered the gray cat, his blue eyes on Amy.

The black cat chuckled. "She's from Old Earth, *poona* brain."

"I have too, just not inside a spacesuit," said Amy. "What am I talking about? I've never seen a cat in a spacesuit, period."

The pair of cats hung the sections of the heavy space suits on hooks along the walls. A low warble sounded and the black cat touched Amy's shoulder.

"Time to stand up, Miss Armstrong. Gently, now. Watch the low ceiling."

Still a bit light-headed, Amy used the walls for support as she got to her feet. The black cat wasn't lying; the room was much smaller than it seemed. Amy had to stoop, and the back of her shoulders pressed against the white ceiling.

The black cat touched a section of wall and a round hatch rolled away with a thunk. A clamor of sound poured into the airlock: the clang of metal on metal, orders shouted from across a room, and the hiss and hammer of hydraulic tools.

Amy squeezed through the hatch after the two cats, and stood to her full height in a long and wide hangar bay. Along the metal bulkhead to her left were several small airlocks like the one she'd just exited, followed by a line of thirty wider hatches. On Amy's right a throng of cats and dogs in colored overalls and protective goggles bent over metal components or stuck their heads inside large black spheres hanging from yellow repair cranes. On the far end of the wide hangar deck, Amy saw a gray craft being pulled into view by a dog driving an electric cart. The wide wings and long, narrow tail made Amy think of a manta ray.

The black cat touched her hand. "This way, Miss Armstrong."

Amy walked behind the two cats as they trotted on all fours toward the gray craft in the distance. The hatches on her left were painted with large red numbers and a screen above each hatch displayed a video feed of empty tubes. Amy felt occasional vibrations in the floor as they walked, and saw the large black spheres dart into the tubes and stop. Cats in bubble helmets and flexible red suits emerged from doors in the spheres, pushed into the adjoining airlocks, and began to remove their pressure suits.

Amy and her escorts walked by hatch numbers that grew smaller and smaller. As they passed the single digits, the hatches clicked and hissed open. The final hatch in the line was labeled with a big red one. It rolled to the side and a familiar orange tabby trotted out.

Amy waved at him. "Sunflower!"

The cat saw her and dodged the other pilots leaving the tubes.

"Amy! Are you okay?"

"I'm fine, thanks to these two."

Sunflower nodded at the pair of cats. "Good job, Lee. Good job, Kira."

"Thank you, Commander."

The cats bowed and trotted away, leaving Amy with Sunflower.

"Are you sure you're feeling fine?" asked the cat. "The Lady was afraid you might die from a pressure blowout or oxygen leak. I'm actually shocked that the plan worked, mainly because Betsy was involved."

Amy squinted at Sunflower. "Wait a second ... How did you rescue me? I was in the middle of a space station slash prison full of creepy lizards slash morons."

"You weren't in the middle, luckily. The sauros thought you were extremely dangerous, and the idiots put you in an isolated section away from guards and other criminals. Sauros may be fierce, but they're also very predictable. We simply scanned the station, cut away the part with you in it, and flew away."

"Cut away the part with me in it? It's outer space! I could have died a million different ways!"

Sunflower blinked. "More like a thousand. Decompression, oxygen loss, laser failure, collision with our bombers, reactor failure, accidental overcharge of a laser, more sauro fighters showing up, Betsy playing her music too loud; the list goes on and on."

"Thanks. I didn't really want to know."

"You're here now and that's the important thing," said Sunflower. "When the sauro battle fleet catches up to us we'll all be dead anyway, but you got to live another five minutes, right?"

"Doesn't the Lady have a plan?"

"That's exactly what I said. Come on, let's see if Betsy is stuck in his cockpit again."

Amy followed the orange tabby past a line of huge rectangular doors with blue numbers painted on the face to the pair of gray craft. Cats and dogs in rubberized suits swarmed over and under the wings, spraying tanks of white steam onto every surface. The clear bubble of the cockpit slid back, and a dog in a blue spacesuit climbed down a ladder. At the bottom waited a beagle wearing manos tools on his paws. He grabbed the pilot's bubble helmet and twisted it off to reveal the brown and white head of a Jack Russell terrier.

"Betsy!"

The dog saw Amy and barked happily. After the blue spacesuit was pulled off his body, the terrier raced up to her.

"We did it!"

"Yes," said Sunflower dryly. "The mission was a success, apart from the fact that you returned in one piece."

Betsy glanced left and right and hung his head.

"Two pieces, actually," whispered the dog. "I had an accident. In my space pants."

"You were supposed to go before we left!"

"I know, I know! Why do you always have to yell?"

"Because it makes me feel better!"

A low-high-low whistle sounded throughout the hanger, and all the pilots and engineering animals froze for a second. Whispers filled the air.

"The Lady!"

"The Lady's coming."

"Impossible. How?"

"Move it! Get in line!"

The animals dropped what they were doing and formed two parallel lines in the center of the hangar bay, leaving five meters of space between the rows. The cat and dog pilots made up one side and engineers and repair techs the other.

Amy stood between Sunflower and Betsy. "What was that whistle? Is the Lady coming?"

"Yes," said Sunflower. "And it's either really, really bad or really, really good. Those are the only times the Lady visits anyone."

"I think it's good!" said Betsy.

"You would, wouldn't you?"

Amy gently nudged the cat with her bare foot. "That silver disc from the Lady--did you listen to it?"

Sunflower bowed his head and replied in a whisper.

"I did. I don't think it was the Lady's fault that Andy disappeared."

The low-high-low sound whistled once more through the speakers and a wide door swished open opposite the hangar from Betsy's manta bomber. A pair of tentacled inspectors floated into the room followed by the Lady, her metal spider legs hammering on the hangar floor like a giant typewriter of doom.

The Lady's wrinkled hands were clasped in front of her as if she were holding a mouse. She wore a long-sleeved blouse of pale blue and a shimmering white robe on her upper torso instead of the striped sweater Amy had last seen her wearing. Her gray braid had been wound into a circle on the top of her head, and a diamond-covered tiara rested on her forehead. The polished obsidian ball of her lower body swiveled and turned with each step of the metal legs.

The Lady stopped in front of Amy and smiled.

"Miss Armstrong. I'm very happy to see you back, safe and sound."

Amy shrugged. "I'm just glad I didn't have to spend one more second with those reptiles."

"I hope they weren't unpleasant with you."

"Nah. More like smelly and boring."

The Lady bowed her head. "An apt description of their race, I'm sorry to say."

An airlock opened beyond the line of fighter tubes and a pair of sauros tumbled out, squealing and clawing at a half-dozen cats in white spacesuits. The inspectors next to the Lady dashed forward and grabbed the two lizard men in their tentacles, lifting both into the air. One sauro wore a long white coat, like a scientist or doctor. The other looked as if he'd spilled an entire cup of coffee down the front of his blue uniform.

"Welcome to the *Dream Tiger*," said the Lady. "To whom do I owe this pleasure?"

Nistra wriggled in the grip of the powerful tentacles, bits of loose change flying from his pockets and bouncing on the metal hangar deck.

"You can't treat an officer of the Empire like this, you monster! You'll pay for this!"

The line of cats and dogs standing proudly at attention winced at the sauro's remarks, but the Lady waved a wrinkled hand.

"How rude," she said. "I thought the most powerful beings in the galaxy would be more polite."

Nistra wrinkled his scaly nose and growled. "Detention Officer First Class Nistra. The spotty-faced *poona* brain beside me is Recruit Officer Flistra."

The Lady tilted her head. "Officer Nistra, today is the most important day of your life."

The sauro bared his teeth. "I will die with honor, Lady! You won't find me begging, no matter how famously cruel you are."

"I haven't saved you from the fragments of your prison station just to execute you! No, you will live today, tomorrow, and the next day. You have many days ahead of you and many grandchildren to whom you may tell this story."

"He ... um, he's already got grandchildren," said Flistra in a squeaky voice.

"Great-grandchildren, then," said the Lady. "For the life of me, I can't tell how old you sauros are, or even one sauro from the next."

"Lizardist," hissed Nistra.

The Lady clapped her hands. "Everyone dismissed! Let Officers Nistra and Flistra go. I will take charge of them."

"Release them from protective custody?" crackled the metallic voice of the inspector holding Flistra in the air.

"Yes, please."

The inspectors released their claws and the two sauros fell several feet to the deck. The assembly of cats and dogs wandered back to their stations or out of the hangar.

Amy watched Nistra and Flistra stand up. “I have a bad feeling about this.”

“Please don’t be worried,” said the Lady. “Both are special individuals, and both have a grand part to play in what happens next.”

“Thank you,” said Nistra. “Finally, some respect.”

Amy sighed. “Miss The Lady or whatever, you keep saying weird things like that, like I’m special, this guy is special, that piece of lint is special. If you’d just spill the beans on what’s going on instead of keeping it a big secret, I think we’d all be happier.”

The Lady smiled. “I understand, Amy Armstrong. For now, please follow me.”

“Isn’t a battle fleet coming to blow us out of space or whatever?”

“Not for a few minutes. Sunflower and Betsy, you must also come.”

“Sure!” barked Betsy.

“Yes, my Lady,” said Sunflower quietly.

Nistra growled and spat on the deck. “In the words of the ancient sauropod Napoleon Bonaparte: ‘Death is nothing, but to live defeated and inglorious is to die daily.’ ”

Amy laughed. “Ancient sauropod? Seriously, Godzuki, you need summer school.”

The small party followed the Lady and her inspector bodyguards across the hangar, through a series of wide airlocks, and down a long corridor to a security door. With a touch of the Lady’s wrinkled hand, the bulky steel door split horizontally and rumbled into the floor and ceiling. Amy followed the Lady into the narrow chamber beyond and squealed with surprise.

A vast field of stars glimmered above her head and below her feet, as clear and real as if she'd stepped outside the ship. Every surface from top to bottom––the floor, the curving walls, the bench seats––were almost completely transparent, turning the chamber into a glistening bead of dew on the black, rocky surface of the Lady's hollowed-out asteroid slash spaceship. The fantastic view, however, was not the sole reason for Amy's sudden outburst.

"Philip!"

Amy jumped at the teenager and hugged him around the neck.

"Nice to see you, too," he said, squirming a bit to keep from being strangled. "It's only been twelve hours. What did those beastly sauros do to you?"

Amy pouted. "Grouchy Gus. I'm just happy to see my favorite English boy."

"Got a hug for me?" asked a high-pitched voice.

Nick landed on Philip's shoulder and curtsied in a purple dress. Amy carefully shook the tiny sprite's hand with her thumb and forefinger.

"What a beautiful dress," she said.

The blonde sprite grinned and twirled, fluttering her skirt.

"Thank you!"

"Can we get to the point of all this?" snarled Nistra. "Someone in this room has a home world that's gone missing. Let's see ... it's me!"

"Kepler Prime will return in eleven point three minutes," said the Lady. "First I must apologize to Amy for the pain and suffering she has experienced from the sauro prison and my rogue inspector in London."

Amy shrugged. “I’m fine. The transmat healed my broken bones, and the sauro prison wasn’t even as scary as summer camp.”

“Summer camp?” asked Recruit Flistra. “What is ... summer camp?”

Nistra slapped the back of the recruit’s scaly head. “You fool! It’s obviously where they train to resist torture! That’s why we failed to penetrate the psychic defenses of this human.”

The Lady smiled at Amy. “As a physical token of my sincerity, I offer any treasure from the vast warehouses of my ship. Perhaps you would like the Daria-i-noor diamond? The British Crown Jewels? The actual Shroud of Turin?”

Amy laughed and rubbed the fur on Betsy’s head. “Thanks, but I don’t need any of that stuff. I’m just happy to be with my friends again.”

A mournful expression crossed the Lady’s face. “Amy Armstrong, you have changed since you arrived on my ship, changed from a young thief to a young woman. My old eyes are dim and clouded over, but I hope that I have helped steer the ship of your life onto a more positive course, and that you have gained honesty and wisdom. Keep your friends close and you will have a long and cheerful existence.”

“What about everyone back on Earth? What about Lucia? She needs me!”

“As I said before, the possibility for returning is small. I have sacrificed much to help you find a way back, Amy Armstrong. Out of all the billions upon billions of people who have ever lived and died in the galaxy, no one wishes you could go back to your stepmother more than me. I have lived for hundreds of years and traveled to more dimensions than you can imagine. Believe me when I wish for your safe return.”

"That's a fine sentiment, your ladyship," said Philip. "But cold comfort to those stranded here."

The Lady turned and gazed at the vast panorama of stars.

"We're all stranded one way or another, young Philip. The life of an individual is a silver thread woven throughout the vast tapestry of the universe. I hope that Amy is much smarter than I was and can find a way to hook the strands of our life back where they belong. That was my hope when she came here."

Amy squinted at her. "Our life? What are you talking about?"

"Sorry for interrupting your tea party," said Nistra. "But nobody seems to be paying attention to the giant missing planet in the room!"

Sunflower cleared his throat. "My Lady, we have battle cruisers approaching."

"Right. I suppose I should speed this up. Nobody likes being late to their own funeral." The Lady pointed above her head. "What's up there?"

"The universe," said Amy.

"Outer space," said Philip.

"Your finger," said Betsy.

Sunflower laughed. "Idiots! It's the *White Star*. The Lady's personal cutter."

The entire group peered up through the dome to a long and narrow craft docked to the side of the asteroid. Mottled silver and gray, the tapering nose and wide engines at the rear made the craft appear strikingly similar to a barracuda, although one that was a hundred meters long, twenty meters high, and happened to swim in space.

"That's impossible!" said Amy. "White Star was the name of my first cat, and I called the second one–"

"Dream Tiger, of course," said the Lady.

Amy clenched her teeth and pointed at her. "I don't believe it! This whole thing has all been a dream. First Lucia's voice in the computer, and now the names of my pets!"

"Whether you believe it's imagined or reality, you must keep going," said the Lady. "What we think about any situation in life is less important than actually what we do about it."

"Great speech. What imagined situation are you going to tell us about now, Miss Lady All-In-My-Head?"

"Amy, please don't fall into that trap again," said Philip. "There is nothing imaginary or false about anything that's happened."

"I understand how confused you must feel," said the Lady quietly. "The *White Star* was my first ship. It's where I grew into a woman, saw the galaxy for the first time, and traveled through dimensions. The important 'thing' I'm going to do is give it to you."

"Give it to me?"

"Many pardons, your ladyship," said Philip. "But you're supposed to be hundreds of years old. By any sort of calculation, that would make it a useless old relic."

The Lady smiled. "Old relics are never useless."

"But the human is right, my Lady," said Sunflower. "Everyone knows the *White Star* is just an old, dusty museum. It was shut down during the building of the *Dream Tiger* and hasn't been used since!"

"That part is correct," said the Lady. "The ship's power core was transferred to the *Dream Tiger* and she lay dormant for many years. In the last day, however, my crew has reactivated her and stocked the ship with supplies. She's a self-repairing mechanical organism older than you can imagine, from a parallel dimension where cats, dogs, sprites, and sauros lived in peace and harmony."

"Katmando," whispered Sunflower, Betsy, and Nick simultaneously.

"Trust me, the *White Star* will be cruising Orion's arm long after the galaxy has forgotten about all of us. She was constructed in a dimension where the level of scientific cooperation between the species allowed them to develop the first transmat drive; although ironically, the success of transmatting the entire ship meant they could never return. The vessel belonged to the very first Lady and has been passed down through the ages."

"That's a cool story," said Amy. "But what am I supposed to do with a spaceship?"

"Search for answers, or even the questions you do not know you will have. You're a very smart girl, and because I never found them doesn't mean you won't. My crew and I have stocked the White Star with every essential, including things that were missing when I flew on her: the components for a basic transmat, a particular video game console from 1995, and toothpaste. There are video diaries to help you in your journey; some from past crews and some from a younger version of me. You may spend your time researching a trip to Old Earth or exploring the galaxy. The choice is yours, as are the friends you take with you."

"Part of me thinks it's a great idea," said Amy. "The rest says it stinks."

"There is a time and a place for everything, Amy Armstrong, but the wheels are already in motion and have been for some time. Whether through your departure or the actions of the quickly approaching battle fleet, all of us standing here will soon be thrown apart."

"She's giving you the *White Star* in working condition," Sunflower whispered to Amy. "That's huge!"

"All right, I'll take it. Who's with me? I know––he's from Yorkshire and his name starts with 'P.' "

Philip blushed and looked away.

"I'd follow you anywhere, Amy. I think you know that."

"Ha! Don't get squishy on me now, Philip. I'll start telling ghost stories."

Betsy barked and jumped in the air. "I want to go! I want to go!"

"Don't leave me here this time," said Nick, her arms crossed.

Amy stared at the orange tabby at her feet. "Sunflower?"

The cat sighed. "Fine. You'll probably need a good pilot, and Betsy couldn't fly a frisbee into the ground. I guess after all the problems I've caused the Lady would be happier with me out of the picture."

"Not at all," said the Lady. "You were an irreplaceable catalyst for Amy's journey, and may choose to stay with the *Dream Tiger* or continue with her on the *White Star*."

Sunflower blinked his green eyes at the Lady. "I'll go with Amy."

"Of course. Now, Amy Armstrong, I failed to mention two caveats in my offer of the *White Star*. First, you must take Officer Nistra."

The sauro stamped his foot on the transparent deck of the viewing chamber. "What? Impossible!"

"I'm not living on a ship with some lizard," growled Sunflower.

"The feeling is mutual, you hairy ball of *poona* droppings!"

The Lady raised a pale hand. "Stop. Officer Nistra is an intelligent and brave officer who is ready to face any situation. He knows much about the galaxy and the sauropod race, and will be a valuable resource on your journey."

"I'm not interested in being a tour guide," hissed the armored sauro.

"Perhaps not, but the secret to finding Kepler Prime and your family lies within that ship. You will need the help of Amy and her friends to discover it."

Nistra swayed back and forth for a few seconds, as if bouncing between decisions. At last he dipped his scaly head and bowed from the waist.

"I accept the challenge."

"Understand, of course, that you will be under Amy's command."

"Ordered about by a disgusting human?" Nistra sighed. "As you wish. I will endure this shame in order to save my people."

"You said 'two conditions,' " said Amy. "What's the other one?"

The Lady smiled. "I don't mean to be mysterious-"

"Bravo," said Philip, and clapped his hands slowly. "You're doing a magnificent job."

"Sorry," said the Lady. "You will discover the last condition, but it will take many, many years. Or five minutes, who can tell?"

Amy shrugged. "Okay, fine. When do we leave?"

"I need to get some things from my apartment," said Nick. "About two dozen suitcases, hat boxes, make up cases, back-up dresses, back-up make up––"

"Your things have already been placed aboard the *White Star* and we haven't a second to spare," said the

Lady. "You must leave immediately, as the sauro battle fleet is entering weapons range. One of the inspectors will escort you to the docking platform."

"My clothes are sprite-clean only!" yelled Nick. "You better not have wrinkled them!"

Philip grabbed the tiny flying woman and sprinted out of the room with Sunflower, Betsy, and Nistra.

Amy gave a mock salute. "Bye, now!"

"Farewell," said the Lady, her eyes tearing up. "Good luck, Amy Armstrong."

"Right back at ya!"

Amy jogged after her friends.

The door closed and the Lady was left alone with Flistra and a single hovering inspector.

"What a view," sighed the lizard man.

"Quiet," ordered the Lady. She held out both arms and a panorama of holographic displays appeared around her. "All stations yellow alert! This is the Lady. All stations yellow alert!"

The faces of cats, dogs, and pale sprites popped onto the screens and acknowledged the command.

"Engineering, prepare for core eject," said the Lady.

The brown eyes of an English bulldog widened on a flickering display.

"We can't do that, My Lady! The entire ship will–"

"Shut up and get ready!"

The Lady swiped her hand across another screen. "Transmat Ops, are you powered on and warmed up?"

An image of a Siamese cat nodded. "Yes, My Lady."

"Good. Be ready for activation in less than sixty seconds."

The Lady followed the progress of Amy and her friends as they rode the express elevator up and sprinted through a docking tube to the *White Star*. The airlock doors closed and a few seconds later, the main engines of the sleek spacecraft flared with blinding white light and pushed the craft rapidly away from the asteroid.

"Transmat Ops, activate now. Engineering, eject the core in 3, 2, 1. Now!"

The *White Star* disappeared in a brilliant flash of sparkling blue. Each of the hundreds of holographic displays around the Lady clicked off and dropped the room into a darkness lit only by starlight.

"I have no idea what's going on right now," said Flistra.

"You'll see, you'll see," said the Lady. "Oh my-- what could that be down below us?"

"Um ... it's the floor. Duh!"

"No, you boob! In space."

The sauro gasped. "Kepler Prime!"

The azure seas and pale clouds of the planet rotated slowly below their feet.

"But how? You said that Nistra would find it on the *White Star*!"

"It IS on the *White Star*. What do you think is powering their engine core?" The Lady clicked a button on a small red box mounted next to the door. "This is the Lady. All hands abandon ship. Repeat, all hands abandon ship. This is not a drill."

"What's going on?"

The Lady pointed a spidery leg at the corridor behind her. "This asteroid no longer has power and will implode in less than thirty seconds. If you want to breathe the air of Kepler Prime again, run down that hall, turn right, and jump into an escape pod. Go! Also, it's not exactly your planet, but one from a parallel dimension. Close enough for sauro work, as your people say!"

She clicked back into the observation room and watched the thousands of tiny white globes of escape craft shoot away from the Dream Tiger, along with shuttles and transport craft. Many of the warehouses had been designed to seal up and eject in the event of power failure, and hundreds of these large metal boxes spun away from the *Dream Tiger*.

Tears filled the Lady's eyes, but not because of the valuable goods spinning away. With the artificial gravity off-line and safety doors unpowered, the giant ship began to rip apart and collapse upon itself. As streams of gas burst into space and explosions rocked the transparent deck, the Lady took a faded photograph from her blouse. Her wrinkled hands shook as she touched the image of a grinning Amy in her twenties, a tiny infant in her arms and Philip kissing her cheek.

"Excuse me!"

Flistra stuck his head into the room. "Sorry to bother, but I'm still confused about everything. Are you Amy's daughter? Are you her mother? Are you made of liquid metal?"

The Lady spun around.

"No, no, and no, you swamp-dwelling cretin. I'm a version of Amy two hundred years in the future! I'm trying to get her back to Earth and change her life so she doesn't end up as a half machine spider woman with no friends!"

"Right! Sorry, back to the escape pod!"

The Lady turned back to the peaceful blue globe of Kepler Prime as escape pods left sparkling trails of exhaust and rocky chunks of the *Dream Tiger* began to break away. Without the captive gravity of an alternate-dimension Kepler Prime, the massive ship was collapsing upon itself like a rotting orange under the tropical sun. In less than ten seconds it would be a dead hulk floating useless in the vacuum of space, and so would the Lady.

"Run for it, Amy Armstrong," she whispered. "Run as far and fast as you can."

END

Further Books in the Amy Armstrong Series

Empire of the Space Cats--To fix her damaged spacecraft, Amy travels to Tau Ceti Epsilon, the center of cat civilization in the year 3317.

Available September 2016 at amishspaceman.com and fine retailers near you!

SpaceBook Awakens--Enemies from the past and across the galaxy follow Amy to California.

Available October 2016!

Contact the Author
stevecolegrove.com
amishspaceman.com
facebook.com/pages/Steve-Colegrove-Author
twitter @stevecolegrove

Other Works by the Author
The Amish Spaceman (2014)
The Roman Spaceman (2014)
A Girl Called Badger (2012)
The Dream Widow (2013)

Made in the USA
Middletown, DE
04 October 2021

49649695R00182